Bethlehem

Bethlehem

Karen Kelly

St. Martin's Press ⚇ New York

BETHLEHEM. Copyright © 2019 by Karen Kelly. All rights reserved. Printed in the United States of America. For information, address St. Martin's Press, 120 Broadway, 25th floor, New York, N.Y. 10271.

www.stmartins.com

The Library of Congress Cataloging-in-Publication Data is available upon request.

ISBN 978-1-250-20149-2 (hardcover)
ISBN 978-1-250-20150-8 (ebook)

Our books may be purchased in bulk for promotional, educational, or business use. Please contact your local bookseller or the Macmillan Corporate and Premium Sales Department at 1-800-221-7945, extension 5442, or by email at MacmillanSpecialMarkets@macmillan.com.

First Edition: July 2019

10 9 8 7 6 5 4 3 2 1

To Susan, for insisting.
And to Mom and Dad,
for providing the music—always.

Acknowledgments

Enormous thanks to Laura Ross—your perception, talent, and kindness are world-class. I would also like to thank Alexa Stark, at Trident Media, and Jennifer Weis, at St. Martin's Press. Most of all, my eternal thanks to the girls who keep me going—my beautiful squad.

PARRISH FAMILY

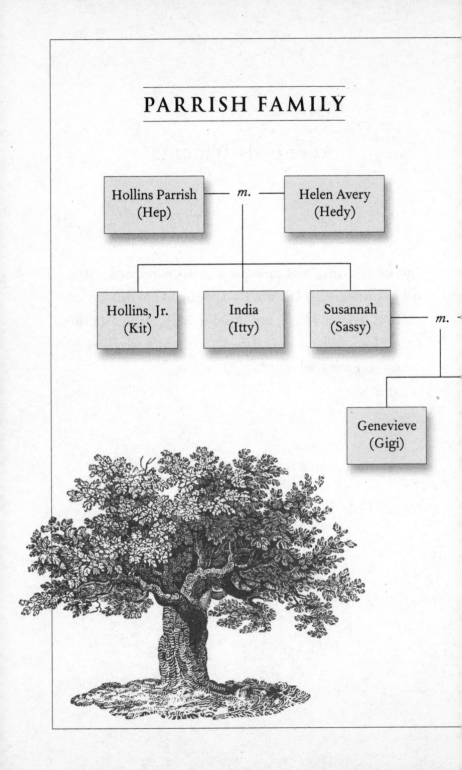

Hollins Parrish (Hep) — *m.* — Helen Avery (Hedy)

Hollins, Jr. (Kit) — India (Itty) — Susannah (Sassy) — *m.*

Genevieve (Gigi)

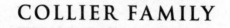

COLLIER FAMILY

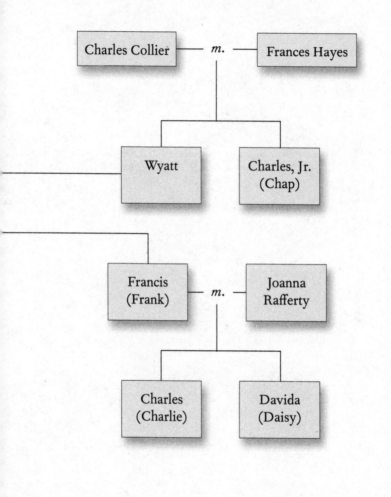

Charles Collier — *m.* — Frances Hayes

Wyatt

Charles, Jr. (Chap)

Francis (Frank) — *m.* — Joanna Rafferty

Charles (Charlie)

Davida (Daisy)

Bethlehem

One

"It's nice to see some live children around here."

The voice came from behind Joanna—unnerving in itself—but as the ghoulish implication settled in, she shivered.

The figure seemed to have appeared out of nowhere—*The Old Woman in the Wood* in a frayed straw hat. There was a trace of dirt on her cheek, and when she smiled, one front tooth pushed just slightly forward, giving her a charming, imperfect appeal. "Welcome to my garden of eternal repose."

Joanna couldn't control it—her eyes ran up and down the woman in a conspicuous once-over. Thick-soled shoes layered with soil, baggy men's dungarees, a canvas apron anchored by four large pockets—all topped by a lined face with crinkled spaniel eyes. A cottony bun peeked out from under the hat. This was a grandmotherly face—not ghoulish, not unearthly. Thoroughly earthly, in fact.

Cautiously, Joanna returned the smile. "I hope it's all right.

I thought we'd just stroll through, but when they saw the swing . . ."

Suspended on thick ropes from an enormous oak tree was a grayed slat of wood, where now perched a young girl, propelled by her brother's indulgent heave-ho.

"It certainly is." Placing her small spade and bucket of weeds on the grass, the woman lowered herself onto the bench. She smiled again at Joanna, patting the seat next to her. "Lovely to have you here. I've been waiting to meet you."

"I'm sorry?"

The woman laughed, clapping both hands on her knees. "Sounded like the grim reaper, did I?" She slipped off a work glove and held her hand out. "Doe Janssen. Proprietress. And you're Joanna Collier."

Clasping the proffered hand somewhat tentatively, Joanna sat down. If she wasn't outright rattled, she was getting there. "How did you know?"

"Wouldn't take a soothsayer to figure it out. One look at that little boy and you know he's a Collier. But I've seen you before—at your father-in-law's funeral last year. And I knew that Frank had moved his family into Brynmor."

Joanna looked over at Charlie, surprised. She hadn't thought he took after her husband whatsoever. "You know the family?"

"Oh yes. Hedy's a dear friend. We go back decades."

Joanna was beginning to wonder if she was hallucinating. Sitting in the middle of a graveyard with this rustic stranger—

a little old lady in trousers who seemed to know a lot about her life—was peculiar enough. But even more bizarre was the idea that her husband's stately, refined grandmother could have somehow befriended a cemetery custodian.

"Do you live in the house?" Joanna nodded toward a hulking brick manor of indeterminate style that sat within the tall iron gates, surrounded by headstones large and small.

"Oh yes . . . it goes with the territory. *In Grange House, we have dwelt—nigh fifty-seven years.*" She recited the line like poetry. "My husband moved me in as a bride, and we've never left." Pausing, she gazed around. "It may seem strange, given the circumstances, but it's turned out to be a lovely life. We've known most everyone in Bethlehem, and those who have moved in here are quite good company."

Curious about the earth-streaked little woman in the tattered hat, Charlie and Daisy had quit the swing and were now hovering at their mother's elbow. Charlie—shy at six but naturally inquisitive—ventured a question: "How many people live here?" He was looking toward the house.

Doe chuckled and gave him a weighty look. "Well . . . there are just three of us actually *living* here . . . but we're surrounded by very interesting neighbors, if you get my meaning."

Increasingly uncomfortable with the slant of the conversation, Joanna tilted it in a more corporeal direction, drawing a handkerchief from her pocketbook to scour at a scuff of dirt on Daisy's knee. "Charlie, Daisy, please say hello to

Mrs. Janssen. This is her yard, and she has been nice enough to let you play on her swing."

One voice was muted and one rang out: "Hello, Mrs. Janssen."

"Hello, little monkeys. You can call me Doe. Everyone does."

"Do you have any children?"

Daisy (she of the bold approach) was hoping to find a friend, Joanna knew. The move to Bethlehem had been exciting at first, but school didn't start for another month, and the kids were getting tired of each other. Their only other playmate over the past weeks had been Harriet, the maid. Dear old Harriet. If she was tired of pretending to look high and low for them as she dusted and polished, she hadn't let on.

"Our little girl is all grown-up and moved away." As Doe gazed at the swing, a shadow drifted across her face. "Her daddy rigged that up, oh . . . I guess it must have been about fifty years ago. But our grandson Daniel replaced the ropes this year." Her expression brightened. "I think that old swing is happy to feel the weight of some real children for a change, and not just that sweet little redheaded fellow who is nothing but air."

Charlie and Daisy were speechless, staring at the woman with expressions that swung from suspicion to wonder.

A little warning signal flashed in the back of Joanna's mind: *Bats in the belfry.* "I'm sure Mrs. Janssen—Doe—is joking," she said evenly, hoping the woman would take the hint and stop sowing nightmares.

But Doe continued with breezy aplomb. "Oh, but I'm not. We have all sorts of souls wandering around here. There is a band of Union soldiers, for instance. And I do mean *band*. Drum . . . bugle . . . banjo. They can make quite a racket." She paused for a beat, looking over at a section across the way. "It's lovely, though, when the young fellow from Easton plays his harmonica. *'Oh Shenandoah . . . I long to hear you. . . .'*" Her voice piped out in warbling vibrato.

Now Daisy was rapt, begging for more. "Who else do you see? Are there any more children?" The macabre implications didn't even register, so giddy was she at the prospect of meeting some new friends. Charlie, however, couldn't hide the cloud of anxiety that drifted across his face. He made a sudden scan of the surrounding headstones, and his hand snaked into his mother's as he pressed against her hip.

"What's this over here?" Joanna was on her feet in a preemptive strike, taking the children in hand to a neighboring headstone, where a small ceramic dachshund stood sentry. As distractions went it was somewhat uninspiring, but at this point Joanna was doing what she could—and was beginning to regret her earlier impulse.

St. Gregory's Cemetery sat high above the Lehigh River, overlooking the voluptuous river valley and beyond to the broad heft of South Mountain. Joanna had been there before, but only under sad circumstances and in a large procession of people. Since moving to Bethlehem, however, she had a new appreciation for its verdant beauty. Each time she walked to town, she passed the gates: despite the irony, there was a quality about the graveyard that was somehow inviting. She couldn't help being drawn to the serenity of what her aunt Martha always referred to as the "marble orchard." And so today, as she and the children were returning from a trip to the five-and-dime, she had decided it couldn't hurt to go in and let them roam. Now she wasn't so sure.

"We do find the occasional memento." Doe had followed them, shifting to a less spectral subject. "There are the usual love letters, rabbit's feet, lockets, and such. A pocket watch here and there. One time there was a plastic snowman, and once, an old musket. Not loaded." She was squinting to re-member. "And there was a stethoscope. That was from poor old Doc Maxwell. He couldn't be convinced his wife had died. He'd walk around town looking high and low, until he remem-bered she was here. Then he'd lie on the grass and listen through his stethoscope for signs of life through the dirt." She shook her head. "His daughter didn't know what to do about it. It was a blessing when he joined Millie here." Remember-ing Joanna's question, she considered the dachshund for a moment. "This one's new, dear. We'll leave it for now. Every dog has his day, as they say. Which reminds me . . ." Leaning forward, she inveigled the children with a dramatic stage whis-per: "If you want to really see something, come with me."

As they wound through canopies of elm and oak, sycamore and dogwood, Joanna trailed behind, taking it all in. The natural beauty was idyllic, and yet somehow the smooth stone of the carved monuments managed to improve upon it—no small feat. Even the plain zinc markers lent an austere, elemental grace. Many dated from before the Civil War, their inscriptions barely legible. Each one seemed to call to Joanna, a faint petition: *Recognize me once more—that I should exist again.* But Doe forged ahead in front of her—inured, probably, to the brief, beckoning narratives—so Joanna passed them by, apologetic at heart.

At a large trapezoidal slab, Doe stopped. On inspection, it would have been easy to pick out the carved image of a noble-looking canine just below the dated inscription. This detail, however, was overwhelmed by the blindsiding distraction of an actual dog, lying motionless across the mounded grass—a German shepherd with glassy eyes and a tattered, mangy coat.

Charlie's face was a study in shock. His eyes opened nearly as wide as his mouth, and he reflexively grabbed at his mother's skirt as he failed to suppress a strangled cry.

Doe was contrite through her laughter. "I guess I should have warned you," she cackled. "This poor soul, Macpherson, loved that dog so much, he hired a taxidermist when he died. His daughter brought Shep over the other day—she was finally cleaning out the shed and found her dad's old companion. She couldn't bear to just throw him away. I didn't have the heart to turn her down. But when Daniel mows this section, old Shep's days are numbered."

Daisy was on the ground, gently stroking the mottled fur, not bothered in the least by the animal's lifelessness. At the mention of Doe's grandson, she turned to ask, "Could Daniel come out and play with us?" Her little face was so beseeching—brows knit and eyes hoping—that Joanna reflexively took a mental snapshot, depositing the small, insignificant moment into her memory bank of images. Oh, how she loved five. Five was wondrous. Five was artless, unaware, wide-open, and heartbreakingly sweet. Five hadn't started school yet, hadn't begun the steady, inevitable journey toward self-consciousness, contrivance, comparison, and all the other encumbrances of growing up. Charlie was only six, yet already she could tell a difference.

Doe looked into the distance. "He's already out here, somewhere. I thought we would have seen him by now." Her face lit up as a figure came into view. "There he is! Yoo-hoo!" she called, waving her hand high in the air.

The man walking across the southern edge of the property—along the ridge overlooking the river and the valley—waved back and started to make his way across the rolling sea of green, pushing a wheelbarrow. Daisy's face fell.

"Daniel came to us six years ago," Doe said, turning to Joanna, confidential. "Our daughter, Sarah, married Amish. She and Samuel live in Lancaster. They have seven children now. Because of their . . . ways . . . we've never been welcome in their lives." The words were coated with a dim patina of pain, but as her grandson drew closer, she brushed her hands together and lifted her chin. "But Daniel was cut from a different bolt. He's independent, that boy. He studied for his diploma when he first got here, and then went to work in the Pittsburgh mines to save. He's going to be an engineer. Takes night classes at Lehigh. In another year, he'll be working his way right up the ladder at Bethlehem Steel, mark my words."

They observed him like spectators as he cut over to the path, finally wheeling up to tip his straw hat. He wiped his brow with a red bandanna, and his manner was almost courtly. "Hello," he said solemnly. "How are you?" Joanna half expected him to make a small bow. He had the clearest, lightest blue eyes she had ever seen. They were nearly translucent. She was reminded of the Siberian husky that had lived down the street when she was a young girl. She had always found that dog's pale eyes slightly disturbing.

Doe made her happy introduction. "This is Joanna Collier, new to town but part of a very old family here."

Daniel hesitated as Joanna extended her hand, looking askance at his own before clasping hers. "Sorry . . . occupational hazard."

Despite the grimy effects of grounds-keeping, his hand felt warm and smooth, and his gaze was so direct and steady that Joanna felt a strange discombobulation. Too abruptly, she pulled her hand back.

Doe didn't seem to notice as she rested her own hands on two small shoulders. "And for our amusement, she has very generously brought us these adorable puppets. They're called Charlie and Daisy." She tugged lightly on their collars as though they had strings.

Though shy, Charlie was sharp. With a deadpan expression, he shot out one arm and one leg, then tilted his head to the side, staring blankly. Joanna was always a little surprised when Charlie did anything goofy—he was usually a pretty serious kid. Daniel laughed and ruffled Charlie's hair. Daisy, for once, was mute, her disappointment momentarily forgotten as she stared up at Daniel's pale eyes.

"Puppets, eh? Well, I wish I had time to stay for the show." He nodded at the wheelbarrow. "A person can't get dinner around here if the job's not done."

This was directed at Doe, and she winked at her grandson. "I bet if you pull the right strings, you could put these little dolls to work."

Daniel squatted down so his forearms rested across his knees. "I could use some help with the pruning. Have you ever given a haircut to a rhododendron before?"

Daisy's face lit up and she looked to her mother hopefully. "Can we do pruning? Please, Mama?" She was inordinately excited about the prospect, given the certainty that she had no idea what pruning was.

Joanna was skeptical. "Wielding a hedge clipper may be a bit above your pay grade." Trailing her fingers through her daughter's neat bangs, she leaned down to kiss the little girl on the forehead. "But I think you two would make excellent assistants."

"Come on, then." Daniel grabbed the handles of the wheelbarrow and started off. "You can be my cleanup crew. Who wants to use the rake?"

The children fell in behind him, loudly vying for the rake and keeping so close, they were practically stepping on his boots. As they moved away, Daniel turned back. "I'll be coming for that dog"—he arched an eyebrow reproachfully at his grandmother—"before old what's-his-name wanders by."

Doe grinned as she watched the small parade cross over to the hedges bordering the tall iron fence. "Mr. Janssen has had it with me, letting people leave their tokens. He says this place would look like a yard sale if he didn't put his foot down."

Joanna looked around and saw a plot with a small figurine of the Virgin Mary leaning against the headstone, but for the most part there were just simple urns of carnations or roses to represent the grieving. She turned back to Doe, who was now pulling a handful of stealthy yarrow from behind a bench. Though *inveterate tease* and *just plain nuts* still vied for the verdict, Joanna was grateful for the woman's kindness. "Thank you. It's getting to be a long summer. We moved in at the beginning of June and they don't have any friends yet. School can't start soon enough."

Doe moved around the bench and then took a seat, patting the spot beside her. For a while they sat in companionable silence, and Joanna luxuriated in the serenity of her surroundings. Eventually she remarked on the fine weather, and Doe declared the necessity of a clear day for making fudge, moving on to the fullness of the late-blooming azaleas, and the recent *Good Housekeeping* article about Mrs. Kennedy. And then she steered the conversation in a more personal direction.

"How is Susannah these days? It was a real shock, Wyatt Collier dying so suddenly like that." She shook her head mournfully.

A shock, yes. Joanna could still see her husband's face as he dragged himself home that night, grief etched in his exhausted eyes. She thought he had been working late again—she hadn't known the past hours had forged a terrible odyssey, that Frank had held his father in the ambulance, refusing to follow in the car, that he had insisted the doctors continue their efforts, despite the obvious futility. At eight o'clock that night, Joanna could not have known that Frank was shuffling up the wide front steps at Brynmor—bearer of tragic news, summoning whatever emotional strength he could as he limped down the long hall to tell his mother that her husband was gone.

"She is amazingly stoic," Joanna replied. "Such a long, devoted marriage . . . and yet she has never shown a crack. I don't know how she does it."

Though sixty's shadow loomed ever larger, Susannah Parrish Collier was still a beautiful woman. Her jawline remained firm, and her eyes were a deep indigo, though her blond hair—

worn in sleek chignon—had softened to a creamy buff. Frank had her fair coloring, but he had his father's cleft chin and hazel-gray eyes. Father and son had also shared an identical build—not tall, but broad-shouldered and solid. But, most distinctive, Frank had his father's demeanor—open, sweet, uncomplicated.

In Joanna's opinion, the word *uncomplicated* would never be used to describe her mother-in-law. It wasn't that she was temperamental or unbalanced or even difficult—but she was private to the point of being enigmatic. Just the other day Joanna and the children had come upon her on the landing of the grand staircase at Brynmor. She seemed frozen there, staring into the distance as she grasped the banister. She didn't even notice the trio coming down the stairs until they were practically on top of her. She flinched when she finally saw them—snapping out of it like a parishioner caught nodding off during the sermon. There was a slightly awkward rite of small exchanges—"how are you today . . . we're off to the library . . . enjoy yourselves"—but her gaze fixed oddly on Charlie. It was strange the way she looked at her small grandson. Joanna had noticed it on some level before—a fleeting, private wistfulness in the wake of an unguarded moment. It had registered with Joanna formlessly, like a low, melancholy chord from some distant requiem.

Doe sighed, pulling Joanna back into the moment. "I suppose we're all tempered by the trials we've faced. . . ." She rested her gaze on a nearby oak, majestic in its twisted expanse, and her next words were uttered almost under her breath: "Some more than others." Rather abruptly, she moved on. "And how do you find living at Brynmor?"

Hesitating slightly, Joanna gave a meek shrug. "I guess I'm still getting used to it. I thought—we thought—that moving here would make things easier, what with the commute and Frank traveling so much. He had been talking about it for a while, and I was starting to see his point. I'd never considered that we wouldn't have a place of our own, but after his father died, Frank felt that he couldn't leave his mother and grandmother in that big house by themselves. It all got decided so fast—" She stopped, mindful of her audience. If Doe was, indeed, a friend of Frank's grandmother, she didn't want to put the wrong foot forward. But she needn't have worried—her new acquaintance was sympathetic.

"I imagine it's not easy. *The position of mistress of the manor has been filled—we are no longer accepting applications,*" Doe intoned dramatically.

Mistress of the manor. Joanna wondered to which mistress Doe was referring. The idea of moving into the family home—the venerable, imposing Brynmor—was overwhelming in itself. But the fact that her curiously unfathomable mother-in-law lived there too, along with Frank's impeccable grandmother, placed Joanna in the tricky situation of living with two mistresses, as it were.

Brynmor was not Susannah's house, not yet. It belonged to her aging mother, Helen—known to close friends as Hedy.

When Hollins Parrish died, Susannah and Wyatt had tried to convince Helen to move in with them. Their own home was only blocks away on Wyandotte Street, and although it did not have the grand privilege of bearing a name, there was more than enough room for all of them. But Helen had refused to leave. She missed her husband terribly—they had been together for nearly sixty years—and the idea of moving out of their home was untenable.

Of course, she wasn't entirely alone. There were still house and grounds staff—maids and gardeners and a cook and a driver . . . but servants notwithstanding, the house was ridiculously large for one elderly woman. And then, the following winter, Helen fell and broke her hip.

Susannah's sister, India, who lived in Baltimore, was the one to suggest that Wyatt and Susannah take over Brynmor instead. India and her husband, Paul, had never had children and they traveled extensively. "We have no intention of returning to Bethlehem," she'd stated emphatically. "And you know Kit has no interest." Their brother, Kit, had long ago moved to South America to run a large iron-mining operation, and had put down deep roots. "Sell your place and take Brynmor," India had insisted. "It's yours. We don't want it." The obvious implication was that neither India nor Kit was particularly eager to suffer the upheaval and shoulder the responsibility of caring for their aging mother, and so the bargain was struck.

It was a cruel twist that left the two women alone together, so to speak, when Wyatt died just three years later. And that was when Frank sat Joanna down one night in their moderate and manageable home in Chestnut Hill and confessed his guilt and worry about leaving his mother all alone with the burden of caring for Helen.

To be fair, Joanna should have seen it coming. Moving to Bethlehem had been a discussion topic for some time, and to say that Brynmor was large enough for all of them was an understatement. Certainly, there were items in the "against" column. All of their furniture—the things she had chosen so carefully to make their house a home, things that had come to represent their history—would have to be sold or stored. And there were Joanna's parents to take into account. John and Eileen Rafferty lived in South Philadelphia—a retired policeman and his devoted wife. They relished the privilege of proximity, and they doted on their grandchildren. It would be a big adjustment for them, but Bethlehem was less than two hours away—it wouldn't be an impossible hardship to visit back and forth.

Well, that was all in the rearview mirror now. But Doe's teasing articulation made a point. Joanna responded with a weak smile: "*Mistress of the manor.* Are you referring to Helen or Susannah?"

Doe chuckled. "You do have a sticky situation, moving into a hive with two queen bees." She gave Joanna a complicit wink. "And it would be an adjustment for most anyone to call a house like Brynmor *home.*"

The words were welcome. It *wasn't* Joanna's home. Her in-laws could never be accused of being unaccepting—they were far too gracious to make Joanna feel like she was less than they were by virtue of her modest background. But there was just a way of being—standards and expectations and assumptions—to which she was alien. She was the daughter of a Philly cop. She was a nurse. She had put herself through school, working in the evenings at Bullock's Drugstore and then at Penn Hospital, where, after graduation, she'd taken a full-time position on staff in the orthopedics ward. That was where she'd met her husband. When Frank was seventeen, his father had taken him on his first assembly-line tour at Bethlehem Steel. Seven years later he'd needed one final surgery to repair the damage done by the steel railcar wheel that had fallen off the conveyance, crushing his foot.

It wasn't long before her patient moved out of bed 2C and began to turn up regularly at apartment 4D. And now here she was, transported from that cozy apartment in Philadelphia to the grand manor that was Brynmor, and despite Frank's repeated assurances that his family—what remained of it—was delighted to have them there, she couldn't help feeling like an outsider.

"The house is lovely, of course, and I'm glad for the chance to get to know Frank's grandmother better while I can. . . ." Too late, she realized the implication, and cringed. Helen and Doe had to be roughly the same age. Sheepishly, she continued. "But I'll admit, I'm finding his mother a bit . . . formidable. I guess I'm a little intimidated. She's just . . . hard to know."

Doe looked pensive. "Scratch the sphinx and spy the sparrow," she said cryptically.

"Excuse me?"

"I've learned a thing or two in my antiquity—chief among them that things are seldom what they seem. Often the person who appears the most . . . impenetrable . . . is, in truth, the most fragile."

Things are seldom what they seem. . . . Joanna could hear the music as plainly as if she were on the gymnasium stage, playing Buttercup in her high school production of *H.M.S. Pinafore*. The lyrics tiptoed through her memory in their ominous, staccato whisper, then swelled to a resonant augury:

Tho' a mystic tone I borrow, you shall learn the truth with sorrow. Suddenly Joanna felt a strange sense of foreboding. With an uneasy glance at the surrounding graves, she straightened her shoulders and changed the subject. "You mentioned a family resemblance in Charlie," she said, clearing her throat as she looked across the expanse toward the distant trio of gardeners. Her head tilted as she regarded her young son—slender and knobby-kneed, dark hair gleaming in the sun. "I've never been able to figure out who he resembles. I can't see myself or Frank."

"Oh, there's a resemblance, all right." Doe nodded. "That

little boy looks exactly like Chap Collier. Anyone who was around way back when would see it."

Joanna tried to remember if she had ever seen a photo of Chap. She knew her father-in-law had a brother who had died young—a brother named Charles but called Chap. When Frank wanted to name their son after his paternal grandfather, Charles, it hadn't occurred to Joanna that the baby would also be named for Frank's long-deceased uncle.

Then she thought of the traces of her own brother, David, in his little namesake. Daisy was actually Davida, in honor of Joanna's only sibling—struck and killed by a car when Joanna was seven. She had felt a wrenching twist in her heart the first time she saw him in her daughter's deep dimples, and the little wrinkle on the bridge of her nose when she smiled. How strange—almost mystical—that each of her children would resemble the ancestors with whom they shared a name.

Looking at her watch, Joanna realized that half an hour had passed since Charlie and Daisy had been foisted—however charmingly—upon Daniel. She thought of Doe's bucket and spade, abandoned by the swing. "My goodness—you must have things to do. And I'm sure Daniel has had enough 'help' by now."

Doe rose slowly, placing a hand on her lower back. "A fine reward for all those years of stooping," she said, turning toward the house. "Looks like he's finally tackling the rose-bushes." She ushered Joanna to a path that led to the backyard of the house, although *yard* wasn't really the word for it, as it wasn't delineated in any proper way from the graveyard itself. There was a barbecue grill just a few paces from a carved statue of a young girl holding a basket of flowers—a graceful tribute to someone once named Gertrude Schaller, who'd died in 1918. Other headstones of varying sizes were sprinkled right up to the house. Charlie was holding a gunnysack as Daniel clipped the thorny stems, but Daisy was off in her own world, kneeling next to a small granite headstone. The little marker was situated right next to a wrought-iron garden table and chairs. As the women approached, she jumped up and ran to her mother.

"Mama, come and see this. I found a little baby grave. It doesn't have a name. Just 'Baby.'"

"It does too have a name," Charlie called over his shoulder. "Just not a first name. It's Baby Hayes." His tone was slightly condescending.

Daisy took her mother's hand, practically pulling her to the marker. Pointing solemnly to the brief epitaph, the little girl leaned down to pat the stone. "Poor Baby Hayes. Didn't you have a mama?"

It *was* strange and sad; the absence of identity struck Joanna. There was no other inscription—no sweet send-off quoting Matthew 19, no carved angels, not even a date.

"Of course it had a mother," Charlie said. "Babies can't be born without a mother, ding-dong."

Concern overrode umbrage, and the mild insult rolled right

off Daisy's back. "I wouldn't like to be called *Baby*. If I had a baby, I would give it a name."

Suddenly Joanna had the pressing urge to move along. The peculiar events of the afternoon had left her feeling disconcerted and vaguely anxious. "I guess we'll never know, but what we do know is that we need to let these nice people get on with their business. You two could use a bath before dinner." She took Charlie's hand as he put down the gunnysack, but Daisy was reaching up to give Doe's gardener's apron a little tug.

"Do *you* know who Baby Hayes is?"

As the words left Daisy's mouth, Doe's open, sunny countenance clouded over. She rested her hand lightly on Daisy's head, and her voice was soft. "In this world, petunia, there are some things we're just not meant to know." She turned away, readjusting her apron, and then said, "I'd better go check on my patient—the boss is down with a cold today." She gave a little wave as she climbed the short stairway to the back door. "Don't be strangers—there's plenty more fun where that came from," she said, nodding at the gunnysack stuffed with bramble.

Joanna and the children waved back as Doe disappeared into the house. Above them, two birds began to quarrel, darting at each other with peppery commotion. Suddenly one of the small, feathered missiles dropped from the sky, saving itself in a last-minute swoop that brushed Joanna's cheek, shivery and repellent. "Oh!" She gave a little shout, instinctively crouching. Charlie reached out to his mother in alarm, but Daisy just laughed at the spectacle.

"There is special providence in the fall of a sparrow." The words came low and portentous. Daniel was watching with serious eyes, but as Joanna straightened and visibly shuddered, he drily raised a brow: *"Hamlet."* Then he tipped his hat with courteous formality, and Joanna was struck again by the unsettling, lucid directness of his gaze. Her back stiffened as she turned away, a reflexive response to the prickly feeling that some private part of her was exposed.

Two

"I could put the worm on by myself."

"No."

"Come on, Kit, just for a little while."

"You said you just wanted to come along and watch. I'm not here to watch *you* drag a line."

Susannah angled her foot to create a wake in the warm August water. "You're just afraid I'll get a bigger fish." She leaned back on her elbows and turned her face to the sun, a sham pose of serenity that she held for only a few moments before her hand shot up and batted the cork handle of the fishing rod.

"Knock it off, Sass." Kit lunged to grab the fishing rod before it sailed into the river. "You're lucky that didn't go in. You'd be next." His patience with his little sister was wearing thin.

"You can hold my pole," Wyatt said from the opposite

corner of the raft, then looked down quickly as his words registered.

Explosive laughter split the heavy summer air as the two older boys slapped their knees and doubled over. "I'll thank you to keep your dirty propositions away from my sister," Kit said, practically choking.

Chap shook his head in disbelief. "Cripes, Wyatt, you say the dumbest things." But he was smiling at his brother, and reached over to give him a fond shove on the shoulder.

A deep shade of red would have been visible to anyone standing on the banks of the river, had they noticed the boy on the front of the raft with his face turned toward the water.

"You two are horrid. Poor Wyatt. Just ignore them." India stood up gingerly, taking a couple of careful steps to the other side. She sat down next to Wyatt and patted his back. "I think that was sweet. I'd like to try my hand, if you don't mind."

This provoked another bout of uncontrollable mirth. Chap had to sit down, holding his shaking sides, and Kit hid his face in the crook of his arm. "Oh dear God." His voice was muffled.

Taking the fishing rod gently from Wyatt's hand, India said, "Don't pay any attention to Kitty. He's just a mean old cat."

Kit bristled. India knew exactly how to get under his skin. "Don't waste a perfectly good night crawler on Itty," he scolded Wyatt. "She wouldn't know she had a bite if it took her arm off."

India turned and raised one eyebrow at her brother. "Meow."

Kit glared at her. "Itty-it."

The Parrish family, with its long history of carrying given names down the line, had a penchant for nicknames. As the fifth Hollins Parrish, Kit's was selected from the rather limited options yet available; and Itty was simply his toddler interpretation of his baby sister's name. Given India's diminutive stature, it stuck. When Susannah came along, it took her almost no time to earn her sobriquet. Emerging from an exile prompted by naughty misbehavior, she had leveled her three-year-old gaze at her mother and demanded an answer: "Are you ready to be nice now?" From the start, Susannah had a bold and disarming sassiness that could charm a Gorgon.

She now pulled her foot out of the water and sat up, stretching and yawning. "I could probably catch a fish with my hand before any of you get even a nibble." She leaned over to dangle her fingers in the water.

Wyatt turned around to watch her, a habit he seemed unable to shake. From the moment he had laid eyes on Susannah, his compass could point in one direction only. He had fixed solidly on his true north, and the arrow hadn't so much as wiggled over the past four years.

The Collier family had come to Bethlehem on the galvanizing thrust of the war in Europe. In 1914, Bethlehem Steel had begun to roar with warfare's terrible bounty—both England and France were placing orders for ordnance, and stock was nearing six hundred dollars a share. At the helm of the company sat Hollins Parrish, who took personal responsibility for ensuring that his new head engineer—one with the best faculty and expertise in the industry—was received with warmth and favor. Welcoming Charles to "the company" meant that he and his wife, Frances, and their sons, Chap and Wyatt, were also welcome to the baronial and bustling Brynmor . . . and to Helen Parrish's splendid table.

In the course of the past few years, the families had become inseparable. Hollins and Charles not only worked side by side, they were dedicated golf and squash partners. Helen and Frances played in the same canasta group and were officers in the Ladies Auxiliary and the Bethlehem Garden Club. But the friendship between Chap Collier and Kit Parrish was closest of all. Each was an eldest child and each bore his father's name—a mantle that came with both enormous privilege and daunting expectation. Perhaps it was this common circumstance that produced the brotherly bond, or perhaps it was the happy fact that they both possessed an easygoing, charismatic confidence. In any case, they shared nearly every experience and the admiration of their friends. These days, however, they also shared a nearly complete disregard for younger sisters. While they were usually good-natured about letting Wyatt tag along, the older boys wanted very little to do with India or Susannah. In fact, at age sixteen they would have more willingly taken the town librarian on their fishing expedition that morning, but they had been blackmailed by a twelve-year-old girl, and Susannah had magnanimously shared the ransom with her sister.

After a few minutes of letting India fish, Wyatt once again gave in to his hectoring heart. Leaning close, he said under his breath, "Maybe we should give Sassy a chance."

India patted his shoulder as she stood—she had a veiled empathy for Wyatt's case. "Here, Sass, it's your turn."

As intermediary, Chap grabbed the pole—inadvertently forcing a blush as his hand brushed India's. Oblivious, he made the toss to Susannah and went back to his captain's shift, guiding the raft with the skill of a seasoned gondolier.

Susannah flicked the line and made a very good cast. She turned to Kit and narrowed her eyes. "Watch and learn."

Kit just shook his head. "If you catch anything, it will be a cold from when I toss you into the river."

The quintet floated in silence for a time as the raft drifted slowly past the leafy banks, lulled to lethargy in the wavy shimmer of the late-summer haze. The Lehigh River wound from the ridges of the Appalachian Mountains through the heart of the Lehigh Valley, zigzagging along the lush gorge until it joined the waters of the Delaware on its path to Cape May. But the soothing somnolence of the river was shattered by a sudden squeal as Susannah jumped to her feet. "I felt something! I felt a tug!"

"Reel it in!"

"Don't reel too fast!"

"Give it a jerk!"

"Use your wrist!"

The instructions were flying fast and furiously, but Susannah was slim and light, and the fish was patently not. She flew off the raft as though the thing were reeling *her* in.

One second later, Wyatt was in the water.

Susannah came up just fine, but she had lost her grip on the rod, which was still attached to the fish and heading west. Sassy Parrish was not a girl who would lose her brother's fishing rod. She had left her stockings and shoes on the riverbank, tucked under a yew, but her skirt was heavy against her legs. Fortunately, she was swimming with the current, and there was a bit of leeway while the fish ran out the reel. She was just within reaching distance when the slack ran out and the pole leaped forward.

Wyatt wasn't far behind, and there was plenty of shouting from the raft.

"Leave her and get the rod!" Kit was cursing under his breath, hoping the cork would keep it afloat, while Chap stood by unhelpfully, calling out feeble advice through gales of laughter.

"Go get 'er, Wyatt! Try the backstroke! Watch out for snapping turtles!"

India had grabbed the barge pole and was stabbing through the water in an attempt to slow down the raft. Kit and Chap had been careful about keeping them close to shore, well within reach of the river bottom, but in the clamor, they had drifted and now they were out of their depth. They were picking up speed as the raft veered into the main current.

In what would have been a stroke of luck, the fish shot under a partially submerged fallen tree, snagging and snapping the line. The fishing rod lodged in a fork. But the raft was enjoying its liberty, and they could only watch the rod disappear as they sailed past the tangled limbs. At that point, Kit evidently reconsidered his priorities and turned his attention to his sister. "Just leave it, Sass!" he had to shout now as the distance grew. "Come on—you're losing ground!"

Susannah could be stubborn, but she wasn't foolish. She struck out after the raft, kicking against her twisting skirt, and as she got close, her brother lay on his stomach and reached out to grab her hand.

Wyatt, however, lagged behind, fighting a helical current that was pulling him toward the bank. Chap had stopped laughing and was standing aft, his hands to his mouth, hollering imperatively at his little brother. "Come on, Wyatt! We can't come back for you! You can make it!"

Susannah threw one leg up onto the old boards and Kit heaved her up, while India wrung her hands and peered worriedly back at Wyatt. "I knew this was a bad idea," she said to no one in particular. "We are going to be in so much trouble."

Wyatt's struggling form was growing smaller and smaller. The group was quiet for a moment, bewildered by the expanding distance, but then they realized with relief that Wyatt was swimming to shore. Chap made one more effort to communicate, cupping his hands to his mouth with a feeble and ridiculous "Don't forget the rod!" The boys looked at each other and broke into laughter again.

"Poor sucker." Kit was shaking his head. "The road to hell is paved with good intentions."

Chap rolled his eyes and turned to take the barge pole from India. "Girl intentions," he said drily.

"He'll have a good walk home from there," Kit said, grinning at the thought. "Maybe he'll dry out by then."

"I don't know what you think is so funny," India said. "You're going to be in worse trouble than any of us. When Hep finds out you took these barrels, you're finished. And look at Sassy's dress." Susannah was wringing out the hem, but the batiste cotton was a dripping morass and had a six-inch tear where it had snagged on one of the rough planks.

India's concern wasn't unfounded. At the beginning of the summer, Kit and Chap had come up with a plan to build a raft. It took some doing, but over the course of a few weeks they had managed to steal eight small oil drums from the steelyard, along with what used to be Henrik Hansen's shed. To be fair, the old toolshed had been abandoned for years. The hardest part was finding a long enough barge pole. They had finally come up with the idea of sneaking into the forging plant to steal a fifteen-foot furnace rod from the No. 2 machine shop.

"The only way he'll find out is if you tell him, Itty," Kit

said accusingly. Then he turned to Susannah and narrowed his eyes. "You'd better think up a whopper, Susannah."

Only in rare circumstances did Kit ever call his youngest sister by her given name, so Susannah knew she was on thin ice. The boys' plan that day had not included the girls. They had made the usual arrangements with Ben Swenson to pick them up two miles downriver, at Bryce's Landing. Ben was a local dairy farmer who had a hay wagon that made a perfect trailer for hauling the raft back to the grove near the flats where they kept it. Most of the time they had to wait awhile, but eventually Ben would get there with his ancient plow horse, Guvner, and for fifty cents he would help them load the raft onto the wagon and pull it to the grove.

That morning, however, the boys made the critical error of retrieving their fishing gear from the shed behind the stables at Brynmor just as Susannah had finished grooming Pericles, her little Arabian gelding. With the stealth of a leopard, she followed them to the river, and—with no real intention of actually blowing the whistle—handily extorted an invitation. Then, pushing her advantage, she ran to get her sister.

As it was turning out, unwanted guests weren't the only challenge of the day. Bryce's Landing was just a sliver of brown on the bank as they tried and failed to navigate the current with no oar. The boys were shirtless already, but now Chap was taking off his belt and rolling up the legs of his pants. He turned to Kit, a grim twist on his lips. "We're gonna have to get in."

The current was moving faster as the river widened, and although the boys kicked furiously as they grasped the edges of the two portside drums, it was nearly impossible even to keep up with the raft, much less steer it. But, in an effort laced with stifled profanities, they somehow managed to push out of the current. Susannah had been testing the depth with the pole, but by the time she felt the river bottom, the boys were making better progress from the water, and they finally shoved the vessel onto a sandy strip about a half mile south of the landing.

With heaving chests, Kit and Chap flopped onto the deck, lying back, their eyes closed to the sun. "Now what?" Kit exhaled the question with a huff of frustration and more than a little annoyance. There was no road through the thick arboreal cover where they had come ashore, and no way Ben could get his wagon through.

"Could we just leave it here?" Susannah asked, wanting to be helpful. She was fully aware of her culpability. "Hep could have a boat come and tow it."

There was no response from either of the boys. Chap had covered his eyes with the crook of his arm, and Kit just groaned. India was looking around futilely, but then she had an idea.

"It looks pretty clear along the shore. Maybe you could walk it back in the water."

The boys sat up and looked upriver. It *did* appear to be pretty smooth going, with no fallen trees in sight, but it wasn't a straight shot and they couldn't see beyond the first bend.

Forty minutes later they were sliding the raft up the apron of the landing. On the way, they had been forced to float it around a tangled strainer of limbs and a rock jetty, but the current was far weaker in the shallow water. As they were pulling the ropes to hoist it onto the bank, they noticed the back of the wagon moving away up the road, and Kit had to run, hollering and waving his arms, to get Ben's attention.

It took some maneuvering to turn Guvner around—in his old age the horse had only left turns remaining—but Ben finally worked his way back to the landing and the three men heaved the raft onto the wagon. Despite his rusticity, Ben was a gentleman. He courteously helped India and Susannah onto the buckboard, but then gave a weary, sour look to the boys, who had hopped up onto the wagon and were sitting on the raft. "You're gonna have to get off. Guv can't take that pile of junk plus the four of you up this hill."

Trudging up the hill behind the wagon, the boys shook their heads and grumbled while the sisters turned around to wave and smile, gleefully rubbing it in with calls of "Nice day for a walk!" and "Such lovely weather we're having." At the top of the rise, Kit hoisted himself onto the back of the wagon and held his hand out to Chap, but Guvner stopped dead and wouldn't budge until they got off again.

At the grove, Ben was awarded a dollar to compensate for his extra time and trouble, and he set off to the left as they tucked the raft away in the underbrush. When India sat down to pull on her lisle stockings, Chap picked up one of her shoes and peered at it intently. "Looks like a doll's shoe. Can you really get your foot into it?" He ran his finger down the long row of small buttons. "This seems like a lot of work."

India was tongue-tied, and a tide of red rolled up her neck and headed for her cheeks. Susannah responded for her sister. "It *is* a lot of work. Especially when we don't have a hook." Exasperated, she left half of the loops on her own shoes hanging open.

Recovering some composure, India found her voice. "I wonder if Wyatt made it back yet. Do you think he'll tell on us?"

"Nah. He's smarter than he looks." The affection in Chap's tone belied the faint praise of his words. "I bet I'll find him on the porch with his face in a book and Hilda serving cake and lemonade."

The girls finally got their shoes buttoned, and they headed up the hill on a dirt path. On a particularly steep pitch, India slipped. As it happened, Chap was behind her. With reflexive ease, he grabbed her by the waist and set her back on leveler ground. "Light as a moth," he remarked. "Maybe those really are doll shoes."

Susannah—who never missed a thing—sidled up to her nearly quivering sister and whispered, "You're the moth and he's the flame." And India slipped again.

They made it through town without fanfare; the streets were fairly empty and they knew the quietest ones. India was still in the stars as they reached the lofty air of Fountain Hill—

the privileged demesne of Bethlehem's most fortunate daughters and sons—but Chap turned off toward Seneca Street, and as they approached Brynmor, she pulled herself back to Earth. "Wait behind the garage," she instructed Susannah, "and don't let Jimmy see you. I'll get another dress."

Susannah skirted the wide cobblestone drive toward the new five-stall garage built in front of the stables. Jimmy, the Parrishes' driver, lived above the garage in the chauffeur quarters, but he was probably down below, polishing the Winton touring car or the Templar roadster. Hollins Parrish had a fondness for automobiles.

Since it was Saturday afternoon, they knew their father would be on the golf course. And, as luck would have it, their mother was preoccupied with the business of grooming. If Helen and Hollins Parrish weren't entertaining guests on a Saturday evening, they had inevitable social obligations and could be found at the Fountain Hill Opera House or a St. Luke's Hospital benefit or—as was the case this evening—a white-tie affair for the executive officers of Bethlehem Steel. In preparation for the event, their mother had been busy in her room with a hair stylist hired in from town and Lydia, the upstairs maid who doubled as a lady's maid. This distraction played well for the erstwhile river rats, who scurried into the shadows of the house without so much as a squeal.

That evening when Elvie rang the dinner bell, they drifted to the breakfast room from their individual innocent occupations. The younger Parrishes were accustomed to being served at the small walnut breakfast table on Saturdays, as the opulent formality of the dining room—with its long, gleaming mahogany table—seemed ridiculous when populated solely by children.

On the way out, their parents appeared in the doorway. "Well, well, Hedy, what have we here?" Hollins said, unwilling to relinquish the teasing tone he'd taken with the children since they were toddlers. "Isn't that the smithy's son from the stables? And what of these pretty little girls? Are these the new housemaids?" He moved around the table, kissing each of them on the top of the head as he spoke. Tall and dignified, Hollins Parrish was imposing to most, but his children found him endearingly harmless. Although he was Dad or Daddy face-to-face, they tended to call him Hep when they were talking about him. It was the name his wife and friends called him—born of his monogram.

Helen was known by her friends as Hedy, but her children only called her Mother. She was a delicately beautiful woman, born in London to a preeminent banking family and raised in the Back Bay of Boston. Because her blue blood ran exceptionally warm, she was beloved by persons stationed high and low. "They are vagrants," she said, smiling as she pulled on her gloves. "We're feeding the needy tonight. I didn't want to, but Elvie insisted." Turning to the children, she said, "Please go to bed at a decent hour, you hooligans. We're leaving promptly at nine for church in the morning, and I don't want a struggle on my hands." Taking her husband's arm, she blew a kiss as they left, trailing a wake of Vetiver and elegance.

As the rumble of the car engine faded away, there was another sound—a tapping at the window. Elvie was serving small tulip cups of tapioca pudding, and Kit had to lean around her to see Chap peering into the room. Kit shook his head and put a finger to his lips, then made a discreet jabbing motion toward Elvie, but she had eyes in the back of her head and spoke without turning. "I suppose you should invite Mister Charles in," she said placidly.

When Kit got to the door, Chap was waiting. His face was drawn and there was a frightful look in his eyes—walking the razor's edge of panic. "Wyatt isn't home. He never came home." His expression spoke loud and clear: *Please tell me nothing has happened to him. Please tell me he's all right. Please don't let it be possible that he's not.*

Without a backward glance, Kit was out the door—taking the wide marble steps two at a time, Chap right beside him. They flew down the hill and crossed the bridge on New Street, instinctively heading for the last place they had seen Wyatt. A short road ran along the ridge above the river; at the end of it they stumbled down through the underbrush and landed on a narrow dirt path that wound through the woods and followed the water. There was still enough daylight to see, but the thick canopy filtered it and the sun was ominously low.

"How far down do you think he was?" Chap asked, breathing hard but moving as fast as he could through the bramble.

"Did you actually see him get out of the water?" His voice rang sharp and imperative; fear had turned him into a drill sergeant, barking out questions.

"He's a good swimmer. He was really close to shore. Of course he made it." Kit was giving his best effort at reassurance, but his words were hollow—he was as worried as his friend. "Wyatt!" he shouted as they rushed through thicket. "Wyatt!" Chap joined in and they continued to call as they pushed along the path, stumbling over tree roots and rocks.

The light was disappearing fast as the sun went down, and darkness settled over them like a hood. Common sense said to get off the river and go for help, but desperation had the upper hand, forcing them forward with the foolish hope that they were going to find Wyatt there on the bank, safe and sound.

As they fought through an especially thick twist of undergrowth, they heard a faint sound. Chap stopped abruptly and held up his hand. "Shhh. What was that? Wyatt?" He craned his neck, listening. "Wyatt?" There it was again. Voices. As they peered through the woods they saw a flickering light in the distance. They moved forward, slower now—instinctually quiet and treading lightly on the sticks and fallen leaves.

"It's a fire," Kit whispered. "Smell the smoke?" He grasped Chap's arm, signaling him to stop. "It might be drifters." Wariness echoed in his voice. As schoolchildren, they had been warned many times to stay away from the tramp camps that dotted the river valley. Local lore about kid stew and roasted babies had disrupted plenty of bedtimes.

But urgency overrode childhood terrors, and they moved forward, straining to see through the dusk. Ridiculous as it was, the thought that Wyatt might somehow be sitting with the hobos, sharing a can of soup, had lodged hopefully in both of their chests.

As they neared the light they could see that it was, indeed, a small group of men, bearded and disheveled, sitting on crates around an oil drum fire. There was a smattering of conversation, but the words were impossible to make out. When the breeze blew east, subtle undertones of whiskey mingled with the smoke.

Suddenly Chap gasped. His eyes were wide and he was looking at a man sitting on the far side of the fire. Kit followed his gaze and swallowed hard. Wyatt hadn't been wearing a shirt when he dove into the river, but he had been wearing suspenders. Chap's outgrown trousers were too big for Wyatt, who at thirteen hadn't hit his growth spurt, but he liked to wear them fishing and he kept them up with a pair of bright yellow suspenders. It was too much to hope that the man holding a brown bottle would have his own yellow suspenders, relatively clean and bright in the light of the fire.

Chap looked to Kit mutely, the color draining from his face. At that moment, Kit heard something else; when he spun around, he was looking straight into a pair of gray pebble-like eyes set in a mud-colored face, framed by lank and matted hair.

A glinting flash revealed a knife poised at the man's side. And below the knife—secured around his waist by a length of twine—were Chap's outgrown trousers.

Grabbing Chap by the shirt, Kit started to run. Chap was quaking, nearly convulsive with blind panic. "Come on, come on!" Kit's command was a whispered hiss. Fueled by adrenaline, he virtually dragged his friend through the woods, scrambling blindly over roots and rocks. Grasping onto limbs and saplings, they somehow made it up the hill—despite the drag caused by Chap, looking wildly back into the darkness. When they came to the road, they had to stop, doubled over and gasping. Chap fell to his knees, shoulders heaving. Kit pulled him by the arm. "Get up! We have to get help!" He was shouting now, but couldn't think where to go.

Frantic, he scanned the road, but there wasn't a soul in sight. The police station was all the way across town on Washington, but he started in that direction—practically hauling Chap—hoping desperately to find help somewhere on the streets.

Suddenly Chap snapped out of it, taking off like a shot dog. He was sprinting with preternatural energy, elbows and knees pumping, heading back toward the bridge. Kit struggled to keep up, and could barely get his next words out: "Where are you going?"

There was no response—Chap flew across the bridge and straight up Broadway. Kit realized then that his friend was making for home. The Collier house on Seneca was much closer than the police station, but Kit knew that no one was there. The Colliers were with his own parents at the Steel Baron's Ball. Then it came to him: Chap was running for a car. Charles Collier did not have the extensive automobile collection that his boss did, but he had a Turnbull runabout that Chap knew how to drive.

Halfway up Broadway, he watched in amazement as Chap stopped dead in his tracks. Reeling back a few steps, he stood frozen on the street, staring at a cluster of cedars.

As Kit reached him—winded beyond sensibility—he heard a muffled shout.

"Over here!"

Though it was just a strangled hiss, they both knew the voice. They peered into the darkness, and after a moment a form stepped out of the cedars. And there was Wyatt, shivering and naked in the flickering gaslight of a streetlamp.

Chap fell backward. He sat straight down in the road, catching himself with his hands behind him. Then, silently, he leaned forward and put his head in his hands.

"HOLY MOTHER OF GOD, WYATT, WHAT HAPPENED?" Kit didn't mean to sound so harsh, but he couldn't control it.

Wyatt started to cry—silent tears rolling down his face— and Kit walked across the grass and put his arm around him. "You're all right. It's over. We'll get those guys. We can go to the cops." He was saying every soothing thing he could think of, but comfort in a situation like this was beyond his sixteen-year-old range, and it felt meaningless to him. He didn't know what had happened to Wyatt, and he wasn't sure he wanted to.

Chap stood up suddenly and took off his shoes and socks. Then he took off his pants and walked the pile over to Wyatt.

"I don't really need the shoes"—Wyatt somehow managed a small, wry smile through a staggered breath—"but thanks." He stepped into the pants, bunching the waistband in his fist. "I could probably make it home now, anyway. I had to hide in the woods until it got dark." He shivered. "Even then, it was hard to get across the bridge."

"Are you all right?" Chap was looking at his little brother with barely concealed dread, skirting the edge of the precipice, the free fall of knowing.

"Yeah, I'm fine. They didn't hurt me. They just wanted my clothes. They didn't even chase me when I ran."

Kit felt something unclench in his chest as he watched his best friend—standing in his undershorts—close his eyes and hang his head. Then Chap stepped forward and wrapped his arms around Wyatt. "You little ninny. You just about did it this time." He rubbed his hand roughly through Wyatt's hair. "You didn't have to go in after her, you know."

Wyatt was quiet for a moment. And then, muffled against his brother's chest, a small sigh escaped, and he responded the only way he could—weary and resigned. "Yes, I did."

Three

"We met a lady named Dough." The dinner roll in Charlie's hand had apparently triggered an association. "I think that's a funny name."

It took Joanna a moment to figure out what he meant. When it came to her, she laughed. "I think it's supposed to be like a mama deer, honey." She spelled it both ways for him.

Helen chuckled—a soft, creaky warble. "It's Dorothy, actually, but no one calls her that. I'm delighted you met! Dear Doe. How is she? Still talking about her ghosts?"

"She has a real dead dog, and a not real little boy who plays on the swing," Daisy said, leaning forward, her eyes wide for emphasis.

Charlie was not to be outdone. "I worked with Daniel," he said importantly. "We trimmed the rhododrumdrums and the roses." He held up his finger, bandaged now from a thorn Joanna had extracted.

"I worked too!" Daisy was determined, as usual, to put herself in league with her brother.

"You didn't work. You just played on that grave. That baby grave."

A sharp clink rang out across the table. Susannah had been pleasantly conversational over the course of dinner, discussing the pretty weather, the news that Justice Frankfurter had resigned, and—closer to home—the progress on the Burns Harbor plant. Frank's chair was empty yet again, and she felt it was important that the children understand why their father was absent. But when Charlie had introduced the topic of St. Gregory's, she became quiet. Now, as she cut a small slice of Cornish game hen, her knife slipped and clattered on the plate.

"I found a baby that doesn't have a name," Daisy said, her words weighty with her discovery. "Doe said, 'There are some things we're just not meant to know.'" She shook her head gravely.

Joanna couldn't help smiling at her daughter's mimicry, until she caught a look passing between Helen and Susannah. It was fleeting, but it registered nonetheless—obscure and covert.

"Daniel is there?" Helen cleared her throat in defiance of her aging vocal cords. "I'm glad to hear it. I never had the chance to meet him before he went to Pittsburgh, but I heard all about it. Doe was over the moon that he had come to them. What a blessing that he's back. Doe isn't much younger than

I, you know. She has been spreading herself thin at that place for too many years to count. Not to mention Nico—he must be eighty-five now. That Nicolaus Janssen is a miracle of nature. He started bringing in help for the digging, but never anyone permanent. I can remember—not long ago—finding him up to his neck in a hole." Her smile was highlighted by a perfect trace of Tea Rose lipstick—the same shade she had worn for fifty years. "Here I am being wheeled about or doing a dicey little dance with my cane, and those two are hopping around like spring chickens."

As Helen's quavering voice rambled along, Joanna thought there was something a bit . . . determined . . . about the discursion. And then Susannah advanced the ostensible campaign, turning to her mother with a question. "Sarah married a Mennonite, didn't she? I thought they were in Lancaster."

"Old Order Amish," Helen corrected her, and then turned to Joanna. "They're forbidden from using any worldly conveniences. Poor Doe and Nico have rarely seen their own grandchildren. But Daniel broke away from the Community—no small thing. He came to Doe and Nico, and then went to work in the coal mines."

"He's going to night school now, at Lehigh," Joanna reported. "He wants to be an engineer."

"Hmm." Susannah expelled a little huff of approval. "Good for him. I've never understood blind acceptance of rigid belief. . . ."

"Now, now, dear . . . judge not, that ye be not judged. . . ."

Helen tilted her head very subtly toward Joanna, but it didn't go unnoticed. That Joanna had been raised in a strict Irish Catholic household was something the Parrishes tended to ignore politely, as though averting their eyes from an embarrassing split seam. Joanna hadn't hesitated to point out to Frank that Episcopalians were only a few obligations shy of Catholic, but as Protestants, his family still viewed her religion with a leery eye. Helen's graciousness extended to all things, however, and the fact that Joanna now attended Sunday services with her husband and children at the Episcopal Church of the Nativity didn't hurt.

Susannah, however, wasn't willing to drop the subject. "Tell that to the German Reformation," she replied, with a wry little arch of the brow.

"What's a German Reformation?" Charlie was predictably curious, and he never settled for anything less than a full explanation.

"Oh my . . . here we go. . . ." Helen made a weak grimace.

"Well, Charlie, the German Reformation is why we're here. I'll give you a simple version." Susannah looked briefly at her mother: "Don't worry, I'm not going to get into selling indulgences and such." There was an intent gleam in her indigo eyes as she turned back to the children. "About five hundred years ago, there was only one Christian religion. It was known as Catholicism, because the word 'Catholic' means something that involves everyone. But the church didn't want people to be able to read the Bible on their own. The priests were afraid to let people have their own interpretations and come to their own conclusions. And most people couldn't speak or read Latin anyway, so even if they tried, they couldn't know for themselves what the Bible said. Then a man named John Wycliffe translated it into English because he thought that people should be able to read the Bible for themselves. For his troubles, he was burned at the stake."

She stated the last as a casual matter of fact, moving ahead as Charlie's and Daisy's eyes grew wide.

"After that, a group of people got together and decided that they would take the Bible as their only standard of faith, without any interpretation from a church. They settled in Germany and were doing just fine until Germany made Catholicism the official state doctrine, and that was the end of religious freedom."

By this point, her aging mother was giving Susannah a sidelong look, surreptitiously waving her hand. If Helen had imparted nothing else to her offspring, she'd taught them that it was in the poorest of taste to hold forth about religion in any social situation—particularly at the dinner table. And with a confirmed Catholic sitting in the next chair!

But Susannah continued, blithely ignoring her mother's signals. "In fact, that wasn't quite the end. There were a few survivors. They called themselves Unitas Fratrum, but they were known as the Hidden Seed. And a man called Count Zinzendorf invited them to live on his lands in Saxony, where they were free to practice individual religious beliefs.

Eventually, Count Zinzendorf came here to America, and brought this group with him. They became known as the Moravians, because Moravia was the place they were from originally. And they settled here in Pennsylvania and called the town Bethlehem."

She sat back, satisfied with her history lesson.

"Susannah, really. Must you?" Helen shook her head, resigned.

"Are we Moravians then?" Charlie asked.

"No. We're Episcopalians." Susannah had the decency to bestow a brief, acknowledging smile on Joanna, an unspoken concession to her forfeiture. "But that's because we get to choose, and that's the important thing." She sat back and took a sip of water, dabbing her mouth delicately with her napkin. "Do you know why this state is called Pennsylvania?" She had decided she wasn't finished after all.

"Because of pencils?" Daisy was eager to win a point.

This earned a smile from her grandmother. "No, because of William Penn. The name comes from his name, plus the word *sylvan*, which means 'woods.' William Penn was the reason Count Zinzendorf came here, because Penn, as a Quaker, believed that all men were equal under God. And that concept is also why we don't have a monarchy in America."

"What's a Quaker?"

Susannah paused, realizing her mistake. This could go on all evening.

Joanna came to the rescue: "Do you remember the picture of the man on the oatmeal container?"

"Yes, Quaker Oats!" Charlie was proud to make the connection.

"Well, that is William Penn, and that is a Quaker." Joanna closed the conversation, shaking out her napkin. But before she could signal Harriet that she had finished her meal, Daisy piped in with her own question.

"What's a monarchy?"

It was clear now that Susannah had launched a sizable armada. Joanna gave her mother-in-law a sympathetic smile, and then saved them all from further didactics with a concluding clap of her hands. "It means a king and a queen, which reminds me that you two have a chess game set up in the playroom. Let's get your pajamas on and we can practice until bedtime." She handed her plate to Harriet, checking herself too late. She may have imagined it, but she thought she saw Helen wince as she politely looked away, folding her hands in her lap and waiting patiently for Harriet to clear from the right.

As Joanna helped the children brush their teeth, she wondered if Frank would make it home in time to kiss them good night. When she had met him, he was a young plant manager at Bethlehem Steel, learning the industry ingot by ingot. The fact that his father was chief-in-command had nothing to do with Frank's career advancement—an engineering degree and compulsory time in the machine-shop trenches proved his bona fides. But Frank's real strength was people, and soon after Daisy was born he was made Director of Personnel. The title came with a cost—some evenings he didn't get back to Chestnut Hill until after nine o'clock. With two babies in her arms, Joanna was usually so exhausted, she didn't even notice that the dinner hour had passed.

For some time, Frank tried to convince her to hire help, presenting it as an opportunity to provide employment. "It isn't slavery, Jo. It's not immoral to pay someone for help. And it doesn't speak to your competence, whatever you've been raised to think. Give yourself a break."

Joanna suspected that in his subconscious, Frank hoped that relieving some of her burden would give him a break too, from the guilt of his familial dereliction, and the worry about his wife's well-being. She finally relented and hired a cleaning woman, but on the days that Dolores was there, Joanna was awkwardly uncomfortable. It felt unnatural to have someone else doing her laundry and washing her floors. One of her mother's best friends had cleaned for people. Joanna would never forget the stories Mrs. McKinney told sitting at Eileen Rafferty's kitchen table with a bottomless cup of coffee: the empty beer bottles hidden under a teenager's bed, the thick ring of grime around someone's bathtub, the mysterious thing in the trash can that made Joanna's mother laugh so hard, she spit out her coffee. . . . On most Tuesdays and Fridays, Joanna would pile the babies into the buggy and escape for as long as they would allow. She couldn't calculate the miles she'd logged wandering around, avoiding Dolores.

One point on which she wouldn't budge, however, was getting a nanny. In Frank's world, it was completely normal to have a couple of them. But Joanna couldn't pry away the steel grip of her mother's opinion. She knew that Eileen Rafferty would have sooner set herself on fire than allow some stranger to care for her babies. And so, Joanna had mutated into a three-headed Hydra, with the children attached to her body for most of the day. When she managed to get them both to nap at the same time, she often fell asleep right on the carpeted floor of the nursery.

And then, in '59, there was a prolonged workers' strike that practically swallowed them whole. And it was during that grueling tribulation that their world nearly collapsed.

It was the coldest night in ten Novembers, with an icy sheet of snow covering every inch—not even the busiest thorough-fares could melt it. Joanna had intended to wait up for her husband. She was worried about the drive from Bethlehem; the radio on the kitchen shelf broadcast repeated warnings about road conditions. Thus—after the crucible that was Daisy's bedtime ritual—she settled into the Eames chair in the living room with Charlie on her lap and a pile of children's books on the table next to them. This arrangement had become quasi-routine. About the time Charlie turned three, he developed a near-obsessive attachment to his father, made achingly poignant by Frank's scant time at home. Many times a day, he would pepper Joanna with the same question: "Is my daddy here?" And so, she sometimes allowed the little boy to wait up with her, reciting together page after page of Mother Goose rhymes and cycling through a stack of Little Golden Books, until Frank finally came through the door, to carry his oft-sleeping son to bed.

The lounge chair was cozy—soft, cushiony leather with a tall headrest and matching ottoman. It was part of a modern design scheme that Joanna had labored over when they first bought the house, filling the rooms with Brazilian rosewood and sleek Danish teak and earthy tones of olive and russet and gold. The clean, spare lines spoke to her—honest and uncontrived. She wasn't attracted to ornate decor. It felt false to her—like wearing a pretend tiara.

But the chair was, perhaps, too comfortable, and the day had taken its toll. On that night, it wasn't Charlie who fell asleep. It was Joanna.

When she awoke, fuzzy and disoriented, it took several moments to realize what was missing. She stretched in the chair, looking absently at the books scattered on floor. Frank must have taken Charlie to bed, but why didn't he wake her? As she rose to check on Charlie in his bedroom, a creeping apprehension began to wrap around her heart. Something wasn't right. Frank would have woken her—he wouldn't have left her to sleep in the chair.

Charlie's bed was empty. Frank wasn't home.

She had opened the front door and was peering frantically into the dark, frigid night, when headlights turned the corner and Frank's car pulled into the driveway. That was when she saw the small footprints in the snow.

They found him by the side of the garage, nearly unconscious, curled in a tight ball between two large yews. When Joanna lifted him, his pajamas stuck to the snow, frozen there. Charlie had gone to look for his father, certain he had heard the car.

Hypothermia and frostbite seemed like a gift. It could have been—it almost was—far worse. The near-catastrophe shook them both to the core. Joanna was sickened with self-incrimination, and the expression that now haunted her husband's features proved that he felt the same way.

That was when Frank started thinking about moving them to Bethlehem. After three months the strike ended, but for the next couple of years Frank continued to bring home mimeographs of real estate listings that his secretary pulled together, and Joanna continued to pretend to study them. One night, late again and wearing his weariness like a yoke, he said they needed to talk. Plans had been announced to build a major plant in Indiana to produce sheet and plate metal. Times were changing and the business had to keep up, so they were beginning to cater to the auto industry. The Burns Harbor plant would be the biggest thing ever to happen to

Bethlehem Steel. He didn't have to say it: he was afraid that the weight of his commitment would crush them. He needed his wife and children in Bethlehem.

And then his father died.

As she was helping Daisy into her nightgown, it occurred to Joanna that looking after Susannah and Helen may not have been Frank's only impetus for moving his family into Brynmor. She saw now what he must have realized right away—that installing them in a new home in Bethlehem would be worse than staying in Philadelphia if he couldn't improve his attendance. And he was right. The responsibilities at the new plant were backbreaking; he was traveling from Pennsylvania to Indiana on a continuum. At least until the Burns Harbor plant was up and running, she was grateful for the ready society of their small colony. Even the presence of the help was oddly comforting. Joanna had struck up a nice rapport with Hazel, the cook, pulling up a chair in the kitchen most mornings for an early cup of coffee; and Harriet—stooped and no longer required to perform anything more strenuous than dinner service and light dusting—had turned out to be the children's favorite fixture. Her good-natured confusion—exaggerated for effect, Joanna hoped—provided endless amusement as they switched the forks around on the table and placed feather dusters in the hat rack.

"Am I black or white?"

Joanna blinked as she tried to interpret Daisy's question. "I'm sorry. What did you say?" She thought fleetingly that the little girl had been watching Walter Cronkite. The last thing she wanted at that hour was to answer questions about civil rights.

"Last time when we played I was white, but Charlie says he's white."

Ah, chess. She took Daisy's hand and led her up the back stairs to the third-floor playroom. "You have to take turns. This time it's Charlie's turn to be white. You get to be black."

In its former capacity, the playroom had been the nursery— nestled between two bedrooms that had been occupied by the nannies of yesteryear. It was a large room—much larger than any of the servants' rooms in the other wing, and it had a lovely arched window set into an alcove with a window seat that overlooked the park-like grounds behind the house. Brynmor was classically symmetrical in design, consisting of a wide central section flanked by two wings. The master bedroom suite was directly below the nursery; a clever intercom of sorts—a conduit in the ceiling—had allowed Helen to hear her babies crying and keep tabs on the alacrity of the nannies. This wing also housed the other family bedrooms on the second floor. The opposite wing, on the east end, was composed of mostly guest rooms on the second floor, with the rooms for the other house servants above.

In the center section of the third floor was the ballroom, situated at the top of the grand staircase, which rose from the enormous center hall. The staircase divided at the first landing, where the attenuated balusters progressed to a second-floor gallery overlooking the reception hall. From there, they merged at another large landing to form a single, wide staircase that led to the ballroom.

The first time Joanna had come to Brynmor had been just after she brought Frank home to meet her parents. The previous week, at the Rafferty's brick row house in Pennsport, they'd sat at the worn maple table for supper, bowing their heads for grace and passing the pot roast family style. The next week, Frank responded in kind, inviting her to his family's weekly Sunday dinner with his grandparents. When they pulled up to the house, Joanna had felt something flip in her stomach. The look she gave Frank was accusing. She couldn't help it—the intimidation made her unreasonably defensive. While he hadn't made a secret of his family's background, he also hadn't quite prepared her for the reality of it. But his painful wince made her laugh, and she realized then that there was nothing she could do about the ocean between them but put a smile on her face and try to keep her head above water.

By luck or mercy, she was seated at dinner between Frank and his father. Wyatt Collier was a warm and inclusive man, welcoming by nature. With authentic interest, he quizzed Joanna about her experiences in the orthopedic ward, her father's life as a policeman, and even her grandfather's barbershop. She became so absorbed in the conversation that she barely noticed the weight of the thick damask napkin and heavy sterling flatware, or the enormous Baccarat chandelier.

After dinner, Frank had given her a tour of the house.

When they finally reached the top floor, he admitted that the ballroom hadn't been used for a party since 1946, when his twin sister, Gigi, had her debutante ball. With a reminiscent smile, he recounted how his grandmother used to let him bring his friends over in the winter to play dodgeball and practice long jumping there. Then he led her across the room to a bank of Palladian-style doors on the north wall that opened to a wide balcony. They stepped outside, and as Joanna regarded the manicured grounds, he pulled her into his arms and proposed.

Now, eight fleeting years later, their own children loved to race around on the expansive, polished floor. A few weeks earlier Frank had had the brilliant idea of moving some old rugs out of storage so they could tumble around. It was a saving grace on rainy days as they practiced their cartwheels and somersaults. And there, instead of at the chessboard in the playroom, was where Joanna and Daisy found Charlie in his pajamas, standing on his head.

"I've been waiting like this for two hours," he said thickly, his face swollen and red.

Joanna laughed and grabbed him by his ankles, lifting him off the ground. "You can join the circus," she said, swinging him around in a circle. "The Amazing Charlendo, upside-down boy." Confronted by the evidence of that dreadful, frozen night nearly three years past, her smile faded. But the frostbite hadn't taken any toes, and scarring was a small price to pay.

Daisy was kicking her legs into the air, and her comic flailing put the smile back on her mother's face. "I don't want to play chess anymore," the little girl said as she tipped onto her elbows. "Let's do gymnastics!"

Although Joanna knew it would only rile them up before bed, she agreed to let them tumble for a few more minutes. She sat down on one of the gilded Chiavari chairs that lined the walls and looked at her watch. Eight o'clock—she hoped again that Frank would get home before she put the children down.

Charlie was trying to help his little sister into a headstand, patiently holding her feet, while Joanna looked absently around the room—admiring the beautiful stained-glass skylights and the ornate bronze balustrade that encircled the orchestra platform. She noted various pieces of furniture that had been moved in over the years—including a barrister's bookcase with leaded glass doors hinged to swing up and slide back. Idly, she stood and walked over to the bookcase, wondering if it might hold something worth reading. She chose a shelf in the middle and lifted the door, pushing it into the case. There were, indeed, books—but they weren't novels. They were photograph albums. It hadn't occurred to her until now that she hadn't noticed any albums around the house. Certainly, there were framed photos displayed on walls and tabletops, but she hadn't thought to wonder where one would keep photo albums in a house like this. If she had, then here was her answer. Pulling one out at random, she carried it back to the chair and sat down.

She opened the old leather cover and turned the velum fly-leaf to the first page of photos. Attached by small corner clips, they were printed on thick paper, like postcards, in muted, se-pia tones. The first one was obviously a Fourth of July pa-rade, with several youngsters dressed up in costumes on a makeshift float—a hay wagon being pulled by two heavyset horses. There were two girls and three boys; Joanna knew it had to be the Parrish and Collier children. At some point, when she and Frank were getting to know each other, he had men-tioned that his parents had grown up together. Looking closer, she could see traces of her mother-in-law in the blond girl wearing a Betsy Ross bonnet, and she assumed the brunette dressed as Lady Liberty must be Susannah's sister, India. She had met India and Paul on a few occasions; she remembered India as having a petite frame and small features—the physi-cal type that was enviable in youth but rushed too quickly into old age.

Joanna could deduce that the smaller boy was a young Wyatt Collier, dressed as a Revolutionary drummer. Under the tricorne hat were the same kind gray eyes with which she was familiar, for the too-few years she had known him.

The two bigger boys she thought had to be Kit Parrish and Chap Collier. She remembered what Doe said about Charlie resembling this long-lost uncle, and she studied the picture, trying to see it. But the boys were dressed as Uncle Sam and George Washington and it was impossible to tell.

The next page held shots of the Parrish children in front of an enormous Christmas tree. Joanna could make out some of the details of the reception hall downstairs. They were dressed formally and looking directly into the camera with serious expressions. She could see Frank's uncle Kit clearly in these—his even countenance resembled Susannah's and they shared the same fair coloring, but his hair was slicked back and the pomade had clearly darkened it. He looked to be about fifteen or so, the girls a few years younger. Susannah had waist-length hair that shone blond even in the sepia print. Joanna recognized her mother-in-law's features, which hadn't changed all that much. Both her brow and her jaw were strong and her face had an appealing symmetry; the overall effect was an all-American, athletic type of beauty, vital and luminous. India's face was pretty but less striking—narrower and delicate, framed by soft brown waves.

Turning the page, Joanna had to sit back a little as she saw what could have been a photo of Charlie in a few years: a young teen in tennis whites, standing by the net with Kit. So, this was Chap. Doe had not been exaggerating the remarkable resemblance. Chap was built differently from his younger brother—lanky and lithe—and his hair was dark. He was smiling in that secretly amused way that Charlie had already acquired—a closed-mouth twist that always made Joanna think he was holding back an ironic comment. Charlie's eyes were an unusual shade—a lambent golden-green; and while she couldn't tell if Chap's were the same color, they were set deep like her son's, over strong cheekbones. She gazed at the photo for a long minute. People had commented on Charlie's striking features since he was a toddler, and here was his mirror image, presented in the form of a ghost from the past. It was more than a little unnerving.

As she leafed through the pages, she began to understand just how close the two families had been. Aside from the few formal Christmas pictures and one with the description *Easter, 1915* etched across the bottom, almost all of the photos were of the Colliers and Parrishes together. It was interesting to see Frank's paternal grandparents, Frances and Charles Collier. Joanna had seen framed photos before, but this gave her a much better picture of who they were. Here were the adults having cocktails on the terrace, toasting the camera with their champagne glasses; here was a large, professional photo of a party in the ballroom, with the orchestra in the background and several white-gloved waiters holding trays; here were the two families in a large skiff on the river, with Hollins and Charles holding oars while the children waved. When she looked closer, she noticed that Frances was lying back on a pillow and Helen was resting a hand on her shoulder. There was an official photograph of a baseball team, with Kit and Chap standing center and back, holding a pennant in the air. Chap was smiling that mischievous, oblique grin, and it took Joanna a moment to realize that his large, floppy baseball mitt was resting directly on the head of the player kneeling in front of him. That player was Wyatt—who looked like he was wearing a big leather bonnet.

There were pages of the children in various activities, and after a while Joanna couldn't help noticing that it was Susannah who captured the camera's eye; her charisma was uncanny. And Joanna noticed another thing: if Wyatt was in the picture, he was usually standing next to her. She smiled at the sweetness of it. Frank's father had been absolutely devoted to his wife, and here was evidence of its origin.

She was studying a frame-worthy photo of a young Susannah in equestrienne attire astride a beautiful horse, when Charlie's shout jolted her.

"Daddy!"

"The king of the castle returns!" Frank's voice boomed loud as he entered the room. "Where are my loyal subjects?"

The children shrieked and ran to their father, throwing themselves at his legs.

"Who are these unruly urchins?" He grabbed Daisy and threw her into the air. "Oh, I remember you." He drew out the words suspiciously, narrowing his eyes. "You're that girl, Daffodil."

"No!" Daisy shrieked through her laughter. "I'm Daisy!"

"What? Are you sure?" Frank looked puzzled and turned the little girl this way and that while she fluttered her feet in the air. He nuzzled his nose into her neck where she was ticklish. "You don't smell like a daisy."

She could hardly get the words out through uncontrollable giggles. "Daisies don't have a smell, silly."

"Daddy, look!" Charlie scrambled to the nearest rug and threw himself into a headstand.

"What ho—there's an acrobat in the room!" Frank got down on his hands and knees and started to tickle Charlie on the stomach where his pajama top had fallen open, then flipped the little boy around and wrestled him to the rug. "Don't worry, Mama," he called as he wrapped his arms around his son, "I've got this handled. We'll rid this place of these pesky acrobats yet!"

Joanna smiled at her husband's antics, but she felt a sharp little sliver of resentment poking at her chest. She invested endless hours finding ways to amuse the children—games and stories, trips to the playground and the library and the park, teaching them to read and play chess . . . and all Frank had to do was walk into the room and they were ecstatic. But then, watching her husband amble around on the floor with both children on his back—still wearing his tie and starched white shirt—a squeezing pinch of shame extracted the sliver and she flicked it away.

Daisy slid off and landed on her brother as their father stood up and brushed his knees. He leaned down to them and said out of the side of his mouth, "See that woman over there? Think she'll give me her phone number?"

Charlie just flashed his knowing grin, but Daisy shouted, "That's Mama!"

Frank strode over and kissed Joanna on the cheek. "Hello, Duchess. How fares the fairest of the fair?" He squeezed her shoulder and sat down.

"Well enough, all things considered." She smiled as she shifted toward him. "We met a very interesting woman in the cemetery today who told us all about her ghosts, and then at dinner your mother gave us a nice lesson about religious freedom."

Frank winced. "Sorry about that. She has a thing about you papists. But on the bright side, it sounds like you met Doe Janssen. She's a character, all right. Maybe a little crazy, but that woman knows more secrets than a priest."

"She has a dead dog!" This contribution came out as a muffled shout as Daisy turned a somersault, trailing her brother across the floor.

Accepting that statement with a shrug, Frank glanced at the album on Joanna's lap. "What's this then?"

"I found some photo albums in the bookcase over there. Look at this one—isn't it something?" Joanna propped up the book, open to the photo of Susannah on the horse.

Frank was quiet for a moment, his brow knit. "That's odd. Mother never mentioned having a horse." He looked at it for another long beat, shaking his head. "Gigi begged for a horse for years. Mother wouldn't even consider it. She said horses were nothing but trouble."

"Didn't you tell me there used to be stables here?"

"Yes, but that was years ago, when they still used horses

for transportation. I don't actually know when they got rid of the stables. I just know they were back behind the garage somewhere. Most of that land was sold off."

"Ow! Daisy kicked my head!"

"It was a accident." Daisy burst into tears as Charlie slapped her leg.

"Okay, the show's over. Who wants a ride to bed?" Frank scooped up one child in each arm and headed for the door, propelling them like airplanes. "Say good night to your mother. She's off the clock."

"Good night, Mama."

"Good night, Mama."

"What's 'off the clock'?"

As the chatter faded down the hall, Joanna sat in the dimming wake, gazing at the photograph of Susannah. Closing the album, she decided to take a nice long bath—after which she thought she might put her silk negligee to good use.

But when she entered the bedroom, powdered and scented, Frank was nowhere to be found. The hallway in the west wing was quiet—she knew Helen would have turned in early, and Susannah was likely in the library, reading. Low light emanated from the children's room, which had once been Kit's. They had tried separate rooms for the kids at first, but Daisy would last only ten minutes before hightailing it to her parents' bed, so she became Charlie's roommate, an arrangement that had worked out fine for everyone.

Joanna peeked around the doorframe and there they

were—all three of them on one twin bed—fast asleep under the light of the nightstand lamp. A book lay open on Frank's chest and a child was propped on each shoulder. Gently, Joanna lifted Daisy and deposited her onto the other bed; then she removed the book. Standing over father and son, she decided she didn't have the heart to separate them. Quietly, she turned out the light and returned to her room, getting into bed alone yet again.

Four

"You're a foxy little thing, aren't you? Yes, you are . . . just a little Arabian fox. . . ." Susannah was murmuring to Pericles as she brushed his sleek chestnut coat. "And now you're a champion—let's see that champion's smile." She cupped her hands around the horse's soft muzzle and pulled back slightly, exposing the big yellow teeth. "There it is—just like a movie star. Just like Douglas Fairbanks. That's what you are, Peri, a star. Twinkle, twinkle, Periwinkle." She nuzzled her face against the soft mane, stroking the gelding's neck.

"Congratulations, Miss," the stable boy said, nodding at Susannah as he passed. A cigarette dangled from the side of his mouth, and he carried two buckets of oats.

"Thank you, Carl, but Peri did it—I was just along for the ride." She picked up a back hoof and examined the shoe. "You charmed those judges all on your own, didn't you, you little flirt!"

Horse and rider had just returned from the Devon Horse Show—the largest outdoor equestrian competition in the country—and Susannah was flying high from a blue-ribbon win in Junior Equitation. The week had been a hectic flurry—moving Pericles to the DuPont barn on the Devon grounds near Philadelphia, working with the horse to relax and perform in the unfamiliar ring, and competing in preliminary events. Susannah's events took place over the course of three days, and instead of going back to the Rittenhouse with her mother at night, she had opted to stay in the stable, sleeping on a cot next to Pericles. Rumors of sabotage were rife and she wasn't taking any chances.

"He's a dandy, but you're givin' 'im too much credit," Carl said. "I know a thing or two about them shows, and dressage is more about the rider than the horse." He smiled through a wraith of smoke, moving away toward a trough in a far stall.

"If that horse knows anything about flirting, he learned it from you." India was stepping delicately across the cobblestones. Manny, the Parrishes' stable manager, kept everything pristine—even applying a fresh coat of paint each spring—but in her blue linen frock and low-heeled spectator pumps, India looked starkly out of place.

"Look who's talking," Susannah replied, shooting a knowing glance at the summer cloche her sister was holding. "Why the new hat, Itty? Going somewhere? Somewhere like . . . oh, I don't know . . . a baseball game?

"Come on, Sass. Please? You said you'd come with me."

"I said I'd think about it. I didn't know Peri was going to get me a blue ribbon. Now I feel like celebrating, not sitting on some hard bench, watching . . . nothing happening. I hate baseball. Why couldn't the boys play something exciting, like polo!" Her face brightened as she slipped a monogrammed blanket up and over the horse's flanks.

"Not everything in the world revolves around horses, you know. Please? Just for a few innings?"

"Oh, all right." Susannah took mercy on her sister, knowing how carefully and devotedly India maneuvered to put herself in the general vicinity of Chap Collier. "Three innings."

"Unless they're short, though. You have to stay for at least an hour. But hurry—it already started."

Susannah unhitched the tie ring and led Pericles to his stall, complimenting him lavishly. On the way up to the house, she made India laugh when she did a little jig on the flagstone path and clicked her heels—still walking on air. In her room, she traded jodhpurs for a summer skirt, leaving the long braid in her hair and grabbing a hat from the antler rack by the terrace door on her way out.

India was waiting under the arbor. Grabbing her sister's arm, she practically pulled her off her feet.

As they passed the garage, Jimmy tipped his hat. "Afternoon, Miss India, Miss Susannah. Is there someplace I can carry you?"

The girls giggled. Jimmy was from Alabama, and they

found his Southern colloquialisms adorable. "No, thank you, Jimmy. We're just going down to the baseball field."

"That's right. I nearly forgot—big game today. I hear those Easton fellas are tough, but they'll just be swattin' gnats with Mister Kit on the mound." Jimmy went back to polishing a fender, and the girls skittered down the hill, swinging their hats by their sides.

South Bethlehem High was only a few blocks away, on Brodhead Avenue. It was new—completed just two years earlier—and had its own baseball field. The bleachers were nearly full when the girls got there, but Susannah sashayed right over and smiled prettily at two men sitting in the middle of the first row. "I think we can squeeze in here, Itty," she called to her sister. "I'm sure there will be room if we all just tighten up a bit."

Had India and Susannah been lepers, the men would willingly have made room for Hollins Parrish's daughters. The population of Bethlehem had grown by 200 percent in the past decade, due entirely to employment by Bethlehem Steel. As the girls were taking their seats, they noticed their parents up in the top row—where the ladies could open their parasols—alongside Charles and Frances Collier.

"Oh, look, Sass—Mrs. Collier is here." There was a tender note in India's voice. "She must be feeling better. I'm glad she'll finally get to see the boys play." As the words left India's mouth, the pale, thin woman coughed delicately into her handkerchief. The girls waved, and were surprised when quite a few people in the stands waved back. It took an embarrassing moment to realize the fans weren't waving at all, but suggesting that India and Susannah sit down.

One of the finer features of the field was a real dugout, and it was easy to spot Wyatt, leaning forward with his elbows on his knees, intently following every play. It wasn't until the teams were switching sides that he noticed Susannah. Grinning sheepishly, he fanned his glove at her and turned his attention back to the game.

"Poor Wyatt. Last game of the season and he won't get in again," Susannah said, adjusting the brim of her hat and squinting into the sun.

"He's only a freshman. He'll get to play once Chap's gone." India's eyes were on the field, centered between first and second base.

Wyatt played backup shortstop, but unfortunately the player he backed up was the star of the team—who also happened to be his brother. An assortment of college ball teams had been after Chap Collier; when he had finally committed to play at Lehigh, it seemed the whole town celebrated. The hometown hero would stay at home.

Bethlehem had been leading by two runs when the girls arrived, and by the bottom of the seventh inning they were up seven to three. Kit was throwing blue streaks from the mound, striking out three in a row in the fifth inning and two more in the sixth. A husky kid from Easton was two strikes in at the plate and it looked like another strikeout, but a cut fastball didn't sink fast enough and the swing made contact, sending the ball at a straight angle toward center field. It looked like it would continue on course right past the outfield, but in the briefest instant of opportunity, Chap managed to launch himself into the air and place his glove directly in the path of the ball, rolling as he landed.

He got to his feet slowly, stumbling on his right ankle and then limping to the sidelines. A huddled conference with the coach resulted in Chap sidelined on the bench, his leg propped up on a rail, and Wyatt scampering onto the field.

India's smile was proud and proprietary. "Did you see that?" she whispered to her sister. "He did that on purpose. That's just the sweetest thing—he got Wyatt into the last game of the season."

India missed the next play because her eyes were glued to the dugout, but Susannah jumped up and squealed as she clapped her hands. "Hurray! Hurray!" Wyatt had lucked into a grounder on his very first play of the season, scooping it up handily and making an easy throw to first base. Susannah bounced on her toes and turned to look up at the Colliers, who were laughing as they cheered for their younger son. Then she looked back at Wyatt, who was trying to keep a self-conscious grin off his face, and blew him a kiss. He flushed and hung his head, scuffing his toe in the grass.

Sitting down, Susannah idly observed her brother on the pitcher's mound, stretching and rotating his shoulder as he warmed up for what might have been a third out, when there was a rustle of collective distraction. The buzz was directed at the outfield. When she turned, she was astonished to see a figure running through left field. He came from the direction of Brodhead Avenue, and he was waving his arms wildly as he dashed across the expanse of grass and straight over the diamond. All eyes were on this strange spectacle as the man wheeled to a stop on the red dirt of the baseline, kicking up a cloud of dust.

"Mr. Parrish! Does anyone see Mr. Parrish?" He was shouting, one hand shielding his eyes as he desperately searched the bleachers. The man was wearing a uniform. It took Susannah a moment to realize it was Jimmy, hatless and dripping sweat, eyes bulging and face contorted.

The girls turned to look for their father, but he was already making his way down, taking the risers two at a time. When Jimmy saw him, he couldn't contain himself: "Fire! Fire!" His shouts cracked with ragged urgency. "Mr. Parrish, the stables are burning!

Susannah didn't remember going back to Brynmor. As Jimmy's words had registered she froze, paralyzed by a reflexive denial—a self-protecting impulse that refused to consider the implications. She felt bizarrely cocooned from reality. A muffled space enveloped her, blotting out the pandemonium as the crowd jostled and clamored around her. And then her eyes met India's, and the mute horror in her sister's expression shattered the bubble. She saw her father racing to the car with Jimmy. Kit was right behind them, abandoning the pitcher's mound without a second's hesitation. She must have been moving, but she was unaware of the ground passing beneath her feet.

There was no sense of time, no awareness of distance crossed. One instant she was sitting on a bench at a baseball game—she would remember it like a scene in one of her mother's German snow globes, a crystallized moment that represented "before"—and the next instant she was flying past fire trucks and men wielding hoses attached to tanks. Flames rose in macabre, dancing tongues from the small iron-barred windows and in mighty towers from the wood-shingle roof. There was roaring in her ears and smoke in her eyes and the blaze of heat on her face. A pair of strong arms grabbed her as she threw herself forward—arms clad in oilskin, anchored by thick canvas gloves. She felt a furious howl leave her chest, but she could hear nothing but one specific sound—the hideous, anguished scream of a horse trapped in his burning stall.

Twisting in the fireman's grasp, she took frantic inventory: There was Manny, nearly indistinguishable under a layer of black soot, head in hands, doubled over in grief and defeat on the far side of the riding ring. There was Carl, desperately trying to control the two Belgians, rearing up in wild-eyed panic as he fought to lead them away from the overwhelming heat. Two other horses were doing a nervous, skittish dance in the yard beyond the ring, trotting in jerky passes around a small area as though confined, watching the fire like spectators with terrified eyes. A palomino, a bay. Juno, the gray Andalusian, was running in crazed, disoriented circles. Farther off, a jet-black thoroughbred was on its own, bucking wildly—her father's stallion, Ahab. Not chestnut. Not Arabian. Her mind raced as she kicked and struggled: One more. Just one more. But it was effort wasted, because she already knew. She already knew.

Peri was dancing. Susannah laughed with delight as the horse two-stepped to the right, and then back again to the left. With the slightest pressure of her right heel, Pericles dipped his shoulder and bowed his head, bending his right foreleg and spinning in place. "You've got it!" Susannah leaned forward and ruffled the horse's mane, tipping farther to give him a quick kiss and press her cheek against his warm neck.

Ever since her father had presented her with her dream gift on her eighth birthday, girl and horse had been connected at the soul. From the moment she had uncovered her eyes to see a spindly one-year-old colt standing alone in the riding ring like a little lad lost, Susannah had spent most of her waking hours with Pericles. In the beginning she would lead the little horse around the yard—jumping beside him over a small course of logs or playing tag in the riding ring or just lolling about with her brown-eyed boy, communing nose to nose in their own special language. Manny teased her that she was going to brush the hair right off the horse as daily she groomed the soft coat to a sheen. He had even discovered them napping together in the stall, Susannah curled up next to Pericles, her head resting snugly on his shoulder. When the colt turned two, Manny started the breaking-in process. He intended to follow the standard practice, beginning with an empty saddle, but Susannah defied him by climbing right onto the gelding's narrow back without so much as a bridle. After a little shimmy and a backward glance, Peri took her for a careful, smooth trot around the ring.

But now there was an awful, clanging noise and Peri's ears twitched as he missed a step. What was it? Susannah couldn't tell where it was coming from. It was incessant now—a smashing, hammering cacophony that was scaring Peri and confusing Susannah. Suddenly she was looking down, and Peri was by himself, but he wasn't in the ring anymore. He was in his stall. She could see him start to shuffle nervously, eyes wide and nostrils flaring.

Manny! Manny! She couldn't move. Without knowing what, she understood with horrifying certainty that something was wrong—something was coming—and she could not get to her horse. *MANNY!!!* She was screaming now. Someone had to let Peri out of the stall. *MANNY!!!* She screamed again—a long, tormented shriek—but for some reason, she had no voice. She tried and tried, but she couldn't make a sound.

And then a terrible, weighty sadness settled upon her, like

an anvil had been placed on her chest—so heavy, she wasn't sure her lungs could breathe or her heart could beat—as she woke to the sound of a dozen sledgehammers smashing brick walls, and the lingering smell of smoke. There was a cool hand on her forehead—it was her mother. She placed something on Susannah's tongue, and then lifted her daughter's head, urging her to take a sip. Susannah swallowed and waited, willing oblivion.

After a few days, the doctor advised discontinuing the sedatives, confident that the cushion of time would do its job. The nausea-inducing smell of smoke had dissipated, and Susannah was able to swallow some broth and even some bread. She didn't come down to dinner, though. In fact, she didn't have any inclination to get out of bed, except to take very hot baths. The near-scalding water fulfilled a strange need—a primal urge to steep away the sorrow that was slicked all over her.

It was more than a week before she ventured out of her bedroom and into the old nursery to sit in the window seat, watching woodenly as the workmen finished hauling away what was left of the stables. That was where her father found her. Gently, he told her that he was considering selling the horses. There wasn't much use for the team of Belgians anymore, and the pleasure horses were rarely mounted. He said he couldn't remember the last time he had ridden Ahab. If not for Manny and Carl, the horses wouldn't feel the weight of a saddle.

And there was another thing—Carl had left. Her father thought she might as well know the truth: Carl had been leading Ahab out of his stall when the stallion reared. Struggling to control the horse, he'd tossed his cigarette through the iron bars of a window. It had landed in an open can of turpentine. That was how the fire had started. Manny didn't have to let Carl go—he'd left on his own, crippled with remorse.

Susannah took it all in without a word, her expression glazed and distant.

Studying her with tender eyes, her father leaned in. "If you think you may want to keep riding," he said, "you could try Juno or Calliope. I know they aren't trained for dressage. . . . If you like, we can find another Arabian. I don't want to rush you, but I want you to know the choice is yours. I can have the workmen rebuild. Something small—a couple of stalls. Just in case you decide you want another horse."

She looked at him then as though he were mad, as though he had suggested she would want another moon, or another head. "There isn't another horse."

And so, as the last cart of stones and bricks rumbled away, it was settled. There would no longer be stables at Brynmor.

The following week her mother found Susannah in her usual place; she had taken to reading on the window seat. The old nursery had become an ivory tower of sorts, cocooning her from real life, fending off a routine that did not include Pericles. And she had discovered that Jane Austen and the Brontë sisters could remove the red-hot poker from her heart, if only for a moment.

"There's someone here to see you, Sassy."

Wyatt was standing behind Helen, looking bashful with a porkpie hat in one hand and a bouquet of daisies in the other. Helen turned and left the room, urging Wyatt forward as she passed him in the doorway.

"I'm sorry about what happened," he said, shyly holding out the flowers. "I thought maybe these would cheer you up."

As Susannah looked at the bouquet, a rogue wave of despondency surged over her. The vast expanse between her grief and a simple bunch of flowers struck her as absurd. She knew that Wyatt's impulse was true and sweet and kind. Rationally, she could appreciate it. But it felt as though someone were offering her incense for her thirst, or a painted fan for her hunger.

Wyatt must have read her expression, because suddenly he seemed to consider the gesture ridiculously feeble. He actually groaned. And that—combined with the mortification on his face—yanked Susannah from the undertow and made her laugh out loud.

Wyatt's smile was hesitant, and when he looked over his shoulder to see if he was missing something, Susannah laughed even harder, an uncontrollable chortle that made her clutch her sides. With a dubious glance at the daisies, Wyatt shrugged and walked to the goldfish bowl on the windowsill, shoving the stems into the watery realm of Gill, the bowl's sole occupant.

Now there were tears streaming down Susannah's face, and she could hardly catch her breath. Wyatt crossed the room and sat down next to her, and Susannah leaned her head onto his shoulder. Cautiously, Wyatt put his arm around her; after a few moments her hysteria subsided to a stuttering, spent sigh. She rested there, silent now as her shoulders trembled and tears continued to roll down her cheeks. And then—very gently—Wyatt kissed her.

Five

"As I live and breathe, if it isn't Hedy Parrish!" Doe threw her hands in the air as she came around the bend. "I was beginning to think I'd have to come up to Fountain Hill and get you myself!" Smiling broadly, she strode to the wheelchair and laid her hands upon Helen's shoulders, leaning down to plant a kiss on her cheek.

"Well, Dorothy, I wouldn't put it past you." Helen smiled and patted Doe's arm. "I believe you could outdo Sisyphus and roll a boulder right up that hill if the spirit moved you."

"Hah!" Doe threw back her head with a sharp laugh. "That's a pithy comparison—Sisyphus, doomed to spend eternity in the kingdom of the dead!" She gave an appreciative wink to Joanna. "Still as sharp as a pin, this one." Stepping back, she took in the impeccable St. John suit and Ferragamo pumps—replete with matching handbag. "Still dressing like a charwoman, I see."

"And you, my dear, are still dressing like a scarecrow." Helen's eyes twinkled at her friend.

Joanna felt a warm appreciation for the ease with which the two old women fell into cozy companionship. She was no longer baffled by the relationship; she knew now how the ranks had come to be leveled.

In the weeks since school started, she had found herself at St. Gregory's on many an afternoon. She had been relieved that the kids were occupied and making friends, but she hadn't realized what a gaping hole their absence would leave. In the mornings, Wayne, the chauffeur, delivered Charlie to school—a scenario that seemed preposterous to Joanna as she watched her little boy slide into the backseat of the old Rolls Royce with his lunch box. But Daisy went to afternoon kindergarten, so most days Joanna walked her to school at noon, and at the end of the day she would walk home with both children. It helped fill her days. She liked to find ways to pass the afternoon hours in town, avoiding the extra hike up the hill and back. If the weather was dreary, she might take in a movie at the Palace, or stop into the Cozy Spot for a cup of coffee or a sandwich, and she wandered regularly into McCrory's for sundries like stockings or lipstick. But there was only so much shopping she could do, and on pretty days she often found herself strolling through the green serenity of the cemetery.

Occasionally she came upon Doe, who always seemed to welcome a break from her gardening. From the beginning,

Joanna had been curious about how a young newlywed couple had become the caretakers of the cemetery, and it wasn't long before she asked Doe about it.

"Well, I guess you could say that Nico had two choices: he could earn a living by coaxing things out of the ground, or he could earn a living by coaxing things *into* the ground." Doe laughed at her own joke, turning sideways on the bench to settle in. "I'll tell you just what happened. Not long after Nico proposed, his uncle died. Until then we'd been planning to scratch out a piece of land and grow barley. We both come from long lines of farmers. But you know, if you're not the oldest son, you're out of luck. My father was the youngest of five, so he left the farm and opened a flower shop. You've probably seen it—Meiers Florist over on Union? That's where I met Nico. He came in to pick up a corsage for another girl and we struck up a nice conversation. After a bit, he left the shop with the box in his hand—but a minute later he turned right around and came back to buy another one. I wore that corsage pinned to my apron for three days." She smiled, shaking her head a little at the memory.

"Nico and I were going to borrow the money for a down payment on a hundred-acre parcel over toward Quakertown. Then fate stepped in, I like to think. Nico's uncle Jakob had taken care of this place for decades—practically from the time the Moravians opened it to the public. He never married— lived in Grange House all by himself. When he died, there wasn't anyone to run the show. One of the deacons had to step

in to bury the gravedigger! After the funeral, we were standing right over there"—she pointed to a copse of beeches—
"and while they lowered his coffin into the ground, I just
looked up and decided I was home." She paused for a moment,
gazing around. "Who better to run the place than a farmer and
a florist's daughter?"

It was such a simple explanation, and Joanna saw that it
made perfect sense. Life for a farmer and his wife could be
brutally harsh. Taking care of the grounds and the burials at
St. Gregory's was a comparatively lovely job, and it came with
the added benefit of a sizable house. Joanna was almost envi-
ous, now that she thought about it.

"How did you come to know Helen?" She hadn't forgotten Doe's easy familiarity with Frank's grandmother, and it
still seemed oddly incongruous to her.

Doe hesitated for a moment, and then gave Joanna a small,
sad smile. "As you may expect, it isn't a happy story. But that
is, after all, the nature of the business. We hadn't been here
more than a few months . . . just starting to get the hang of it,
as they say"—she clasped Joanna's forearm companionably—
"when a man showed up one cold afternoon. He was tall and
distinguished-looking, quite handsome in a homburg and a
cashmere coat—I'll never forget it. And he was very young,
not much older than we were." She looked into the distance,
thinking for a moment. "Twenty-eight, as it turned out.
But, oh . . . that face was sad. It had what I call the deep
blues. There's a sort of shadow that sorrow casts—it's hard

to describe." She shook her head slowly. "He needed a burial plot, of course. Nico usually showed people around the grounds to pick out a grave site—I didn't get involved in that. But that day something made me follow along. I don't know why. I guess I just felt sorry for the poor man, and thought maybe I could help. Anyway, Nico showed him several nice plots, but the poor fellow wouldn't say a thing; he just walked along silently with his hands in his pockets. Eventually we came to that rise over there." She pointed toward a group of headstones overlooking the river valley. "And he stopped. I can still see the look on his face. It was like he was lost. It nearly broke my heart. I was such a greenhorn. I've seen that look a hundred times since.

"I felt like I should say something to make it easier, but I had no idea what. So I just started rambling on about the view and the trees, and I said something silly about having plenty of room. Oh, I felt so foolish, and he just hung his head. There we stood—Nico and I—shivering in the wind and waiting. Finally he spoke. He didn't look up; he just stared at a spot on the ground, and then he said the saddest thing: 'We don't need a lot of room. It's for a baby.'"

That was how Joanna learned that Hollins and Helen Parrish had buried their first child. The little girl's sweet headstone was the first in the row of family markers. Doe pointed it out—a delicate alabaster marble, carved with the name CECILIA PARRISH over the face of a cherub, and a heartbreaking five months between the dates of birth and death.

According to Doe, Helen became a near-permanent fixture in the cemetery that year, sitting for hours by Cecilia's grave, watching the distant waters of the river, or simply closing her eyes and listening to the birds sing. It was during that time that the two young women had forged a bond, and the ensuing years had seen them lean on each other through births and deaths, and—though she didn't specify what—much that happened in between.

Now Joanna watched as the old friends clasped hands and beamed at each other. She could feel their kinship like a vibration. Doe sat down on the bench next to Helen's wheelchair and patted Joanna's leg. "I've been getting to know this lovely girl," she said. "She's a keeper, Hedy. And if she's willing to cart you down here, all the better." She narrowed her eyes admonishingly. "Be careful you don't scare her off with your bossy demands, now."

Joanna laughed. When Helen had called her aside after dinner the night before and asked if she wouldn't mind taking her to the cemetery, Joanna had been more than happy to oblige. Helen's hip had healed and she could walk with her cane, but she didn't trust herself on uneven ground—and when she learned that Joanna was becoming a regular, she seized the opportunity. Joanna could see the old woman's face light up as they made it a date.

Wayne had driven them as far as the gates—folding the wheelchair into the trunk of the Silver Cloud—and would wait while they visited the Parrish section of the cemetery. It did have a lovely view, with the valley spread out below them like a ribbon unfurling, and the river sparkling in the mellow autumn sun. Little Cecilia's headstone had company now: Her father was there next to her. Frances and Charles Collier were in the next row, as were both of their sons, now that Wyatt had died. Someone had had the foresight to keep the two families in close proximity. Joanna had noted the extra space reserved next to Hollins for his wife, and there was room by Wyatt's headstone for Susannah's. It was a little un-settling. . . . She couldn't avoid a grim extrapolation.

But the impalpable graces of autumn were weaving their magic, and she pushed the morbid speculation out of her head with a deep, luxuriating sigh. The warmth of the fading sun on an early October afternoon and the smell of drying leaves had an ethereal effect on her, bringing forth a sublime feeling of nostalgic longing—soft and sweet and sad—combined with a thrilling, unspecific anticipation. An anticipation that had nothing to do, she told herself, with the sight of Daniel carrying a ladder over his shoulder as he moved toward an ailing willow.

Doe beckoned him over with a wave. "You'll finally get to meet my grandson," she told Helen. "He's been a lifesaver around here."

"I'm delighted for you, my dear. I've been remiss. Until Joanna told us, I had no idea he was back. What a help it must be." Helen smiled across the lawn at the young man as he set-tled the ladder under the tree.

Daniel pulled a kerchief from his back pocket and wiped his hands with it as he strode toward the women—a gesture that had become familiar to Joanna. "Good afternoon, ladies." He wore his customary solemn expression, but Joanna knew now that it was misleading.

It had been on her first afternoon without the children that she had quite literally stumbled across Daniel cutting back plants by the gate on Church Street. She had just delivered Daisy to her first day of kindergarten, and the goodbye had gone swimmingly. Joanna had been prepared for a teary last-minute change of heart, but Daisy was so preoccupied by the playmate potential that she didn't even notice her mother leaving. And so, it was with a very light heart that Joanna strolled down the sidewalks, exulting in the solitude. She couldn't remember the last time she had been out on her own. The idea that she could do anything she wanted for the next three hours—without having to consider another single soul—made her almost giddy. She couldn't even bring herself to go into any of the shops; the requirements of social propriety would have been too imposing. She wanted to wander at will, with nothing to compromise her freedom.

North Bethlehem was a lovely part of town, with its cobblestones and leafy boulevards. She strolled down High Street—the grand Colonial homes arrayed on sprawling, manicured lawns—and then turned onto Church Street, where the narrow brick row houses were perched right up to the ancient, heaving pavers of the sidewalk. She wandered past the

Widows' House and the Old Chapel, stopping occasionally to read a plaque on a doorway or a historical marker on a small plot of grass. Many of the old buildings were pre-Revolutionary—erected by the first Moravian settlers—and to Joanna there was elegance in their rustic stone simplicity.

Crossing Main Street, she descended a steep, winding hill, and then climbed back up again, treading carefully on the buckled paving stones. A couple of blocks farther up the street leveled out and she found herself looking across at Grange House—so stately behind the tall iron fence. And there she saw Daniel, kneeling by the Avonlea lilies that bordered the gate. At that moment she stepped on a crooked, jutting paver, and with the twist of an ankle she folded to the ground.

She hadn't had time to pick herself up when he appeared at her side, crouching to offer his hand. "May I help you?" The question was posed with the same placid formality she remembered from before.

More embarrassed than injured, Joanna blushed at her clumsy display. "You're very kind, thank you. . . . I'm just fine." She shifted to one knee to push herself up, and he clasped her elbow, pulling her easily off the ground. She winced a little when the weight settled on her ankle, but the pain was minor and by wiggling her foot a little she knew she could work it out. She brushed her hands together and dusted off her skirt.

"I have it on good authority that the sidewalks in Bethlehem are in collusion with the cemetery." The comment was delivered with solemn gravity, and it took Joanna a moment to realize Daniel was making a joke.

She smiled up at him, noting again the startling translucency of his eyes. "Are you giving away trade secrets?"

He gazed at her for a moment and then his serious countenance broke into a charming, transforming grin. And there was something in the combination of the gaze and the grin that made Joanna look away.

Since that day, there had been several chance meetings among the tombstones. She wasn't seeking him out, of course, but it was only natural that she would linger for a moment to visit. It was only being friendly. At first she was disconcerted by his quietness, but in time she learned that he wasn't shy or aloof; he simply lacked the impetus to make small talk. She found that she could sit near him as he worked and feel as if an entire conversation had taken place, though neither of them had uttered more than a few words.

Joanna had come to understand that it was Daniel's austere upbringing that had molded his behavior. Doe had commented on it one day, as she told Joanna about an incident that had happened that morning. Her grandson had been installing the pedestal of a limestone monument when it started to slip off the base. He had to wedge his hand under the sharp, chiseled edge to save it. Before anyone could come to the rescue, he managed to heave it upright with his shoulder, never uttering a sound. She told Joanna that it was a quality imbued from his childhood—a preternatural composure that the Amish referred to as *gelassenheit*.

Joanna had also learned that he could be startlingly direct, a trait that could still catch her off guard. Just the other day, as she sat in the sun near the hole he was digging, Daniel had turned to her and said, "Does your husband know you're here?"

Something in the way he said it made her chest contract. He was looking at her in that unflinching way, and for a moment she was struck dumb. As she struggled to form a response, something in him changed. His eyes shifted away, and when he looked back at her, there was the slightest trace of an amused smile on his lips. He raised one eyebrow and said, "Because according to my grandmother, this place is crawling with spooks."

That was when she started to notice that Daniel had inherited something of Doe's teasing nature. Later, when she told him she could never tell when he was kidding, he looked down at her and, in his typically measured way, said, "A grave demeanor is a job requirement."

Now, as Doe made the introductions, Daniel tilted his head in a small, respectful bow and cradled Helen's hand. "Very pleased to meet you, ma'am."

"Dear boy, you are a godsend to your grandmother," Helen said, smiling up at him. "I've been receiving excellent reports."

His glance landed on Joanna for the briefest second before

he turned to his grandmother. "Have you been spreading rumors again?"

"Don't look at me," Doe replied. "I only said there was an extra mouth at the table and a trail of broken shovels on the ground."

Helen patted Daniel's hand and turned toward Joanna. "You've met my grandson's wife, I understand."

He looked straight at her but didn't say a thing. By now Joanna knew that was just his way, his nature . . . but it felt so personal, so intimate that she felt a warm flush cover her face.

"Oh, they're becoming fast friends," Doe interjected before Daniel could respond. "Joanna has been keeping us both company."

"Isn't that lovely?" Helen looked evenly from Joanna to Daniel. "I'm so glad Joanna is getting out and meeting people. I'm sure Frank is happy to know that his wife is making friends."

Was Joanna imagining it, or was the reference to her husband made by design?

Daniel met Helen's gaze with his trademark equanimity, and the corners of his eyes crinkled almost imperceptibly as he gave her a slight nod. "I aim to please."

He excused himself then, referencing the waiting willow, and bid them all a polite goodbye.

Helen's eyes followed as he moved toward the tree, and after a few moments she spoke to Doe without turning her head. "I imagine that boy gave Sarah a run for her money."

"That he did." Doe nodded slowly. "You know what they say about still waters."

"Indeed." Helen continued to gaze across the rows at the figure now up on the ladder. "But while deep water is often still"—she shifted slightly in her chair, clearing her throat—"it is also true that the deepest part of a river is where the current is most dangerous."

Joanna wondered if it was possible she had heard correctly. The moderate warmth of the afternoon had suddenly produced a thin sheen of perspiration that covered her entire body.

"You'll remember, Dorothy," Helen continued, "that when the children were young, I was always very careful to warn them: It is futile to fight a strong current. The best course is to avoid swimming in the river at all."

With that she turned and gave Joanna a bright smile. "I believe I'm ready to go back, dear, if you would be so kind as to push me. I'm sure Wayne has finished the entire newspaper by now. We wouldn't want to be responsible for a rendezvous with detective fiction."

Wordlessly, Joanna stood and grasped the handles of the chair. As she maneuvered to turn it around, the wheels rumbled over a small cluster of exposed tree roots and Helen's exclamation reverberated: "My goodness, had we known how rough the going would be, you might have thought twice about bringing me!"

There it was again. Joanna was beginning to read subtext in everything the woman said, and it was making her insides twist. She couldn't find a single response as she pushed the chair up a small incline to the nearest path.

Doe walked next to her, and when they reached the car, she squeezed Joanna's shoulder. "Thank you for bringing the old girl to see me. It wouldn't be easy come winter—you'd have to put snow tires on this rattletrap!" She gave a little kick to one of the wheels on the chair, then leaned down and kissed Helen again on the cheek. "Goodbye, Hedy. Come and see us in the spring—we'll have lilacs in all of the urns."

Wayne helped the frail little woman into the backseat and Joanna climbed in next to her. As the car swung around, Helen called to Doe through the open window, "I'll be back again, Dodo. Keep a close eye out for lost souls and way-ward spirits—we wouldn't want any mischief or mayhem." She gave a little wave with her crisp white glove, and Joanna swallowed hard as the Rolls glided away.

Six

"Please stand still, Miss." The seamstress was kneeling next to the wooden box on which Susannah stood in a beaded ivory gown.

"Sassy, why are you so fidgety? Poor Louisa can hardly get a pin into the fabric." Helen was standing a few feet away, her arms crossed, eyeglasses perched on the end of her nose.

"Wyatt's leaving at noon. I told him I'd go see him off," Susannah said, twisting at the waist and tugging the slinky fabric down at the hips.

"Well, things would go a lot faster if you'd just let Louisa do her job."

Squaring her shoulders, Susannah looked straight ahead. "Chap is taking him to the station soon. They can't wait for me—Wyatt will miss the train."

"It's a shame he has to go so soon. My goodness, it isn't even Labor Day."

"The crew is back and starting up already. They barely took a break after Paris."

"Our little Wyatt—on the Yale crew." Helen shook her head. "It seems like just yesterday he was trailing around behind Kit and Chap, hoping to shag balls in the outfield." Her words were tinged slightly blue as they trailed off. "Wouldn't Frances just love to see him now?"

It was true that no one had ever expected Wyatt to become a rower—except perhaps his mother. Everyone assumed he would step right into Chap's cleats as shortstop on the base-ball team, but Frances had convinced her husband to buy their son a single-seat shell for his sixteenth birthday. From that moment, Wyatt was on the river. Over the next few years, he became so skilled at sculling that he was invited to practice with one of the best boat clubs in Philadelphia. Almost every weekend found him on the Schuylkill with the rowers from Vesper. Wyatt knew he would have to break his back if he ever hoped to make the eight-man heavyweight crew at Yale—just the month before, they had won an Olympic gold medal in Paris—but it was both the opportunity and the honor of a life-time. The only cloud in the sky was that his mother wasn't there to see the glistening fruit born from the little seed she had planted three summers before.

"We stopped at the cemetery before dinner last night. Did you know it's her birthday next week? Wyatt brought flowers to put on the grave." As she spoke, Susannah arched her back and looked behind her. "Louisa, I want it shorter than that."

Helen was looking out the window. "I would never forget her birthday." Her eyes were miles away. "Remember how we would take the train into Philadelphia and make a day of it? Oh, how we loved to lunch at Bookbinder's. The oysters!" She laughed out loud, tipping her forehead onto her fingertips. "It took Frances several tries to develop a taste for them, but bless her heart, she just kept at it, making the most terrible faces! That girl was a sport." She had become a little teary, but as her gaze drifted back to the dress, her eyebrows shot up. "My goodness, I do think that is quite short enough, Susannah. Any higher and your knees will show." She squinted disapprovingly at the hem.

"Your mother is right." Louisa sat back on her heels, tilting her head. "This gown needs to fall just exactly where it does. You don't want to interfere with the drape of the silk when it's cut on the bias." She took a pin from the cushion on her wrist and made one final fix, and then stood up and looked it over with a critical eye. "It really is the most marvelous thing. The beading is exquisite, and it fits you like a glove. Paris, did you say?"

"Yes, India got it for me when she went last year. It's dreamy, isn't it?" Susannah gave a little shimmy, and a thousand strands of tiny glass beads moved like a wave across her body. The bias-cut silk hung straight and narrow from slender straps, clinging like mist in all the right places. It was a dress unlike any that had debuted before, at least on any Bethlehem debutantes. "I wish Wyatt could see it. I still think we should have just had the party sooner."

"You know perfectly well that you cannot be presented before your eighteenth birthday. There's not much we could do about that." Helen reached over lightly and adjusted one of the dress straps. She ran her hand softly across her daughter's shoulders, gazing at her in the mirror. "Your hair looks very pretty this way. I like the new short style."

The week before, Susannah had astounded her parents when she came home with her long, flaxen hair sheared to a bouncy, wavy bob. It had taken them a day or two to adjust to it, but they knew their daughter, and they understood that she was—by nature—modern. Neither of her parents could deny that the style suited her. It wasn't just that the soft chin-length waves flattered her features, framing her face with a halo of gold, but also that the progressive aspect of it matched her spirit.

"I want it marcelled for the ball." Susannah swiveled her head in the mirror, considering the angles. "We'll have to tell Lucy to bring her irons."

"I daresay we should tell Lucy to bring her shackles." Her father had appeared in the doorway, wearing golf knickers and argyle socks above his brogues. "I would be remiss if I allowed any daughter of mine to roam free among the hounds of Bethlehem looking like that."

Susannah twirled around. "Hello, Daddy." As customary when she encountered her father, her smile was wide. "Does that mean you like it?" She wiggled her shoulders and the beads swayed.

His gaze was a study in affection and approval. "I think we should send condolences to the dressmaker. All that hard work, only to have his dazzling creation put to shame by the girl in it."

He turned to Helen with a brief, acknowledging bow of his head. "Queen of Troy, I beg your leave. We're only playing nine holes this afternoon—I will be at your service for whatever the evening holds."

"You know perfectly well what the evening holds," Helen scolded him lightly as he turned to go. "You bought the tickets yourself."

"That's right." Hollins snapped his fingers and turned around. "I remember now. There was a voice haranguing me like a raven sitting on my shoulder: 'Chekhov! Chekhov!' I thought I'd better get those tickets before I was pecked to death."

Susannah and Louisa giggled as Helen grabbed an embroidered pillow from a nearby slipper chair and threw it at him. "You're incorrigible. You will thank me later for the cultural enlightenment."

"Ah yes—culture." Hollins looked to the ceiling and squinted. "Something about a family bickering over selling the farm, as I understand it. Enlightening stuff, indeed."

"It's a cherry orchard. And you are a philistine." She was shaking her head, but then she conceded a wry smile. "But I suppose that *is* the gist of it."

He blew her a kiss as he turned to go, and she called after him: "You're playing with Charles, I hope?"

"Yes, the usual foursome."

"Oh good. I'm glad he's getting out. Wyatt is leaving for New Haven at noon, and I know that will be hard."

Hollins stopped in the doorway and looked at Susannah. "He's leaving today? Isn't the showcase for that little frock next weekend?"

She nodded forlornly. "The crew is in practice already. That's why we had the dinner for him last night."

"Well, that's a crying shame." Hollins shook his head. "He doesn't know what he's missing. Who's the lucky escort?"

"Chap has very generously agreed to be Sassy's date for the party," Helen answered on behalf of her daughter.

"Well, good! He's had plenty of practice. First India, now Susannah . . . hmmm . . . we could be on to something. I wonder if he'd be interested in a ticket to *The Cherry Orchard* tonight?" He walked away to the sound of his wife's exasperated huff, waving a hand behind his head.

By the time Jimmy delivered Susannah to the Collier house on Seneca Street, Chap was helping Wyatt load his suitcases into the rumble seat of the Dodge. Since his wife had died,

Charles Collier had a newfound interest in cars. With Hollins's expert guidance, he had acquired the shining maroon touring car for his sons to drive. It was a beauty, with polished maple spokes, a black ragtop, and a gleaming silver hood ornament. On the running board was a wicker hamper, held in place by a wooden accordion gate.

As Susannah stepped out of her father's own new prize—a pearl-white Stutz—Chap gave a perfunctory wave and headed into the house. "Five minutes," he called to his brother. "That train isn't going to wait."

Wyatt looked down and shoved his hands into his pockets, scuffing his shoe on the driveway as Susannah approached. Despite the years they had known each other, the sight of her still caused his blood to hurry a little—if not outright rush—and he was always afraid it would show on his face.

"Someone told me there was a shifty, delinquent-type around these parts, fixing to hop the next train out of town," she quipped, sauntering up to him. She carried a basket of cookies, still warm from the oven.

He peeked under the checkered linen cloth. "Mmmm, Elvie's snickerdoodles." He picked one up and took a bite. "They can hunt me down with a pack of bloodhounds, but they won't get these cookies." He brushed a crumb from the corner of his mouth. "Be sure to tell Elvie thanks. I'm going to miss her baking most of all."

"Is that right?" Susannah raised an eyebrow. "If I had known her cookies were so important to you, I could have saved myself some trouble and just sent the basket with Jimmy."

Wyatt set the basket on the hood of the car and gave her an impetuous and slightly awkward hug. It was a rare display of public affection; he stepped back with a self-conscious smile. "I'll tell you what's important to me—knowing you're going to be here when I get home at Christmas."

Although Wyatt's shoulders were wide and his frame sturdy, he wasn't a lot taller than Susannah; she had only to lift onto her toes a little to give him a bright kiss on the cheek. "I'll be right here where you left me, sitting in the same old boring classrooms at Bishopthorpe, surrounded by all the same old dreary faces."

But her reassurance didn't quite do the trick. He looked off and down, blinking a staccato refrain, and there seemed to be a stone in his throat as he swallowed. "I don't know how I'm going to do it. After everything that happened . . . You know . . ." He paused and drew a quick breath. "I don't know what I would have done without you."

The bond between Wyatt and Susannah that had begun in childhood had been annealed by tragedy. After Wyatt had shown up in the nursery that day with his bunch of wilted daisies, Susannah began turning to him regularly, relying on him to carry her through the worst of her grieving. And then the tables turned.

Like most men who have a disposition for devotion, Wyatt's had started with his mother. Chap had always been his father's shining star, firstborn and first at everything. Although Charles loved both of his sons equally, by the time Wyatt got around to any milestone, his brother had been there already. But, from the moment Wyatt made his second chair entrance into the world, Frances had taken pains to make sure he sat first fiddle for at least some performances, and so—from the very beginning—Wyatt was mad about his mama.

A year before she died, Frances was essentially gone. The Trudeau Sanatorium in New York was one of the foremost tuberculosis hospitals in the world, but the tiny village of Saranac Lake was isolated and the journey was arduous. The boys traveled to see their mother only once. The cold mountain air of the Adirondacks was considered restorative, but in the winter the roads were impassable. When it became clear that Frances was not improving, her husband made one last journey—without his sons this time—to bring her home while he still could.

For eleven days Wyatt hardly left her side. His mother had a breathing apparatus to prevent contamination that reminded Wyatt of the gas masks he had seen in photos of the war. She only had to wear it when others were close, but she wasn't strong enough to manage it on her own. Wyatt found that he could hold it to her face with one arm as he carried her in the other—she was as light as a feather. He would pick her up from the bed in the parlor and move her to the chaise longue on the porch without even disturbing the tuck of the quilt wrapped around her. Of course, he wasn't the only one in attendance—Charles was there as much as he could be, and Chap would sit with her in the evenings when he got back from his summer job at the plant. But over the course of that wistful, watchful interlude, Wyatt stayed off the river, rowing instead against the current of time.

The last day was no different than the others—he was reading to her from Jules Verne, the same wondrous adventures that she had read to him as a young boy. From across the porch he could see a small, appreciative smile form whenever he read a particularly familiar line. The day before, he had started on *Mysterious Island*, and that morning he picked up where he had left off. After a time, he came to the lines:

> *"What a big book, captain, might be made with*
> *all that is known!"*
> *"And what a much bigger book still with all that is*
> *not known!"*

He looked at his mother, remembering. She was gazing at him, her head to the side, and he could see a tear trailing down her cheek. She remembered too. When he was ten years old, this passage had inspired him to make his own book. It was a cardboard-bound compendium of everything he didn't know, page after page, all blank but for the headings of subjects he was determined to master. The pages were alphabetized: Salt Water; Scars; Sky; Sleep; Stars. He had shown the book to his mother with solemn resolution. "This is all I could think of that I don't know about. I'm going to fill in all the pages and then I'll give it to you." He'd wanted to give her everything; that was the best way he could think of to do it.

As Wyatt paused in his reading, Frances made a small beckoning motion with her hand. He started across the porch, but she wasn't wearing the mask and when he was a few feet away, she moved her wrist weakly, stopping him. Her voice was just a whisper, fighting through consumed lungs: "Fill your pages, my sweet boy." She closed her eyes then, and there was a soft rattle from her chest.

After his father and Chap had rushed home, and calls and arrangements had been made, and the mortician had come and gone, Wyatt sat on the porch for a long time. As dusk fell he took up the book and began to read, his voice quiet in the stillness. He was alone now, but when he looked across the room, he saw a young mother with a little boy nestled close in the curve of her arm; and it was her voice he heard murmuring the words of the final chapter—a gentle, lulling cadence that enveloped him like a soft blanket.

In the weeks and months that followed, it was Susannah's turn to provide the support that kept the structure from crashing down. She was tender with Wyatt, but it was her effervescence—her artless, natural sparkle—that buoyed him, carrying him over the rock-filled rapids of his grief like his rowing shell. And she didn't work alone. Wyatt became a regular at the Parrish table, where Helen fussed over him like he was a ghost orchid. Where Helen left off, Elvie took up. It was a welcome arrangement—Kit was in his junior year at Princeton that fall and India had started at Barnard, so Wyatt's presence helped fill the nearly empty dining room. Some evenings, when Charles could no longer stand the silence in his own home, he would join them. But Chap, although just a stone's throw away at Lehigh, was wrapped up in campus life. Unless Kit happened to be home, he occupied a chair for only the occasional Sunday supper.

Everyone had been present the previous evening for Wyatt's farewell dinner, however. Elvie had made Wyatt's favorites—lamb roast with mint jelly, scalloped potatoes, and chocolate cake. As she was serving coffee, Charles gave a toast. "I'd like to take this opportunity to offer my most humble and heartfelt thanks. The debt of gratitude that I, and my sons"—he nodded at Chap and Wyatt—"owe to our hosts—this evening and for many evenings past—is immeasurable. Without the Parrish family, we would have foundered on the rocks. Your generosity, your unfailingly open arms, and your warm, gracious household have given us the strength we needed to get through . . ." He drew a deep breath, squeezing his eyes shut briefly. "Well . . . to get through everything. Frances always knew how special this family was. More than anyone, she would want you to know what your friendship has meant to all of us."

At this point, there were several handkerchiefs dabbing at cheeks, and the other men at the table gazed down with blinking eyes.

Hollins raised his glass and spoke up. "To many years of friendship, both in the past and yet to come. And, lest we forget the purpose of this little gathering, I offer a toast to the young man across the table. Who could have predicted that the runt of the litter would turn out to be a veritable Viking?" There was laughter all around as Wyatt grinned and shrugged. Hollins waved his glass in a semicircle, engaging the table. "Congratulations on a most spectacular accomplishment, and a toast to your future—on the water and off. To Wyatt!"

Now, standing in the driveway, Wyatt tucked the cookies into the wicker hamper as Chap came out of the house.

"Not so fast," Chap said, reaching under the napkin to grab a snickerdoodle before his brother could close the lid. With a crunch, he hopped into the driver's seat.

Wyatt walked with Susannah to the Stutz, where Jimmy was waiting. He opened the door, and as she slid into the backseat he leaned forward to plant a quick peck on her cheek.

"Time's up, lover boy. Let's go." Chap was looking at his watch as he hollered out the window.

Wyatt shot a hot look over his shoulder, but his expression softened as he turned back to Susannah. "Don't let him boss you around next Saturday. I'm sorry I can't be there."

"Don't you worry; I can take care of myself. Besides, India's new beau can't make it . . . so I may as well just hand her my dance card at the outset." They both knew it—despite India's love interest in New York, her heart still beat true for Chap. But, although Chap had been her accommodating escort for her own debutante ball, he always managed to keep a brotherly distance. India had fretted about it untold times, late at night on Susannah's bed. "I can tell he just thinks of me as Kit's sister," she lamented once. "Maybe even his *own* sister."

"Oh, I hope not." Susannah had grimaced. "That would make Wyatt quite the case."

Sitting now on the edge of the deep leather car seat, Susannah gently brushed her hand against Wyatt's cheek. "Row your boat, hotshot."

Reluctantly, Wyatt stepped back from the car. "I'll write when I get there. And I'll be back in four months. It's not that long. It will go fast."

He looked so bereft standing there that Susannah was reminded of a little boy left alone for the first time, convincing himself that his mother would be home any minute. She blew a kiss out the window as Jimmy pulled away, and Wyatt gave her a small, desultory wave before turning toward his brother, who was honking the horn in the driveway.

Seven

"This weather is marvelous. I can't remember a nicer November. I believe I'll ask Harriet to set the table for dinner on the terrace."

It was unseasonably warm, as it had been all autumn. Susannah had just returned from a short trip to New York and found the others in the conservatory, where Charlie was practicing scales on the Steinway. Daisy was sprawled on the terrazzo floor with a coloring book while Joanna stood behind her son, checking his fingering.

Although the old upright in the Raffertys' living room had a few chipped keys and a squeaky pedal, Joanna would be forever grateful that her mother had insisted on piano lessons. At least she could claim that refinement, and she knew her husband's family approved of her accomplishment. Neither Frank nor his sister, Gigi, had stayed with their childhood lessons, and their mother didn't hesitate to admit she couldn't play a note. The piano had been India's territory.

In her day, Helen had been quite proficient, but her arthritic fingers no longer complied and she often asked Joanna to play for her while she rested in one of the deep bergère chairs by the tall windows. She even enjoyed looking on while Joanna gave Charlie his lessons, smiling fondly at her great-grandson as he stumbled through "Shortnin' Bread."

"A candlelight dinner under the stars. Lovely idea."

As Helen's voice rose from the depths of the chair, Susannah started, putting a hand to her heart. "Heavens, Mother, you are like a cat in the shadows over there." She shook her head briskly, recovering her composure. "I may have to put a bell around your neck." She moved to the piano and smoothed her hand lightly over her grandson's hair. "Very fine playing, maestro. Please continue."

With rote and even precision, Charlie shifted from minor to diminished, while Daisy slinked over on her hands and knees, softly meowing and rubbing her shoulder against her grandmother's calf.

Susannah looked down in mock dismay. "Yet another cat!" She furrowed her brow, leaning down to pat the little girl's head. "Just a kitten, though—it must be a stray. It certainly looks hungry." Her hand came away quickly as Daisy tried to lick it, and Joanna had to suppress a laugh.

"How did the meetings go, dear?" Helen was standing shakily, leaning on her cane for support.

"Nothing out of the ordinary. Walter and Richard send their best." Susannah had adjusted very well to her role as financial manager after her husband died. She now sat at the head of the family foundation, meeting with the advisors regularly. "The city was a zoo. You can't imagine the traffic, and no place to park. Poor Wayne had to make circles around the block during dinner, and to get from Delmonico's to the Waldorf took forty-five minutes."

"It's a new day. I'm afraid I wouldn't care for it anymore." Helen made her way toward the French doors, patting her daughter's arm as she passed. "You must be worn-out from all that hubbub. Go and draw yourself a nice hot bath, and I'll tell Harriet to set up the terrace."

"I had a thought," Joanna spoke up as it occurred to her. "Let's have dinner in the courtyard. It's so pretty, and no one ever uses it."

The courtyard—enclosed on three sides—was situated in the center of the house, just behind the staircase. There were double doors on either side leading to a beautiful stone square with a trickling fountain in the center. It was featured picturesquely from the enormous leaded glass window on the first landing of the staircase, but Joanna had never seen anyone in it but the gardener, tending to the potted wisteria and orange trees. She had noticed a round marble table with curved benches surrounding it that would seat the small group perfectly.

But her suggestion was met with silence, and then Susannah

turned and moved toward the door, her voice oddly distant. "I think I'll take your advice, Mother. A bath sounds like just the thing."

As her daughter left the room, Helen wore an inscrutable expression—vaguely troubled and somehow shrouded. "I think the terrace would be best," she said softly. "It's closer to the kitchen."

With that, she tottered away, and Charlie launched into his arpeggios.

In summer, the broad terrace on the west side of the house was graced with lingering light, but this far into the year the sun had set well before the dinner hour. Flickering illumination glowed from tall candelabra, and a cavalcade of gas lamps flanked the wide steps descending to the lawn. Because it was a school night, the children had been fed an early dinner and tucked into bed. Frank was in Burns Harbor again, so the dinner party consisted of the usual threesome—what Frank called "the unholy trinity." While Joanna could still appreciate having companions for dinner, the burden of sustained conversation was getting heavy, and she sometimes thought longingly about taking a TV tray into the library, with only Ed Sullivan for company. The children usually provided a reliable topic, but that evening it wasn't necessarily a safe one.

Charlie and Daisy had been born a year and three days apart, and Joanna had always taken great care that each

birthday be celebrated individually. A few days earlier, however, her mother-in-law had suggested a single party at Brynmor with a carnival theme and a hired magician. Later that
night Joanna had discussed it with Frank. It was a rare opportunity for pillow talk, so instead of responding to her
husband's . . . less prosaic overtures . . . she responded to the
small shoot of resentment that was growing rapidly into a
reedy stalk. Sitting up in bed, she clutched a pillow across her
lap. "It's a little over-the-top, don't you think? They're awfully
young for that kind of extravagance. And besides, I'm not sure
how they'll feel about sharing the spotlight."

Frank reached over to tug on the pillow. "I don't think it
will do any harm. Gigi and I shared a birthday every year.
Mother has always been a good party planner."

The pillow stayed put. "I guess I never envisioned raising
children who had a private circus at their disposal. That seems
like a good recipe for distorted values."

Frank let go of the pillow and sat up, giving his wife a long,
cautionary look. "I would think twice before saying something
like that. There are people around you who may take offense."

Joanna sighed and closed her eyes briefly. "I'm sorry. Of
course I wasn't thinking of you. But look at Gigi. I mean, she
isn't exactly a model of discipline and self-reliance."

Frank chuckled. "Well, you've got me there. But that's just
Gigi. She would have been a hedonist even if she'd been raised
in a convent."

Frank's twin sister was an inveterate globetrotter who

traveled in illustrious circles, and from Joanna's perspective it was an existence that was, indeed, circular. Gigi never seemed to actually get anywhere—she wasn't grounded in any sense of the word. Frank referred to his sister's pattern of behavior as "impulse slavery," shaking his head at the long parade of whimsy, featuring spectacles like the time she followed the man of her dreams to Thailand, only to find that he ran an opium den.

"Could we discuss this later?" Frank asked wearily as he leaned back on his pillow. "I'm bushed and I'd like to kiss my wife, if she would just stop talking."

But Joanna couldn't let it go. The months of living at Brynmor in forced companionship and congeniality, largely without Frank by her side, were taking their toll. The pressure was subtle, but nonetheless it had built up a good head of steam. She looked around slowly. It was a beautiful bedroom— the largest of the guest rooms in the east wing—with gilded Louis XV furniture and fringed silk taffeta draperies on tall, leaded windows—but the absence of anything that would identify it as her own hit her with sudden force. It was a breathless, bewildering moment, and a feeling like fear pushed at her heart.

"Later . . . like, next year? Their birthdays are coming up. If we don't stop this train before it leaves the station . . ." Joanna wiped the sleeve of her nightgown brusquely across her eyes, further frustrated by her tears. They were born not only of the feeling that she was losing her identity and control of her life, but also—and even more acute—of the threat to a sacred expectation: if there was going to be a power struggle in the household, she needed to know that her husband would stand behind her.

Whether the want was in the ken or the caring, Frank effectively put up his own roadblock when he rolled his eyes with a small, exasperated huff. "It's a birthday party. What's not to like about magic? I think you may be contriving problems where there aren't any."

"Contriving?"

And that was that. Joanna reached over to switch off the lamp on the nightstand, and turned toward the wall—still clutching the pillow.

Under the moonlight and unaware, Susannah broached the topic again. "I found a wonderful magician in New York. He does a children's show with rabbits and doves, the usual things. And he can bring an apparatus to make cotton candy. I think the children would love that, don't you?" The question was clearly just rhetoric; she took a dainty bite of tomato aspic and looked to Joanna for agreement.

Joanna could have kicked herself for not having a ready response. In the dim recesses of her subconscious, she wanted to kick Frank, too. He had left very early the morning after their conversation and they hadn't spoken since. Although the stew had been simmering for several days, she wasn't ready to serve it yet. She needed his backup. As usual, he wasn't there.

"Well, I'm not sure they need all of that. . . ." Joanna could hear the meek hesitancy in her voice. She straightened her back, forcing a light laugh. "The most they've experienced so far has been pin the tail on the donkey. Maybe just some games and cake . . . We could let them each have their own little party with their classmates." She took a sip of water; as a diversion, it was a feeble resort.

"Nonsense. The entertainment of children is best left to professionals." Susannah made the pronouncement as a matter of fact. "And it isn't as though we're bringing in acrobats and ponies. Just a simple magician. Efficient and effective." She snapped her fingers, her smile beneficent.

In its dismissive, patronizing, revealing resonance the word rang in Joanna's ears: *nonsense*. She looked down at her hands, clenched in her lap. She could see she was defeated—any attempt to put forth an argument would make her look peevish and ungrateful, or worse, rigid and neurotic. There was no real option to stand her ground. She was in the strange, winless position of having to cede control so as not to seem unreasonably controlling.

She drew a deep breath. "Yes, I see your point. Just a simple magician. They'll be thrilled." Her smile was tight and the tone of her voice was at distinct odds with the words, but the other women at the table didn't seem to notice as they moved on to the news of Eleanor Roosevelt's recent death.

"I read that she had requested a small, private funeral, but it turned out to be quite the affair." Despite the mournful topic, Helen was smiling. "Both President Kennedy and Vice President Johnson were there, can you imagine? Eisenhower and Truman, too. A remarkable show of respect! She was an astounding woman." Helen looked to Joanna. "Did you know that Hep and I had dinner with President and Mrs. Roosevelt when they were in the White House? It was in appreciation for the company's contribution to the war."

Joanna was mute. She should have been accustomed by now to the rarefied air of her new surroundings, but at times like this it could still make her feel faintly dizzy.

Her dismayed silence didn't seem to register, however, as the old woman continued. "Mrs. Roosevelt was a splendid conversationalist. She was just full of curiosity about the industry. She knew quite a bit about the company's curriculum vitae—the buildings and the bridges and such—but she wanted to hear all about the defense contracts . . . the tank arsenals and bomber plants and armor-plate operations. What a curious, bright mind!"

"Good lord, that sounds absolutely dreadful." Susannah shook her head in distaste. "I can't imagine a more tedious topic. I was always thankful that neither my father nor my husband was inclined to talk shop at the dinner table. Raw-steel production capacity does not a dazzling discussion make."

Helen chuckled as Harriet cleared the dinner plates. "At any rate, I held that woman in the highest esteem, and I'm sorry to hear she's gone. It's a loss to our country."

"I can't think of the name of that compound—the Roosevelt home. I remember seeing a photograph and thinking the house resembled Brynmor." Susannah dipped her spoon into a small ramekin of chocolate mousse.

"Yes, Springwood. It is remarkably similar in style. It's on the Hudson, in New York. She's buried there now, with her husband." Helen's eyes traveled the distance of decades. "Do you recall that darling little Scottie, Fala?" It had become evident of late that Helen was forgetting things in the day to day, but her memory for times past was as clear as glass. "He never left the president's side. Mrs. Roosevelt said the poor thing wasn't the same after her husband died. And do you know that dear little dog is buried there too? Right next to his master."

With these words, the image of a grave marker—small, plain, practically hidden from view—came to Joanna. Leaning back in her chair, she gazed absently at the flame of a candle, drifting to a day in October.

She was walking behind Daniel as he pushed a handcart laden with a heavy granite headstone. Suddenly he stopped and put one knee to the ground, laying his hand on something Joanna couldn't see. Looking down, he spoke in a subdued, measured cadence:

"Soon will be growing
Green blades from her mound,
And daisies be showing
Like stars on the ground,
Till she form part of them—
Ay—the sweet heart of them,
Loved beyond measure
With a child's pleasure
All her life's round."

Joanna had stared at him, moved beyond words. Stepping forward, she saw a small stone marker in the grass.

Daniel looked up at her. "Thomas Hardy. You probably know it."

She shook her head. "I don't. It's beautiful." She couldn't see the inscription, and was almost afraid to ask. "Who is it?"

Rising, he brushed his hand over the grass—a quick back and forth, like a rough caress. "This is the very unauthorized grave of a very good dog."

Before she had really gotten to know him, Joanna knew just a little about how Daniel had come to Bethlehem. Doe had given her a briefing shortly after they'd met. She began by explaining that it would have been entirely plausible that she'd have failed to recognize her own grandson. Although her daughter, Sarah, had written with the birth of each child, every time the Janssens made the two-hour drive to Lancaster, they were placidly but resolutely turned away at the door. Non-essential association with the outside world was forbidden by the tenets of the Community. The appearance of their old Dodge in front of the neat, white clapboard farmhouse was looked upon as the worst kind of breach—as if someone had parked a plague cart in a schoolyard. And so, Doe and Nico would head home heartsick—with nothing to show for their efforts but a glimpse of small, serious faces peering out the windows.

But Doe told Joanna that the moment she laid eyes on the strapping young man standing on her doorstep, she knew exactly who he was. Without question, she embraced the boy and pulled him in. She also welcomed the silky sable border collie that sat, absent any tether, pressed against Daniel's leg. In her typically cryptic manner, Doe told Joanna that it was the dog that had led Daniel to Bethlehem, but she didn't elaborate, saying it was a story for another time.

That October day, as Joanna read the name on the stone—*Lottie*—she thought it could be that time. "I heard you weren't alone when you came here." Looking at the simple inscription, she gently asked what happened.

"Not long after we got here she started having some trouble. It turned out to be a tumor. There was nothing to do."

"I'm sorry."

He didn't say anything for a few moments, and then—forcing a puff of breath though pursed lips—he sat down. With a tilt of his head, he indicated the ground beside him. As

Joanna arranged her skirt on the soft, sun-splashed grass, Daniel leaned back on his elbows and began what would be a full and detailed accounting of the reason he'd finally left everyone and everything he had ever known behind him.

Joanna had known that, despite his reserve, Daniel was uncommonly forthright. Now, as he sketched a portrait of his life in the Community, she discovered that he could also be forthcoming. In the course of a long, quiet narrative, she learned that it wasn't so much the absence of mechanical progress and modern convenience that he had chaffed at. It was the idea—no, the rule—that individuality was a sin. He told her about the inexorable yearning he had felt—the need to act as his own agent, to live life according to his own beliefs, his own relationship with his own God. Since he could remember, he had been fighting an internal battle against something he didn't have a name for. Even as he came to understand that selflessness and commitment to the greater good of the Community were perhaps the nobler ambitions, he could never stifle the earsplitting independent streak that whistled through his soul.

But even that existential, conflicted struggle was overshadowed by the incident that finally pushed him over the line.

He explained that his father, Samuel, had an arrangement with the neighbor to the east, a man called Amos Lapp. Lapp and his wife had no children of their own. In exchange for the use of what would eventually be twenty-five acres to augment his corn crops, Samuel would provide his sons to help with the milking of Lapp's dairy cows. Starting at eight years old, Daniel had risen at five in the morning to go over to the Lapp barn, and would go back again after supper.

With his face to the sun, he closed his eyes as he told Joanna how he had come to love the early mornings. He described the way the horizon made a subtle shift before the sun came up, and the smell of fresh dew in the distant tobacco fields, and the soft whisper of the cornstalks. But he hated the milking. "I had to go there by myself until my brothers were old enough to help. And old man Lapp was an ornery cuss." He turned to Joanna with a grim smile. "It took me a while to get the hang of it, and he used to stand behind me and yank on my hair right here"—he reached over and grasped a bit of hair just behind Joanna's temple, giving a light tug—"if I wasn't doing it right. After a while, it makes your whole head ache."

When he was fourteen, Daniel told her, he and two of his brothers arrived for the evening milking after supper one night to find Amos pounding in the final post of a wire dog run. Tied to a rail inside the barn was a sweet, lonely-looking border collie with eyes like a fawn's. Amos Lapp was not the type who went in for pets. Knowing there was a fair market for herding dogs among the many beef cattle farms in the region, Lapp had decided to start a small breeding business.

Daniel had just finished his last year of school—eighth grade was the end of the line—and had moved into his predetermined role in the cornfields. With Lapp's grudging permission, he began taking Lottie with him as he walked the rows, flushing out crows and any unlucky rodents within her scent. She became his daily companion and he loved her like she was his.

When Lottie had her first litter, Amos Lapp was pleased with the results. So pleased, in fact, that he put her on a severe and exhausting breeding schedule that pushed the little collie to the limits. "She would whelp a litter only to be bred again before she could turn around. For four years running, she had two litters a year. That's hard on a dog. And I felt so sorry for her when the pups would go. She would sniff around the pen, looking for them. She always seemed so frantic—I swear it broke her heart every time." Daniel shifted to lean on one arm, straightening out his legs and crossing his ankles. He picked a blade of grass and studied it for a moment.

"One day I had to go over for the second milking by myself. Everyone else was at a barn raising, but I volunteered to go because Lottie was about to have another litter." He paused, and his shoulders sank a little. "I heard her cry. I thought, you know, something was going wrong with the labor. It was just a sharp, painful-sounding yelp. When I got there, she had only delivered two pups. And they weren't moving. She was licking them like crazy—trying to get them to move, trying to save them. And then Lapp kicked her. And I knew that was what I'd heard before." He shook his head, looking directly at Joanna. "I swung at him. I don't even know how hard I hit him, but I turned back to Lottie, and the next thing I knew I was lying on the floor looking up at Lapp's wife."

Joanna sat up straight. "What happened?"

"He knocked me out with a two-by-four. He said I attacked him." He thought for a moment. "I guess I did. But I wasn't the one with the wood plank."

As Daniel described them, the events that happened next were those that decided his future. The incident became a matter for the church deacon, who insisted that Daniel repent. The Community valued penitence over all, regardless of impetus or even—in Daniel's opinion—logic. But he refused to apologize, and at the end of church the following Sunday, Deacon Wasserman asked Daniel to stand. In public, he asked him to repent for the sin of anger and raising a hand in violence against a neighbor. Again, Daniel refused. The punishment was a six-week shunning.

At this point in the telling, Daniel raised his brow ironically. "Turns out, I didn't really mind it. I still had to work the crops, but I got to sleep on the porch . . . eat alone . . . and I didn't have to go back to Lapp's. No more milking. It was funny—my 'punishment' had the opposite effect. It was a relief. I'd never really believed in the Ordnung, and I think I knew for a long time I wasn't going to be baptized. After a few weeks, it came to me that I had to leave." His eyes were remote, and Joanna could see his Adam's apple move as he swallowed hard. "So, I got a few things together and said goodbye. My family still couldn't speak to me. They just cried. Silently." He took a deep breath. "And when I left, I took Lottie with me."

And that, in his own succinct words, was it. He never said it, but Joanna knew the cost of leaving his family—and the only life he knew—was greater than any she would ever know. "Did they know where you went? Did they ever come to see you?"

"They can't. Leaving the Community is the one sin that's unforgivable. It means a permanent shunning. Old man Lapp managed to make his way up, looking for his dog, but my grandfather told him there was no such animal here. And then he told him where to go."

Lost in reverie, Joanna suddenly heard her name. Susannah was looking at her quizzically.

Sitting up straight, Joanna blinked at her mother-in-law. She had been miles away. Or more accurately, about a mile away. "I'm sorry . . . what did you say?"

"I asked how your day was. Did you have a good afternoon?"

Picking up her spoon, she gave her attention to the dessert. "Yes, lovely, thanks. On a day like this, who could complain?" She hoped the generality of her response would suffice, but Helen—as though complicit with her daughter—pressed the subject.

"I imagine you took a nice walk to enjoy the weather?"

A vague, unsanctioned instinct warned Joanna to answer carefully. She had no reason to lie, but for some reason she hadn't felt entirely comfortable revealing the progression of her friendship with Daniel. "Yes, I couldn't bring myself to stay inside. The maples are absolutely on fire. I walked along the bluff over the river—the water looked like it was running through flames."

There was a small pause before Helen responded. "Have you seen much of Doe lately?" Her tone was casual, but there was a measured, intent look in her eye.

Joanna swallowed before the spoon could reach her lips, and then bought a little time following through with the bite. "Ah no, not really . . ." In truth, Joanna hadn't seen Doe at all for the past several weeks. Without acknowledging it, she had been avoiding Daniel's grandmother ever since the day she'd taken Helen to the cemetery. She had discovered a distant path that curved along the river, and a gate on the far end that was just as convenient if she took a different route from the school. . . .

"I've been busy with the reading circle, and I volunteered to play for the holiday sing-along." Joanna had been helping out with the advanced reading group in Charlie's first-grade class, and she could now add piano accompanist to her small list of productive activity, but those things didn't really account for as much time as she hoped they implied. She was still spending some of her afternoons at the cemetery. She'd been there that very day, in fact, and, as it was a Tuesday, Doe had been busy with her knitting group and shopping. Doe didn't drive, so Nico was generally out on Tuesday afternoons as well, running errands or sitting with the men at the barbershop, playing cards and spitting sunflower seeds while he waited to pick up his wife. "I did see Mr. Janssen coming out of the hardware store today," she continued. "He sends his regards."

Joanna had, indeed, bumped into Nico. Even though—to all outward appearances—she was simply walking down Broad Street, she had felt an unreasonable panic. She had looked over her shoulder all the way to the cemetery to see if the Janssens might be pulling up behind her.

"I wonder if he's still doing the heavy work, now that his grandson is there. What was that boy's name?" Susannah asked with vague disinterest. As far as Joanna could tell, she was simply making small talk.

"It's Daniel." Helen's frail voice was surprisingly strong. "I finally met him last month when Joanna took me to the cemetery. He seemed very . . . capable." She was looking directly at Joanna, and the word hung in the air.

Capable. Ah, yes. Capable. But of what? Of hoisting stone and scaling heights and cultivating a perfect rose? Of escaping a forbidding life and carving out a new one? Of making Joanna laugh . . . of listening . . . of really seeing her? Joanna pulled her shawl close—the evening air had taken on a sudden chill. "It's getting a little cold out here," she remarked, hunching her shoulders with a shiver. "I think I may follow your lead and take a nice warm bath."

She stood and carefully placed her napkin to the left of her dessert cup—all too aware now of the gaucherie of leaving it on the chair. Bidding the women good night, she made an even exit; but she didn't need eyes in the back of her head to know that two steady gazes followed.

Eight

"Now, aren't you glad we're hosting our daughter's coming-out at home, and not at some hotel in New York or Philadelphia? Or Pittsburgh, for God's sake?" Hollins Parrish came into his wife's dressing room, fumbling with a cufflink, giving his arm an impatient shake before refolding the cuff to try again. "Blasted things—I can never get the right sleeve."

Helen stood up from her dressing table. "I'll do it. Stand still."

"I still don't see why Susannah would want to be just one more goose in the flock. You would think she'd prefer to be the lone swan, gliding in her own pond."

"My heavens." Helen screwed the back onto the cufflink and patted the pleats on her husband's shirt, then turned back to the dressing table. "You're a veritable poet! I think it was admirable of Sassy to think about the charitable aspect. Some of these balls raise quite a bit of money for good causes."

Hollins shook his head as he adjusted the chain of his pocket watch. "Charitable causes, my foot. That Bix Buggyback orchestra had more to do with it."

Helen laughed out loud. "That is the worst name mangling I've ever heard. It's *Beiderbecke*, which I think you already knew." She sat down and leaned toward the mirror to apply a careful tracing of lipstick. "But I'm afraid you're right. I hate to break it to you, dear, but your youngest daughter is a would-be flapper."

As Susannah's eighteenth birthday had approached, Helen and Hollins had started making plans to host their daughter's debut at Brynmor, as they had for India two years prior. But the arrival of engraved invitations to be presented at some of society's most prestigious affairs piqued Susannah's interest in a way they had not for India. Her argument stressed the higher purpose of philanthropy, but it wasn't hard to detect an ulterior, less altruistic motive: jazz. For her sixteenth birthday, her parents had taken her to see *Liza* on Broadway, and the seed was sown. After that, Susannah followed the Harlem scene with the dogged devotion of a religious postulate. The next year, she finagled another trip to the Great White Way to see *Runnin' Wild*, and studied every dance move as if her life depended on it. She pursued her new passion with the same intensity she had previously dedicated to riding, moving the family gramophone into her bedroom to practice the Charleston and the Black Bottom in front of a long mirror, wearing out needles on recordings of Fats Waller and Louis Armstrong, Sidney Bechet and Bessie Smith.

The invitation to be presented at the Philadelphia Charity Ball arrived first, and right away Susannah checked to see which orchestra would be playing. It was Fletcher Henderson's group—the thought of it gave her goose bumps. As icing on the cake, all Philadelphia debs would be required to participate in a choreographed "kick chorus" at presentation. That meant Susannah would have to take the train to Philadelphia every Tuesday for six weeks to practice. But one man's bonus is another man's burden: Susannah's "fun opportunity" was her mother's "inconvenient imposition."

Next came the invitation to the Cinderella Ball in Pittsburgh. Although Helen considered the beneficiary of this one—the Children's Home—an excellent example of a higher purpose, her husband squelched the idea immediately. "That's an eight-hour train ride. And the concept is rather absurd, I must say. *The Cinderella Ball.*" He pronounced the title with a scoff. "Do all of these girls expect to find their Prince Charming there? Must we keep a sharp eye on Sassy lest she abscond in a pumpkin coach?" Pittsburgh was out.

The final invitation was for the Mayflower Ball in New York. When Susannah learned that it would feature Bix Beiderbecke and the Wolverines, she mounted an all-out campaign, starry-eyed with visions of the Roseland Ballroom. The designated charity was the Soldiers Fund, which she was certain would appeal to her father. For a day or two it seemed she might be making some headway—it had come to Hollins's attention that his good friend Warren Birkland, the chairman of the New York Stock Exchange, would be presenting his daughter there. Susannah hoped that the promise of camaraderie would be extra motivation, but when Hollins saw the itinerary—which required arriving two days early for a host of procedural instructions and practice for the Grand March presentation—he stood firm. "How hard could it be to walk twenty paces with a girl on your arm? All that ridiculous fuss and rigmarole! I can't see why anyone would want to be part of such a silly production anyway—just another pair of lemmings going over the cliff. No, we'll have the party here, as we did for Itty. And if it makes you feel better," he said drily, "I will make a generous donation to the charity of your choice."

Susannah sulked for several days, but then, at dinner one night, Hollins pulled an ace out of his sleeve. "I've been making some inquiries about musicians for the party." He cleared his throat and there was a telling gleam in his eye. "There's a group that's available for the date and willing to come to us—for a price, of course. . . ." He grimaced in exaggerated resignation. "They're called the Wildecats. Ever heard of them?"

Fortunately, Susannah hadn't yet taken a bite of her food, because her mouth dropped open. "That's Harry Wilde's band! You're not serious?" She had completely forgotten she was holding her fork and it fell out of her hand and clattered onto her plate.

"Yes, well, I had to promise my firstborn son, but I think you're worth it."

Kit, home from Princeton on a break, happened to be sitting across from his father. "So glad to see that nothing has changed around here," he said dourly, giving his sister a long-suffering look. "When I turned eighteen, I remember getting a handshake."

"Poor old Kit." Susannah made a pitying little moue. "Subsisting on table scraps and the charity of strangers all this time. As I remember it, that handshake was over a signature on a stock certificate."

"All right, enough." Their mother's mouth was set in a stern line. "We all have more than we need. If I have raised children who are insensitive to that, I don't want to know about it." Helen never liked talk of money or acquisitions—it was in the poorest of taste, and she was ever vigilant that her children not take their privileges for granted.

Societal mindfulness notwithstanding, Helen's nonchalance was positively queenly as she opened her jewelry box and selected a fulgent bracelet of canary yellow diamonds set in platinum. "Could you latch this, please?" She held her wrist out to her husband.

As Hollins fixed the clasp, their younger daughter appeared

in the doorway. "Well, look who's here—the flapper herself!" Hollins took in the finished product, giving his daughter a wink as he checked his watch and slid it into his vest pocket. "I do hope you'll get cleaned up soon. We are due in the foyer in ten minutes."

Susannah shot him an indignant glare, then made a small spin, patting her hair. "What do you really think? Acceptable?" She was dressed and ready in the beaded silk gown, with white satin gloves rising past the elbow and a slender diamond band settled over her marcelled waves.

"My dear, if you will please excuse my French, I must say you are wearing the hell out of that dress."

"Honestly, Hep! Couldn't you think of a more couth way to give the compliment? For goodness sake, we aren't on the docks." Helen picked up her gloves, then turned to Susannah. "You look beautiful, darling—*la belle de la balle, certainement.* No need to make any excuses for *my* French."

The receiving line took form just as the guests started to arrive, with Kit dashing down at the last minute, shrugging into his tailcoat. The expansive double doors were thrown open and the family stood to the side in the center hall, greeting the guests as Alvin—the butler retained for events—ushered them in. India wore a smashing emerald satin number that draped low on her back and complemented her coloring perfectly. Because she was somewhat shorter than her younger sister, she had to rise onto her toes as she whispered to Susannah, "Where's Chap? He should be here by now."

Susannah was well aware that India had dressed specifically for Chap. She felt a tug of sympathy for her sister's obvious efforts. "You know Chap—always up to the brim of his hat in something to do with a ball or a bat." *Or a girl,* she didn't add, although it was no secret that Chap was as adept playing that field as he was on the ballfield.

Sighing, India smiled forlornly at her sister. "Wyatt would have been here an hour ago, offering to carry up champagne or pitch in parking cars with Jimmy. I guess you got the good one."

The gravel on the drive crunched pleasantly as cars delivered guests to Brynmor's august entrance. Susannah had always loved that sound—it was the sound of anticipation, of arrival. Most of the guests employed drivers, but for those who drove themselves, Jimmy acted as valet, standing erectly at the bottom of the broad stone steps, uniform pressed and buttons shining.

Of the 150 invitations extended, there were 124 acceptances. Kit and India had each invited a few friends and old schoolmates, and Susannah had included any of her classmates who had already made their debuts. In their parents' set, there were friends from Bethlehem, Allentown, and Easton, as well as some from as far away as Greenwich and Grosse Pointe. Even Vance Wright, Hollins's archrival at U.S. Steel, made the trip with his wife, Agnes—a friend of Helen's from finishing school. And, of course, there were the relatives: Helen's family from Boston and both of Hollins's sisters with their husbands, traveling from Chicago and Cincinnati, along with several cousins who were of age.

During the reception, guests milled about in the grand hall, spilling through the tandem French doors to the courtyard, where flickering torches cast dancing light across the flagstones. In addition to serving champagne, waiters circulated with silver trays of oysters and caviar on tiny toast points, accompanied by monogrammed linen napkins.

As the stream of haut monde was beginning to taper off, a tall, striking figure with dark hair slid past a group in the doorway and hurried toward the family. "Sorry—had to take care of a bunch of babies all day." Chap kissed Helen lightly on the cheek and shook Hollins's hand, holding his tie in the other. "The new recruits got to campus last night. Can someone please help me with this?" He held the tie out with a defeated look, and India stepped right up. Moving him into the shadow of the staircase, she proceeded to make the bow. Susannah couldn't help noticing her sister's hands shaking just a little. They stepped back into line just in time to greet Clement Clark, the president of Bethlehem Savings and Loan. A confirmed bachelor, he had arrived alone. After paying the requisite respects, he clapped Chap on the back and pulled him aside to enthuse about next spring's prospects for the Lehigh baseball team. It was common knowledge that Mr. Clark was Chap's biggest fan.

When it appeared that all of the guests had arrived, Hollins took a position halfway up the stairs, Helen at his side. "If I may have your attention, please." He waited a moment for the chatter to subside. "I'd like to welcome you all to Brynmor, and thank you for being part of this little celebration in honor of our youngest daughter's eighteenth birthday." With a bittersweet smile, he tipped his glass to Susannah. "It seems like just yesterday she was trying to convince me to let her run the elevator at Bethlehem Steel. She even showed up one day with her own white gloves, ready to take Dickie's place in the cage." He paused briefly. "She was five years old." The crowd laughed and Susannah made a curving motion with her fist, working an invisible lever. Hollins gazed at his daughter for a long moment; there was a revealing sheen in his eyes. "As anyone who knows Susannah can attest, she has been—and will be—an astounding success at whatever she does. But, while she is certainly capable of getting a rise out of a room"—his brow lifted significantly—"something tells me she will never be an elevator operator." There was more laughter, and Hollins raised his glass high. "So please join me in a toast to this beautiful creature as she crosses the threshold to adulthood. We may be losing a little girl, but we are gaining an exceptional young woman."

The guests held their glasses up in tribute. As strains of music drifted from above, Hollins enjoined them to move to the ballroom. "The band is starting without us. We will reconvene here for midnight supper." He held his hand out toward Susannah, and proceeded to escort his wife and his daughter up the grand staircase.

The crowd followed, with Kit and India ushering from the rear. Kit was in charge of Grandmother Avery, who had traveled from Boston with Helen's brother and family. She grasped his arm tightly as she made her way up, one step at a time. Her gown—a high-necked creation with sleeves that ran past her wrists—was in distinct contrast to the modern dresses her granddaughters wore, and she had the old-order Victorian demeanor to match. "My dear boy—I'm relieved to see you haven't succumbed to that dreadful new trend." She gave a disdainful sniff up the stairway at a young man in a tuxedo. "A dinner coat at a formal affair! What's next . . . a dressing gown and slippers?" Her British accent had not dimmed after thirty-seven years on American soil, and it imbued her every pronouncement with commanding authority.

Kit grinned when he saw that Chap—sporting a jaunty white dinner jacket—was the object of his grandmother's outrage. His friend was still monopolized by Clement Clark, who was clutching Chap's arm in exactly the same manner as Grandmother Avery was grasping his own.

The orchestra was in full swing as they reached the third landing. Hollins and Susannah were christening the floor with a father-daughter dance as the guests looked on, applauding as Hollins swept his daughter in broad circles. He couldn't begin to comprehend the newest dance crazes, but Hollins Parrish was an ace waltzer.

As the dance ended, Susannah happily accepted another glass of champagne from a passing waiter. Hollins led his wife onto the dance floor, and Susannah looked around expectantly for her escort. She spotted him against the wall, still trapped in conversation with Mr. Clark. He was casting covertly around for help, and when she caught his eye, he gave a small, relieved wave. Extricating himself from the large hand on his shoulder, he crossed the floor to Susannah.

"Hello, old Chap," she said, in a perfect imitation of her grandmother's Belgravia accent. "I thought perhaps you'd taken a fancy to Lord Fiddleladdie over there. Quite cozy, you two seemed."

Placing his hand lightly on her waist, Chap looked down with a suspicious squint. "It sounds like someone has been into the champagne. Have you been misbehaving, little girl?"

Susannah giggled and set her glass down as he led her onto the dance floor. "My behavior has been impeccable." She stifled a hiccup, grasping his shoulder as he pulled her close. "I have been into the stars. Lovely, twinkling flutes of stars, which sparkle all the way down."

Chap gave a low laugh as he moved her across the floor in a fluid fox-trot. "I wonder if you father is aware you're making such an excellent effort to empty his cellar."

"It's my birthday—I'm entitled to swallow some brilliance." Despite the free-flowing "brilliance," Susannah was following Chap's every step as naturally as breathing. "And don't worry about the supply—Hep bought out every vineyard in France. Not to mention all the hard liquor he could get his hands on. Especially gin."

The wine cellars at Brynmor had been deep to begin with, but with the passing of the Volstead Act, Hollins had ordered as many cases of wine and champagne as he could flush out of France and Italy. He also claimed the whiskey and gin stock of almost every distributor in the region. Tonight he was serving Pol Roger by the case-full, as well as single-malt scotch whiskey for the men.

"You're familiar with Hep's ginventory, aren't you?" She gave Chap a knowing look. "It is truly a triumph."

"I don't know what you're talking about." An oblique smile tugged at Chap's lips as he fixed his gaze over her shoulder.

"Right." She drew the word out. "Certainly, Kit has no idea where the key is. The two of you have never . . . let's say . . . borrowed a bottle or two."

Chap narrowed his gold-green eyes at her. "A shameless spy. Nothing has changed since you were eight years old."

"Shameless, I am." She grinned as she plucked a flute from a passing tray. "Shamelessly thirsty." Her eyes danced as she raised the stem. "Bottoms up!" She took a sip, but that was all; Chap took the glass from her hand and set it on the nearest ledge. Susannah dropped her chin with a protesting huff. "Wyatt said I shouldn't let you boss me around."

Chap grinned. "You are a handful, Sassy Parrish." He moved her toward the center of the ballroom, dancing through the throng that now crowded the floor. "How does Wyatt manage?"

The orchestra was playing "Dreamy Melody"; as it came

to an end, Susannah pouted a little. "I wish they would get to the good stuff."

As though he had heard her, the bandleader struck up a lively rendition of "Do It Again." Susannah squealed and squeezed Chap's hand, her smile radiating like Vega. "That's more like it! Come on." With a shimmy, she scooted toward the bandstand, pulling Chap behind her as she threw a wink over her shoulder. "Time to show me what you've got, old man."

Her hands and feet moved in rhythmic syncopation, and the beads on her dress shimmered and swayed as she led Chap into a swinging Black Bottom. Some of the younger set stayed on the dance floor, doing their best to keep up, but there wasn't anyone who could dance like Susannah. It was as if the brilliance she had been drinking shone through her skin—she sparkled like a prized Grand Cru.

Chap was a quick study, but when the band broke into "Charleston," he generously abdicated to Gerald Barnwell, an old classmate who could match Susannah's every step, throwing himself into it like a cyclone.

A group of young men were sipping scotch by the bar, and Chap joined them. "Couldn't keep up, eh?" Kit ribbed his friend as he handed him a drink.

Chap shook his head. "She's something, your little sis." His gaze was directed in the vicinity of the orchestra platform, as Susannah—in a move all her own—made a nimble pirouette, swiveling her hips in an undulating fishtail.

The boys were debating the chances of the Senators versus the Giants going into the World Series, and although this was a topic Chap knew something about, he was oddly distracted. When he failed to respond to a question repeated three times, George Steichen slugged him in the arm. "Didn't know you were such a jazz fan, Chappie. Don't mind us—we're just having a discussion here."

As the song ended, Chap handed his glass to George. "Duty calls." He gave his friend an irritated look. "And don't call me Chappie." Making his way back to center floor, he stepped in front of his gangly replacement. "Sorry, Gerald, that's all you get."

Gerald pulled out his handkerchief and mopped his brow. "Thanks for the dance!" Unusually large front teeth saddled his smile with an unfortunate goofiness. "I'll be back for more!" He did a little jive step as he scuttled away, and certainly didn't hear it when Chap muttered to himself, "Not likely."

The band had reverted to a slow waltz, and Susannah smiled teasingly as Chap took her hand. "You're back! I thought I'd lost you." Although her last partner had come out looking decidedly worse for wear, the effects of exertion had only enhanced Susannah's glow.

He looked away with studied detachment. "Wyatt expects me to do my job. I wouldn't want to let him down."

They moved together with an ease that was preternaturally

effortless—like birds flying in formation—and stayed on the floor as the Wildecats segued into a wistful rendition of "What'll I Do." Susannah had become curiously quiet, and when the next number proved to be another slow one, Chap didn't let go of her hand.

The band was taking a break. It was hard to know how many songs they had played—for some reason time had become formless and indefinite. But now the music had stopped, and for the first time since Chap had elbowed Gerald out of the way, his eyes met Susannah's.

In that infinite instant, they saw it. The look they exchanged wasn't questioning or confounded. It wasn't awkward or abashed. It was helpless and horrified and empirically certain. Somewhere, in the lilting measures of the music, everything had changed. The algorithm that had been calculated years before—the accepted premise that it would always be Susannah and Wyatt, that Chap was not just Kit's best friend but the established object of India's heartbroken desire—was suddenly, shockingly, shattered. It was Hippasus discovering that the square root of two is an irrational number: the math had been wrong all along.

"Would you like to get some air?"

Susannah simply nodded, and with his hand on the small of her back, Chap ushered her toward the open doors across the room. As they passed through the crowd, Susannah saw her sister standing with several of her old friends from Bishopthorpe. India was giving her a purposeful, imploring look.

They stepped onto the balcony and Susannah drew a deep breath. "You should dance with Itty." Her tone was oddly wooden. "She would like that."

Chap was looking into the distance, and he replied without turning his head. "I don't want to dance with Itty." His words were soft and strained—betrayed by a raspy catch.

After a moment of silence, they heard a cough.

"Hello there."

Susannah jumped and Chap wheeled around. Charles Collier was standing in the shadows, alone with a glass of whisky. "It's a nice night, isn't it?" He waved his glass lightly through the air, as if to demonstrate the pleasing accommodation of the atmosphere.

"Yes." It took Chap an extra beat to respond, and the word hung there for a moment. "It, uh, feels good to get some fresh air. It was getting a little warm in there."

"I imagine it was particularly warm on the dance floor." Charles rattled the ice in his glass and took a sip. Although the moon cast a pale yellow glow across the smooth limestone, he was leaning back on the balustrade with the light behind him; it was impossible to see his expression.

Susannah suddenly felt something like nausea, and she turned abruptly toward the door. "If you'll excuse me please, I need to powder my nose."

An endless procession of faces floated past as she skirted the edge of the ballroom. Her smile was frozen in place and she nodded in numb response to greetings and birthday wishes from well-meaning guests, but she didn't stop. The ladies' powder room was just to the right, but there was a group of women clustered there and Susannah turned left, heading for the back stairway. She rushed down the stairs, nearly landing on her seat as the smooth leather of her soles slipped over the carpet; in the west wing hall, she practically ran to her bedroom. Shutting the door, she stopped short and leaned back with a ragged breath. Then she closed her eyes and stayed there, propped against the mahogany panels, hands over her face.

The Earth hadn't tilted on its axis—it had tipped over completely. She replayed the stunning instant she had known. There was something happening as they danced—she floated in Chap's arms like a feather in a stream, with a strange, transcendental feeling of utter fulfillment, made more bewildering by the fact that she hadn't realized it had been missing before. She hadn't known what was happening—only that she didn't want it to end. And then he'd looked at her, and it was suddenly crystal clear. Her mind's eye fixed on that moment: the sure knowledge . . . the crushing remorse . . . the essential, soul-bequeathing acceptance. And through the shock of that recognition, really *seeing* him for the first time—tall, dark, cataclysmically attractive. Panther eyes and a sybarite mouth. The memory took her breath away.

But in the next moment she felt a wrenching twist in her heart. Oh—Wyatt. Sweet, tender Wyatt, who had been at her side for what felt like her entire life. A tear slipped down her cheek and she bent over with the weight of it. Wyatt—who had written her the moment he had arrived on campus, beseeching her to respond right away, signing off with a reference to the days on the calendar: *1 down, 106 to go.* She couldn't bear to think of the ways that this would hurt him.

But, like any epiphany, the knowledge had been immediate and absolute: it was Chap. If she could have called back the echoing peal as it rippled across the universe, she would have, only there wasn't any way to unring a bell. She knew—with the clarity of a copper chime—it would only ever be Chap.

She nearly jumped out of her skin at a staccato rap. "Susannah?" It was her mother's voice, concern radiating through the wood.

Stepping back quickly, Susannah smoothed her hands over her dress and her hair, plastering a smile on her face as she opened the door.

"Hello!" She blinked brightly at her mother.

Helen looked quizzical. "I noticed you rushing out—I wondered if everything was all right."

"Oh yes . . . just fine. I think the champagne may have gone to my head. I needed a bit of a break."

A small frown appeared. "Susannah, I'm surprised at you.

I would think you'd know better. Ladies never have more than one drink."

Susannah patted her mother's shoulder and turned conveniently away. "Oh, Mother, it wasn't that much. Just a couple of glasses. More likely, I overdid it a bit on the dance floor." As the words left her mouth, she felt a flush race from her chest to her cheeks. "I'll be there in a tick—I need to touch up my lipstick." She moved toward her dressing table, step measured and spine straight.

From the doorway, Helen gazed at her daughter's back with a thoughtful expression. And then, with a slight shake of her head, she turned and left.

Susannah reentered the ballroom to the strains of the orchestra—back on the bandstand again—playing "I Cried for You." She had no idea what would happen next. She had a fleeting memory of being at a carnival fun house when she was four years old, nervous and a little dizzied by the distorted images in the wavy mirror. It was exactly how she felt now.

Chap was dancing with India. Susannah's eyes landed on him without even trying, as if there were a lighthouse on the dance floor. At the exact moment she found him, he found her, too, his eyes settling into hers with a certitude—sure and unwavering—that steadied the reeling yaw.

"There she is! We thought maybe the girl of the hour had

decided this motley crew wasn't worth the bother!" It was her uncle Ronald, her mother's brother from Boston, standing nearby with a clutch of aunts and cousins.

"Dear Susannah—you're as glamorous as a movie star!" Aunt Tabitha was clearly feeling the effusive effects of the Pol Roger. "I just have to compliment that dress—it's simply stunning. Where on earth did you find something like that? I've always said, Helen Avery Parrish sets the bar high, but my goodness, I think she has broken it tonight! What an affair!"

"Hello, Sassafras." Hollins walked up and gave his daughter a light kiss on the cheek. Taking a sip of scotch, he put a fraternal arm around Ronald's shoulders. "Are these people bothering you? I told Hedy we should have a special section for the Bostonians. They're a sordid bunch." Although he addressed Susannah, his smile was cast teasingly around the circle of his wife's family.

En masse, the clan burst into a spirited defense of the superior qualities of Beantown, while over their clamor a gong sounded. Alvin was standing in the wide center archway, holding a brass cymbal. Hollins glanced over his shoulder at the butler, and then checked his watch. "I believe that's our signal—dinner shall be served."

The band had taken the cue and started in on "Goodnight, Ladies" as people moved toward the stairway, fanning out to the sides to wait for the host to lead the way. Helen appeared at her husband's side, and Susannah looked around hesitantly—

hovering in a brief, nervous limbo. Hollins waved his arm high as he spotted Chap across the room. "If Itty will relinquish her hold on your escort's arm," he murmured, "we can proceed."

Chap made his way over and Susannah hoped she was the only one to notice the slight tremor of strain in his upper lip as he smiled amicably at her parents. He bowed his head slightly as he held his arm out to Susannah.

She clasped a gloved hand to his forearm and they fell into step behind her mother and father. The pressure of her hand was light, and there were several layers of fabric separating skin from skin, but there was no mistaking the surge of twin pulses beating in rapid, reverberant accord.

Nine

"What do you do when the ground is frozen?" Joanna watched as Daniel rocked the shovel back and forth with the heel of his work boot, chipping away at clumps of frosty topsoil to get to the more pliable earth below the surface.

"It isn't too bad until about January. They've started using a backhoe over at Greenwood, but we aren't that fancy here. Just good old elbow grease." He pitched a wedge of packed dirt onto a small pile. "Sounding can be a little tough if the frost goes deep. But I've got a couple of tricks up my sleeve, passed down from the tribe elders." He straightened and rested his arm on the handle of the shovel, exhaling a puff of steam in the cold afternoon air.

"Sounding?" The stone obelisk at Joanna's back was tall and narrow—its base providing the perfect width and angle to lean against, feet pulled up and arms wrapped around her knees. Her wool coat was long enough to cover her legs, and her hands were snuggled into a fur muff like a pair of small rabbits in a burrow.

"If there are any other graves nearby, you have to poke around with a rod before you dig to be sure nothing has shifted over. Wouldn't want to disturb anyone's sleep."

Joanna smiled at the typically droll explanation. "What are your tricks?"

Letting the shovel drop, Daniel stepped over to the monument and stood at her feet. "I could tell you," he said, his voice low and serious, "but I'd rather show you."

A confluent ripple, emanating from the separate origins of Joanna's knees and shoulders, rushed to meet in the middle as she looked straight into the depths of his crystalline eyes. He gazed at her, and in that long moment the brisk white day and the bare trees and the chipped earth all disappeared. Then he turned and went to the flatbed cart parked a few yards to the south.

Heaving a large sack of charcoal over his shoulder, he moved back to the dig site and dropped it to the ground. He went back for another bag, and one more after that. Then he pulled a box of long matches from one of the deep pockets in his canvas jacket and gave it a little rattle as he looked back at Joanna. "One of my most effective tools." He threw several lit matches onto the bags, and when they began to take, he got onto his hands and knees to blow lightly at the smoke. Then he sat back on his heels and held his hands over the heat. "Come over here." He twisted around and motioned

Joanna toward him. "I have to watch it for few minutes before I put the cover on."

Joanna stood and stepped lightly to his side, then dropped to her knees, hands still tucked into the muff. They sat in silence, absorbing a warmth that had little to do with the coal. After a while, Daniel asked quietly, "How did the party go?"

It had been a week since Joanna had been to St. Gregory's. The last time had been just before the children's birthday party, and she hadn't been able to contain her exasperation. She had found herself, once again, opening up to Daniel. Something in the way he listened made her feel safe with her confidences. And there was something else. It had become increasingly undeniable—she felt a certain contentment when she was with him.

"It was fine, I suppose. I was a little appalled that Daisy took to it all like a fish to water—*presiding* over everything like some kind of pint-sized empress." Joanna laughed and rolled her eyes, sweeping her arm out as she demonstrated, with a spot-on imitation of Daisy's lisp: "Please be seated. The show will begin soon. Refreshments will be served after. There are very many delicious treats."

She went on to describe the authority with which her daughter took the stage as Fredo's assistant, crestfallen and a bit put out when the magician didn't have the required props to saw her in half. "And then one little boy got sick from too much cotton candy, and Charlie started to cry because he was worried the rabbit might have died. When it finally reappeared,

Charlie was so embarrassed that *he* disappeared. I found him in his room, sulking."

"Did your husband make it back?" The question was delivered with careful neutrality.

"Yes. As a matter of fact, he was home by Friday night. He was nearly as excited as Charlie and Daisy were about the party. After the magician left, he came up with his own tricks. I think the kids were as taken with him as they were with Fredo." She pictured Frank in the center of the room, making a quarter disappear and then pulling it from the nearest child's ear, and she could hear the echo of squeals as he seemingly made a Dixie cup float through the air. The previous night, when Joanna had come into the bedroom, he'd been standing there with his thumb poked through the paper cup, practicing his technique.

Daniel stood to fetch the long metal lid that would contain the heat, and while he was positioning it over the bags of charcoal, he glanced at his watch. "Don't you have to play the piano this afternoon?"

An appreciative smiled curved Joanna's lips. The fact that he knew and remembered her mundane schedule never failed to please her. He paid attention to everything she told him, processing and storing each detail as though it were important. He knew the ins and outs of the children's lives—their latest interests and developments and challenges. He knew that Daisy's best friend was named Rosie. He called them "the flower girls," remembering to ask—with some amusement—if they had worked things out after last week's spat. He knew that Charlie liked to watch *McHale's Navy* and that he had gotten 100 percent on his latest math test. He knew that the little boy missed his father when he was gone.

"Yes. I guess I should go." With the holiday sing-along approaching, the students at Trinity were practicing twice a week now after school. The acoustics were very good in the gymnasium, but Joanna had to roll the old upright out of the music room and down the hall, so she needed to get there early. As she started to stand, Daniel took her arm, helping her up just as he had that day in early September when she had tripped on the sidewalk. It was the first physical contact they'd had since then, and she felt something like an electrical current zip through her arm where he grasped it, straight to an area dangerously close to her heart. His face was near enough that she could feel the warmth of his breath on her cheek, but when she looked up at him, he turned away.

Taking a couple of paces toward the path, Daniel began to whistle a quiet tune. It was just a few notes, but Joanna recognized it as one of the carols the kids were practicing. As he grasped the handles of the cart, he turned back. For a couple of beats he just stood there, with a look she couldn't define. And then he asked her a question, so quiet that she almost didn't catch it.

"Do you see what I see?"

He walked away before she could respond, and it wasn't

until he was gone that she realized it was only a line from the song.

After dinner, the children wanted to play in the ballroom. It hadn't quite been restored from the party—balloons and streamers lingered like persistent, bedraggled revelers, and there was some leftover delight to be had there. The other pressing incentive was Daisy's newly acquired skill. With patient coaching from her brother, she had finally mastered a headstand, and the need to show it off was unrelenting. Joanna knew her hope for a quiet evening with Jack London was a lost cause.

She took her usual seat on a Chiavari chair, making a mental note to haul up something more comfortable for the future. It was becoming clear she would be spending a fair amount of time in the capacious opulence of the third-floor space. After compulsory attention to dual headstand performances, Joanna remembered the photo albums in the bookcase. As Charlie and Daisy hurled themselves over the old Persian carpets, Joanna wandered across the room and selected another volume, settling back in her chair with the heavy leatherbound pages.

The pictures didn't seem to be in any particular order. It appeared that someone had finally responded to some nagging impulse for tidiness or historical obligation, mounting a disorganized stack of photos onto the pages. The first one was of a young man in a graduation cap and gown, tassel hanging on the left and diploma in hand. An older man in a dark suit stood next to him. Both had serious expressions and cleft chins. Joanna recognized them as Wyatt Collier and his father, Charles. She could see the name and emblem of Yale University on the folio cover of the diploma, and she could make out an ivy-covered building in the background.

Next, there were several pictures of a party in the ballroom where Joanna sat. Frank's aunt India was the center of attention, wearing a full-skirted white gown that looked something like a wedding dress. She was posed formally in front of one of the balcony doors, and the tall young man standing at her side was Charlie in about thirteen years. Of course, it was Wyatt's brother, Chap . . . but the likeness was so uncanny that it rattled her again.

There were a few photos of a young Kit Parrish—dangling keys next to a shining convertible with huge, curving fenders; grinning with a Princeton pennant; waving from the deck of an ocean liner—and then Joanna turned the page to photos of another party, this time in evident celebration of Susannah. In one, she stood on the landing of the grand stairway in a dress that produced a swell of admiration in Joanna's chest. She recognized the style as that of the flapper era, beaded and perfectly draped, as if it had been made for her. Studying this young version of her mother-in-law, Joanna felt something like pride. Susannah had been stunning.

As she took in the details of the photo, Joanna noticed something strange. Susannah was posed in front of the large, segmented window that overlooked the courtyard, but instead of intricate rows of clear beveled panels set in slender leaded joints, the window consisted of an elaborate peacock-themed mosaic. Although the photo was in black and white, Joanna could tell by the tonality that there were deep variations of color in the glass. She couldn't imagine why anyone would want to replace it. Perhaps the landing needed more light, or a better view of the courtyard . . . or maybe some decorator had deemed the design out of style. Whatever the case, Joanna thought it was a shame. The window was beautiful.

Looking through the rest of the party pictures, she discovered that the curiosities didn't end there. The photographer had taken quite a few candid shots. In addition to the pictures of the ballroom, there were several that featured the courtyard and the great hall, with tables of guests in formal attire, laughing and conversing over china and crystal and elaborate floral arrangements. From previous experience, Joanna expected to see a young Wyatt Collier somewhere in close proximity to Susannah. But when she spotted the debutante at the head of a long linen-draped table, she noticed that the young man sitting to her right wasn't Wyatt; it was his brother. She peered at the photo, studying the other faces at the table. Although several heads were turned away, she didn't think Wyatt was among them. After a moment she turned the page with a shrug, relegating the question to the murky depths of life's insignificant and forgettable mysteries.

Hollins Parrish was the subject of the next few pages—holding a bottle of champagne against the hull of a ship, at a ribbon-cutting ceremony on some unrecognizable construction site, at a podium in what was probably a boardroom. And then there was an image of Hollins and Helen Parrish, seated with two other people at one end of an enormous, gleaming mahogany table. It didn't take more than a split second for Joanna to recognize the other couple. At the head was Franklin Roosevelt, and next to him, his wife, Eleanor. Looking closer, Joanna could make out the famous Gilbert Stuart portrait of George Washington hanging on the wall behind the president. This was the dinner at the White House that Helen had mentioned. Joanna had been flummoxed then by the very idea of it; seeing it was stranger still.

She was shaking her head a little at the bizarre path her life had taken when, out of the corner of her eye, she noticed a figure coming through the archway.

"Grandmother, watch what I can do!"

As Daisy clamored for her attention, Susannah added to the surprises of the evening by crossing the floor and pulling a chair up next to Joanna. The rumpus of the ersatz gymnasium was under Joanna's purview, and the last thing she expected was that her mother-in-law would join her in the ballroom that evening. "My amazement is at the ready, and I'm prepared to be impressed. Show me what you've got, Davida." Expectantly erect, she gave her granddaughter her full consideration.

Because of her mother-in-law's restrained manner, Joanna had not expected her to be particularly hands-on with Charlie and Daisy. But Susannah had proven to be a mischievously playful grandmother. She treated them like small adults, advocating free will in regard to eating vegetables, and flexible bedtimes. On school nights, Joanna held firm at eight o'clock, but on weekends Susannah prevailed in her belief that "It's more important to spend time in the company of those with whom one lives than it is to follow a silly schedule. Children will go to bed when they're tired."

It had been Susannah's idea for the children to learn to play chess, and she often played with them, offering sly, cryptic suggestions—"Her majesty is very fond of dancing, but she never gets to lead"—and applauding high in the air if they found the move. Charlie almost always won, so Susannah had lately been rooting for Daisy. During one particularly spirited game, she had sweetened the incentive by vowing somberly to come to dinner wearing a lampshade on her head if Daisy won the day. Charlie didn't waste a minute sacrificing his king, and that evening Susannah showed up in the dining room with the small, fringed shade from the floor lamp in the nursery perched on her head like the latest fashion from Paris. The children giggled throughout the meal while their grandmother comported herself with sublime sangfroid.

But after living for nearly half a year under the same roof as Frank's mother, Joanna was learning for herself what her husband had tried to explain, on the rare occasions that he talked about it. Incidental whimsy aside, there was a quality about Susannah that could only be called guarded. She was contained and private—in stark contrast to Joanna's own mother, who had a natural warmth that extended to complete strangers. Eileen Rafferty took a worried, proprietary interest in anyone who wandered across her path, digging out details like a world-class archeologist; but Joanna had never had anything even remotely resembling a personal conversation with her mother-in-law.

She knew that Frank's childhood had been a happy one—that his mother had been active and involved with her children—but he'd shared that he had always found her, in some way, unknowable. He'd said it was as though she had some private, inner realm to which he would never be admitted.

Except once.

One evening during their courtship, Frank and Joanna were in his car, prolonging the sweet good night, when a song came on the radio. After a moment Frank sat back with a puzzled look, then turned to peer out the window as if he were trying to see something in the distance. As it turned out, he was trying to see something in the past.

"I know this song. . . ." It was almost a question—the words slowed by foggy recollection. "One time—I must have

been about ten years old—I was working on a model airplane, and the song was playing on the radio." Frank gave
Joanna a self-deprecating smile. "I went through a big model
airplane phase." Turning back to the window, he continued,
thoughtful. "I was in my dad's study, sort of hidden behind
his desk. I had a newspaper spread out on the floor, and I was
lying on my stomach, working on that block of balsa they
used to give you."

As Frank told it, the big Crosley radio in the corner was
tuned to the weekly broadcast of *Jack Armstrong, the All American Boy*. That was why he was in the study to begin with.
But it hadn't started yet. There was music piping softly through
the mesh fabric of the console—someone crooning an old Ir-
ving Berlin tune: "What'll I Do." As he began to carve the
fuselage, his mother passed the open door and stopped suddenly. From Frank's position on the far side of the large partners' desk, he could see only her legs as she took a few steps
into the study. And then, very slowly, she sank onto the
horsehair chair at her side, grasping the stuffed arm like it was
a crutch.

"There was something about it that was just . . . well . . .
different. She was always pretty purposeful and focused—she
wasn't the type to just drift around. But it was like she was in
a kind of trance or something. So I just stayed quiet. I think I
wanted to see what she would do next. It was so strange.
And then I leaned forward and I could see her face, and I had
never seen her look like that. She was just staring at the radio,

and there was this . . . sadness . . . I mean, it was like she was looking at something really tragic. I remember it sort of scared me. I didn't want her to know I was there. Not just because it would have been awkward, but also because it was, well . . . fascinating. I had always sort of sensed that there was something there, you know, something she wouldn't share with anyone." He paused for a moment, remembering. "And then she started to cry." He gave Joanna a weighty look. "I'm sure you've figured out by now that my mother does not cry."

"And then what happened?" Joanna was as fascinated now as Frank had been then.

"I sat up." Frank shrugged. "I guess I forgot I was hiding. She looked at me like a deer in the headlights—frozen there with tears running down her cheeks. And then she just stood up and walked away."

"Did you ever ask her about it?" Compassion was Joanna's immediate sentiment, but she was also just plain curious.

"No." With a short laugh, he raised a skeptical brow. "Would you have?"

With appropriate applause for Daisy's headstand, Susannah now settled back on the chair, crossing her legs and angling her shoulders toward Joanna. "What have we here?" Reaching over, she tilted the album. "Ah, the vaunted presidential dinner." She looked at the photo for a moment. "To hear mother tell it, Eleanor Roosevelt was her doppelgänger. I think she felt they were spiritually kindred. She talked about that meeting for weeks."

"It really is incredible," Joanna responded, "to think that Beth Steel held such a prominent position in the ranks of industry." When they were first married, Frank had taken Joanna to New York to see *The Pajama Game* on Broadway. Walking down the avenues, he could point to practically any structure—the Chrysler Building, Rockefeller Center, the Waldorf-Astoria—and proudly claim it as one of the company's own. She knew, of course, that the business her husband's grandfather had built was the largest forging operation in the country, but until more recently she had been unaware of just what Hollins Parrish had accomplished.

"Yes, my father was something of a visionary." There was pride in Susannah's voice, as well as tenderness. "Much of it was timing, of course; first there were the railways and the ships, but then—with the wars—the armor plate, the guns, the shells, the submarines . . . they made it all. At one point, the stock went from thirty dollars to seven hundred in the span of three years." She shook her head at the idea of it, and then raised her brow and leveled a significant look at Joanna. "And then came the H beam. The best move my father ever made was to hire Charles Collier. He came up with the wide-flange beam, and that changed everything. Nobody else had it. You can thank Charles for the skyscraper. And for long-span bridges—the Golden Gate, the George Washington . . ." She paused and recrossed her legs, glancing absently at the children as she continued. "After Wyatt took over, there was the business of heavy forging and nuclear power, and things just continued to"—she smiled wryly—"explode."

Joanna was beginning to notice that when it came to matters of historical explication, whether the topic was religious freedom or structural steel, her mother-in-law could be positively loquacious. "I guess Frank's career was a foregone conclusion, what with it coming down both lines like that." She couldn't quite disguise the resignation in her voice. Although it had never been specifically stated, Joanna had been aware, from the earliest days of their marriage, that her husband was being groomed to step into his father's shoes, just as Wyatt had done when his father-in-law retired. But Frank was far from ready when Wyatt died so unexpectedly, and for the first time in sixty years, someone from outside the family was now in charge.

"It doesn't always work that way," Susannah replied. "My brother, Kit, was bitten by the travel bug at an early age, and when he finally settled down in Peru, we knew he wouldn't be back. He wanted to make his own way, on his own terms." Her brow furrowed a little as she paused to consider the facts. "Well . . . perhaps there is something in the bloodline after all. He ended up running an iron mine."

Joanna laughed, then looked at her mother-in-law thoughtfully. It occurred to her that the board of directors might have missed the mark when they named Wyatt Collier's replacement. "It seems to me you could have run the company yourself."

"Believe me, I wanted to . . . when I was about six years old," Susannah said. She wore an amused, faraway look. "For a brief time when I was a little girl, I went down to my father's office nearly every day, hoping to get a job. What I really wanted to do was run the elevator. I just couldn't believe that a person could step into a small room, close the door, and magically come out in a different place." She gazed distantly across the room. "And I loved the dining room. My father used to let me come to lunch every now and then—all those waiters, making a big fuss about the little girl at the big table in her very best dress." She turned to Joanna. "Have you been to the executive dining rooms?"

For those who dwelt in the hallowed halls of the executive offices, the exalted dining rooms at Bethlehem Steel served elaborate five-course meals on white linen tablecloths—not just at lunch, but breakfast and dinner, too. Joanna shook her head. "No. With babies at home . . . and the drive from Chestnut Hill . . . it just wasn't practical. I suppose I could go now, if I had an invitation, but I don't think it has ever occurred to Frank to ask me. Lately he's in Burns Harbor most of the time, anyway."

Susannah dropped her eyes to her lap. There was a momentary lull as she seemed to be deliberating. She looked up at the children for a minute, and then—keeping her eyes on their flailing limbs—came to the point.

"I was wondering . . . if there's anything you might like to talk about . . . in regard to, perhaps, the challenges of your . . . situation . . . here?"

Joanna was nearly speechless. Hesitation and concerned intimacy were not qualities she would ever have assigned to her mother-in-law. The question seemed dangerously loaded, and her mind reeled as she considered her response. She thought immediately about all the afternoons at the cemetery. Had Helen's remarks been as pointed as Joanna had feared—and did the woman say something to her daughter to plant a seed of speculation?

Her response matched Susannah's in its stammering reluctance. "I . . . I'm not sure . . . what you mean. I mean . . . it's difficult, yes, with Frank so busy at work . . . and the travel on top of it . . . I guess I have been a little . . . frustrated. . . ." She let the sentence trail off, unsure of the direction she should take.

Her mother-in-law looked at her now, direct and deliberate. "Yes, I can imagine you would be. I remember those days well—I was all too familiar with the role of corporate widow before becoming an actual one. But your . . . trials . . . are compounded, certainly, by the fact that your life has been uprooted, and then replanted in a place that is not your own, among people who are not your own. And I imagine that presents an entirely separate set of challenges."

A small relief settled through Joanna's shoulders. This seemed like fairly safe ground—Susannah was simply offering sympathy, not warning or reproach. But the subject was somewhat delicate, nonetheless, and Joanna felt a bit awkward. "Well, yes, I guess it has been something of an adjustment. But the kids are as happy as can be. . . ." She glanced over at them bouncing around like puppies, then made a sweeping scan of the room. "And we certainly can't complain about the lodgings." She gave a little laugh—an effort to keep things light.

For a few moments there was nothing but the peal of the children's voices, but then Susannah cleared her throat and—straightforward but careful—asked another question: "Are you aware that there's an old, rudimentary sort of intercom in the nursery? I mean, in what is now the playroom?"

It was an odd segue, and it took Joanna a minute to recall that Frank had, indeed, pointed it out when he first showed her around the house. "Oh yes. I'd forgotten. Frank mentioned it once. I thought it was a very smart idea in a house of this size. I know I would have wanted to keep an ear tuned for babies crying." While she couldn't think why Susannah would suddenly bring it up, Joanna was happy for a safe subject.

Susannah looked away again as she spoke, a telling sign. "I'm not sure you realize that it doesn't necessarily turn off. There isn't anything electronic about it—just simple mechanics. Over the years, Mother has had the supreme privilege of sitting in audience to the fascinating goings-on of the children's hour, should she be in proximity of the speaker."

Something like shame surged through Joanna's veins as the tumbler clicked over, unlocking the riddle of her mother-in-law's visit to the ballroom. She and Frank had been arguing the night before—in fact, it was the biggest fight they'd ever had—and it just so happened they had been standing in the playroom. After saying good night to Charlie and Daisy, Joanna had spoken on the phone with her mother for a while, and then gone to the playroom to tidy up. Normally, she was adamant that the children pick up their own toys and games. She still wasn't comfortable with the presumption that a maid would do it. But that night their father had arrived home in time to read them a bedtime story, so she let them off the hook.

After he had tucked the kids in, Frank had come to find her. Picking up a couple of books from the floor, he casually (too casually) mentioned that his sister, Gigi, would be coming home for Christmas that year. He knew very well that Joanna had been counting the days until they packed up the car and headed off for the holidays with her family. Since moving to Bethlehem, she had only seen her parents twice—both times for short weekend visits with the children. That Eileen and John Rafferty had declined any invitations to come to Brynmor did not surprise Joanna in the least. They knew they would be completely out of their element, and Joanna had no desire to put them in that position. And so, she went to them—but the visits were too infrequent. For weeks now she had been making excited plans with the children about going to see Meemaw and Pops for Christmas.

"I was thinking about it," Frank said. "I know we planned to go to Pennsport, but what if we just rearranged things a little? We could go after the fact, and celebrate Christmas with your parents a few days later." He didn't give Joanna a chance to respond, rushing to advance the argument. "Gigi is afraid this could be the last holiday she'll be able to spend with all of us, and I think she makes a good point. I mean, my grandmother isn't getting any younger, and who knows when Gigi will next decide to grace us with her presence? I really think it would mean a lot—to my mother, too—to have us all here this year." He was pacing in a small circle, looking nervously around the floor for more things to pick up.

For a moment Joanna just stared at him. The hot indignation swelling in her chest was expanding so fast, she thought she might explode. And then she did—in a steaming combination of burning outrage and icy resentment that erupted like a geyser. "Gigi? Really? You are going to let her to do this to me? To our children? Why is she always allowed to have it her way? It's Christmas for God's sake! She could come back anytime she wanted, but leave it to Gigi to pick the single time it would cause a problem. If you want to celebrate Christmas on the wrong day, then why don't we just do that here? Why should my parents have to sacrifice the rare time they get to be with their only grandchildren and their only daughter—on a holiday that means everything to them—just because of your crazy sister? I will not allow her to do this. No. No. Absolutely not." She was flushed and nearly hyperventilating, but she wasn't finished. "What is wrong with you? Why would you even consider it? Here I am, stuck in this . . . this . . . feudal castle like Rapunzel, with nothing but small talk *all the time*—God forbid your mother should want to actually get to know me—and you popping in once in a while to say hello. Well, you can forget it. I'm taking the kids to my parents' house for Christmas. You can stay here with your dear sister, if that's what you want to do." Her lips were pressed tightly together as she took a stuttering breath through her nose, eyes narrowed and glowering.

Frank was looking at her with his mouth open, stunned, but there was also a wary, assessing quality in his eyes as he gave her an uneasy once-over—manifestly worried that his wife had gone over the edge.

In the end, he tried to right the mast by vowing to speak to Gigi about it. But he didn't venture into the dangerous waters of the deeper implications, and when he reached for Joanna in the dark, she turned away. In the aftermath of the storm, she couldn't see her way back to shore—she had drifted too far out and it felt like the tide was against her.

Now she felt a gut-clenching mortification as she mentally replayed her outburst, trying to recall exactly what she had said. But before she could come up with any kind of response, Susannah reached out to lay a hand lightly on her knee.

"I'm sorry your privacy was imposed upon like that. Frankly, I can't imagine anything worse. After Mother shared her . . . concerns . . . I was very reluctant to say anything.

After all, it wasn't information to which we were entitled. But in the end, I decided to be forthright. Not only because it's the decent thing, but also because I want you to know that I'm very pleased to have you here. I realize this can't be easy for you, and I clearly haven't succeeded in making you feel at home. I regret that. I'd like you to think of this as your own home, as much as it is mine, or even Mother's." She paused briefly, and then went on in a more ruminative tone. "I never intended to be here, myself. I loved the home where we raised our family. But life is nothing if not unpredictable." She looked at the children, now playing leapfrog. "And who knew I'd have the privilege of watching these two wildflowers grow, right in my own garden?" She turned back to give Joanna a kind smile. "And their lovely mother here too, to make us all a family."

Joanna felt tears welling. She would have been moved in any case, but the fact that the show of sentiment was so unexpected, and (it was undeniable) so rare, added emotional heft.

Folding her hands in her lap, Susannah continued. "Again, I truly apologize for the means, but since I am—however inappropriately—privy, I insist you go to your family for the holidays. I'll handle Genevieve. She can certainly wait to see you all. Heaven knows we've waited long enough to see her, and she owes us more than just a few days. We will accommodate whatever your schedule requires."

"Thank you." Joanna swallowed a lump in her throat. "I guess it's no secret that it means a lot to me. And I'm sorry if

I said anything . . . well, anything . . . ungracious last night. I was a little . . ." She couldn't find the right words, and once again Susannah patted her.

"Nothing more need be said. You certainly have the right to speak to your own husband without being spied on. Let's just call it an aberrant opportunity . . . and in the future, you will know better: any conversation not intended for Mother's ears shouldn't take place in the nursery."

Joanna smiled, relieved to have that particular dialogue behind her. She had to admit, though, she wasn't entirely sorry about the whole thing. If it had served to establish a better connection to her mother-in-law, maybe it was—as Susannah said—a strange sort of opportunity. She shifted in her chair and realized she was still holding the photo album open on her lap. Idly flipping the pages back, she remembered her curiosity about the window on the landing. She found the picture and was just holding it up to show Susannah when Charlie's voice rang from across the room.

"Grandmother, look!"

He was balanced on the bronze rail of the orchestra platform, poised to launch himself forward in what would be a daring attempt at a flip. But at the very moment the women turned their heads, his foot slipped and he fell backward. Surreally, he seemed to hover in the air—all animation suspended. And then they watched helplessly as his body toppled in a twist, landing with a sickening crack and his right arm splayed at an impossible angle.

For a paralyzing moment he didn't make a sound; but by the time Joanna reached his side, he had started to wail, and it wasn't more than a second before Daisy joined him. It had been seven years since Joanna had worn a nurse's uniform, but professional instincts trumped motherly panic as she bent over her son, blocking out the howls of pain as she moved him—as carefully as possible—off his arm. Cradling him on the floor, she cast around the room for Susannah, fully expecting to find her mother-in-law at her side. Charlie continued to moan and Daisy continued to shriek, but Susannah was nowhere near. Joanna finally saw her—backed against the wall, hand to her mouth, white as a sheet. There was a stunned, fractured look in her eyes. And then, with the strange, absent aspect of a somnambulist, she turned dumbly and walked out of the room.

Ten

"You smell like cherries . . . and a sunny day . . . and a good dream . . ." Chap was pressing his nose against Susannah's neck, murmuring close to her ear. "And a perfect throw to first."

Susannah laughed as his lips grazed her skin. "I'm wearing a new scent—it's called Eau de Throw. I thought you would like it."

"How do you know me so well?" He smiled—a contained, teasing twist that produced a slight crescent in his right cheek and a tingling in Susannah's veins.

The sensation wasn't new—in fact, it was becoming very familiar. Earlier, as she'd waited for him on a weathered wooden bench by the boathouse, the anticipation alone had caused a dizzying rush that made her wonder if she had a fever. And when she spotted him moving toward her on the rocky path—agile, masculine, indescribably desirable—

she had the overwhelming sensation that her pulse was fighting to push out of her skin.

The boathouse was abandoned—it had been used by the local rowers' club for several decades, but it now sat derelict and decaying, replaced by a new fieldstone building on the other side of the river. Despite the queasy association with Wyatt, it had become their regular meeting place by virtue of the fact that it provided complete privacy and—after Chap broke a small glass pane to unlatch the window—a roof over their heads. The amenities were somewhat less than luxurious—a wooden bench surrounding the room, a few decrepit oars, empty pegs on the walls, and a sooty wood stove in the corner. Also, the requisite evidence of squirrels, mice, and some very industrious spiders. But it was hidden and dry and—for the time being—theirs.

In the days following the party, Susannah had been lost in a muddled fog—drifting aimlessly through the house as the maids set things back in order, waving a distracted farewell as Kit and India packed up and left for their respective schools, and asking for a tray in her room when she realized conversational participation at the dinner table would now be compulsory. In the savory grip of fixation, she replayed the evening a thousand times.

Naturally, Chap had been placed at her right for the midnight supper. They'd sat beside each other in near complete silence, neither of them taking more than a bite of the turbot aux beurre blanc set before them. When the evening finally crawled to an end, Susannah stood with her parents at the door, thanking the guests with rote formality. Chap took leave with his father, waiting silently near the cloakroom while Charles bantered with Hollins about an upcoming golf game. In the prolonged awkwardness, another group of exiting guests brushed past, distracting the family with goodbyes. In that moment, Chap caught Susannah's eye, and, again—with unfaltering certainty—affirmed what she already knew.

Her final year at Bishopthorpe began in buffered oblivion—instructors soundless, studies neglected, friends perplexed. And then, one damp and dreary September afternoon, she found herself walking in the wrong direction. Without conscious intent, she turned down Summit toward Brodhead Avenue, compelled by something like gravitational force toward the leafy, gothic environs of the Lehigh University campus.

From the moment she stepped onto the grounds, Susannah knew she would be conspicuous. Except for visitors, there were no women on campus. Beyond that, she was only too distinguishable to many of the men there. In a town the size of Bethlehem, Susannah would have been recognized had she been the daughter of the local wheelwright; but at Lehigh—where her father was on the board of trustees—anonymity was nothing more than a distant dream. The university had been established as an engineering school—a place to prepare the sons of Bethlehem to follow in their fathers' footsteps at Bethlehem Steel. By association, Susannah was playing to a particularly discerning crowd.

And so it wasn't unexpected when a group of young men on their way to class tipped their caps to her. She recognized three of them as classmates of Kit (and—more disquietingly—Chap). In fact, one of them was Gerald Barnwell, her frenetic Charleston partner.

"Well, hello there! Fancy seeing you here!" Gerald beamed as he stepped ahead of the pack, sweeping his arm out in presentation. "For those of you who don't know it, this is Sassy Parrish—it was her party I was telling you about!" He gave Susannah his woodchuck grin, chest puffing a little with proprietary pride. "Just the other day I was saying what a smash it was!" Turning again to his chums, he reiterated what they had already heard several times. "She had the Wildecats." He dropped the name with relish, basking in reflected glory. "They were the berries!" His enthusiasm continued to spill over as he elaborated every salient detail, finally winding down with the question Susannah had hoped to avoid. "So, what brings you to this lawless neck of the woods?"

With a bright smile, Susannah laid her hand on Gerald's arm, sprinkling charm all over him through a bald-face lie. "Big game coming up!" Her enthusiasm was implicit as she nodded at the group. "My father sent me over to pick up the tickets—we wouldn't miss it." The Lehigh-Lafayette game was the longest-standing football rivalry in the country, and the Parrishes had, indeed, been attending since Susannah could remember. "I'm just on my way to the stadium—must dash." She moved off with a cheery wave, calling back over her shoulder: "Fingers crossed for a pretty day and a big win!"

The stadium was on Taylor Street, so she headed in that direction, purposeful and intent; but at the first obscuring bend in the road, she made a quick, wary survey. Then, instead of turning left at the corner, she turned right.

The Lehigh campus, sprawled on the north face of South Mountain, was relatively level at the base, where the stadium and main academic buildings were situated. There were paved paths that crisscrossed the smooth lawns, leading to an impressive assortment of noble, Romanesque edifices; but to reach the resplendent Linderman Library or the towering grandeur of Packer Hall required an uphill climb. And past these, high on the hill, was the lofty domain of the university's three fraternity houses.

Susannah had to stop to catch her breath as she made her way up a ruthless series of chipped stone steps. She passed a few more students hustling down the hill, but—to her relief—she recognized none of them. Finally, at the top of a particularly punishing incline, she came to a winding road. When she looked up, she could see the stately trio of fraternity row. The first building, a stone Georgian colonial with a colossal federal-style portico supported by soaring columns, was the Chi Psi house.

The dismal gray of the day worked in her favor—there wasn't a soul in sight. Somewhere on the side of the hill, her blithe charade had been abandoned; it may have been the close heaviness in the air or the taxing exertion of the climb, but something had caused a clammy flush on her skin and a loud banging in her chest. In the solitary stillness, Susannah stood on the edge of the road and looked up at the house, one hand grasping a steadying sapling, the other holding out her heart. And when the front door opened and a figure stepped out, she wasn't at all surprised.

He paused on the front step for a moment, settling his eyes on her in calm avouchment; and then, slowly and deliberately, he descended the stairway and the canted front walk. When he reached her, he stood very close, his voice low and solemn. "A guy could grow old waiting for you."

And then he smiled softly, and the clamor her in chest was instantly stilled, replaced with an ease essential and full.

But the house looming over them had eyes that lurked, and Chap threw a cautious glance over his shoulder. "Go up the road about forty yards or so. There's a path on the left. If you follow it into the woods, you'll see a lean-to where we keep firewood. Wait for me—I'll be there in a minute." His hand brushed hers—quick and covert—and he set off in the direction of Packer Hall.

The precaution would be the first of many; a winding trail of careful contrivances as they played for time, steeped in denial, desperate to elude the hovering specter that followed them everywhere, whispering Wyatt's name.

But the potential hazards were boundless. Helen continued to extend regular dinner invitations to both Charles and Chap, insisting they fill the places vacated by Kit and India, and Wyatt as well. In every instance, Chap found a reason to decline, pleading studies and meetings and campus activities— but it was clear that Charles was becoming impatient with his son's perpetual absence. It had started to smell unappreciative and heedless. Arriving alone on a recent Sunday, he shook his head as he handed his hat to Harriet, explaining that Chap's attendance was required yet again at some university function or another.

However—as Susannah was to find that same evening— there was an unexpected advantage to the slippery jeopardy of the situation. Although she had known Chap for most of her life, the knowing had been peripheral, indirect. It was becoming more apparent with every hushed, revealing exchange that she hadn't really known him at all. Her image of him as Kit's perennial partner in crime; as Wyatt's breezy, effortlessly charmed older brother; and as India's moony obsession was proving shamefully shallow. Recently, Susannah had been surprised when—during a long, quiet conversation in their musty hideaway—he admitted a bleak ambivalence about studying engineering, and described the heavy, pressing weight of the shadow cast by his father's genius. More enlightening still, she learned that he had taken every literature course available at the university, and that he sometimes wished he had followed his instincts to enroll in a liberal arts program. With a small, rueful laugh, he told her that in his heart he was an English major.

This admission was certified in black and white as Charles settled into his favorite wing chair for a pre-dinner cocktail that Sunday evening. As Hollins handed him a glass of whiskey, Charles patted the front of his jacket, and then pulled a slim, rolled-up magazine from the inside pocket. Smoothing it out, he offered it to Helen. "I thought you might like to see this."

She accepted it quizzically—it was a literary quarterly called the *Keystone Review*. "Why, thank you, Charles. I'll take that as a compliment." Riffling the pages, she gave him a teasing smile. "A unique and thoughtful gift—I'll have to invite you to dinner more often!"

He chuckled at the absurdity therein. "It arrived in the mail the other day. I thought it was odd that I should receive something like that—I've never been one for magazine subscriptions. But there was a letter included. It seemed my essay had been selected for publication." He raised his brow. "You can imagine my surprise. It took me a minute to remember there was more than one Charles Collier at that address." He nodded at the journal in Helen's hands. "Turn to page seven."

As Helen paged forward, Hollins squinted over. "Are you talking about Chap?"

Susannah was seated on the davenport, politely present and accounted for, doing her participatory duty . . . but she hadn't exactly been participating. In fact, she was paging through her own magazine—the latest *McCall's*—looking at the fashions and considering a new coat. But now she sat up straight and the *McCall's* fell to the floor.

"Dear heavens, it *is* Chap!" Helen had found the page and was looking at the byline with eyes wide. "When did he become a writer?" Her voice echoed the astonishment on her face.

"That's what I said." Charles was shaking his head. "I made some inquiries—that little journal has quite an impressive pedigree. But it was odd . . . when I congratulated him on it, he wasn't as pleased as I expected. I pointed out the fact that he might now—to an extent—be counted in the ranks of DuBois and Adams, but his response was . . . well . . . I guess you could say tepid." He paused for a moment, and then his voice wavered slightly as his eyes focused on the pages. "I think the subject matter made him uncomfortable. It's very . . . tender." He cleared his throat. "I thought you, Hedy, would appreciate it. He agreed to let me keep this copy—I don't think he would mind if you read it."

Looking down at the page, Helen read aloud: "He Wanted to Build Her a Boat." She drew a sharp breath. "Oh. Oh my." She looked up at Charles. "It's about Frances?" Everyone in the room knew the provenance of the title. It was a fond, teasing reference that Frances would on occasion make, illustrating the sweet devotion of her youngest son. As the story went, she was reading to Wyatt one evening—a children's tale of a voyage at sea. As she turned the last page, she wistfully remarked how exciting and wonderful it would be to sail around the world. Gazing up at his mother with all the fervor that his heart could muster, the little boy solemnly promised that when he grew up he would build her a boat. He wanted nothing more in the world than to make her dreams come true.

Charles nodded. "Yes, about Frances . . . and Wyatt." He took a sip of his drink and gave Helen a small, sad smile. "Don't feel obliged to read it now. I think it would be best left for later." And then he turned to Susannah, pausing for an extra beat before he spoke: "I thought you might appreciate it, as well."

She could feel a hot flush on her cheeks. Appreciate it because of . . . the author? Or was he thinking of the subject? Naturally, she would have an interest in something about Wyatt. . . . Through a frozen smile, she stuttered a response: "I. . . . Yes. Of course. I would love to read it. Thank you." She leaned down to retrieve the *McCall's*, and in a stroke of excellent timing, Helen stood and suggested they go to the table.

It was nine o'clock before Susannah was alone in her room, curled up on the bed with the essay finally and firmly in hand. It had been the longest dinner she could ever remember. Charles had lingered past the port, clearly reluctant to head back to the lonely emptiness of his home on Seneca Street. When he finally made his way out into the night, Helen had taken the magazine into the library and settled into the wing chair in the corner with her ritual evening brew—a cup of peppermint tea. Susannah must have strolled by the door at least four times, making a ridiculous effort to seem purposeful and casual. At last she saw that her mother had removed her reading glasses and was holding them in her lap, atop the closed magazine. Her head was tipped back and her eyes closed, but in the lamplight Susannah could see a reflective shimmer on her face.

Raising her head, Helen noticed her daughter in the doorway. "If only Frances could see this." She looked down at the journal. "It's so lovely. I had no idea. . . ." Stifling a small gulp, she sighed. "The things we don't know about the workings of the heart are fathomless." She stood and moved toward Susannah, holding out the slender volume. "But I expect you know that. Good night, Sass. Enjoy the reading."

Susannah just stared, openmouthed, as her mother moved away.

Thirty minutes later her own cheeks were wet as she gently closed the journal, running her hand absently over the cover. Again, she was struck by the breadth and depth of what she had never known about Chap. The essay was, as much as anything, a reverent tribute to Wyatt, in his devotion to their mother. It was authentic and unguarded, and what struck Susannah most was the generosity of Chap's observant, abiding love, in its appreciation of the special bond between his mother and his brother. She wiped a tear away as the last lines echoed in her mind:

He never got to build her a boat, but he plies the water with all

his might, skimming across the waves in his hero's quest, follow-
ing her dream in his way. And I know she is there—his constant
coxswain—calling encouragement in the wind and laughing
with the sheer joy of watching him soar.

Susanna closed her eyes as a wave of queasy remorse
covered her like hot, sticky tar. For his entire life, Chap had
loved Wyatt in the best way a brother could. She knew that
whatever torment she felt was eclipsed exponentially by
his own. But it was inescapable. To pretend that this . . .
reality . . . didn't exist would be unforgivably fraudulent. It
was like a terrible accident had happened, and now the only
choice was to try to live with the damage and go forward.

But—like the victim of a real fatality—Wyatt didn't know
it had happened. Susannah looked across the room at a pile of
letters, nearly overflowing from the small basket next to her
writing table. They had arrived in a steady stream, stacked on
a silver tray with the other correspondence of the day. She had
come to dread the presentation of the mail tray, and her
mother's chirpy announcement that there was "yet another one
for you, dear."

The first one had come just days after the party. He had
written to ask how it had gone.

Did Chap behave himself? I have to laugh when I picture him
trying to match you on the dance floor. He really didn't know what
he was in for. I'll bet you showed him a thing or two.

The next one was almost as wrenching.

We've been training hard. I'm lifting weights these days—I bet

I could press you over my head. If you see my brother, tell him I want an arm wrestling rematch when I get home. Last time I had a sore wrist—he won't be able to take advantage of me now.

And nearly all of them held a subtle, wounded reproach about her spare replies. The most recent made her wince.

I guess nobody's perfect, so I'll forgive you for not being a very good correspondent. You make up for it in plenty of other ways. But you're not off the hook—I'll take what I can get. I had them in a box under my bed, but a mouse chewed through the cardboard and started to build a nest, so now they're in a drawer. I just wish there were more.

Susannah could barely make herself pick up a pen. She had somehow managed to fill her paltry pages with gossipy items, like the scandalous behavior of her friend Evelyn Smythe, who came to class wearing trousers and a sailor's cap and refused to return home and put on a skirt until the headmistress threatened expulsion. And she could usually rely on some kind of family doings—such as the news that Kit had decided to spend the spring semester traveling abroad. But the effort was murder.

With a sharp shake of her head, she stood and crossed the room. She couldn't stand to think about it. There hadn't been any need to discuss it with Chap—the understanding was implicit: they would wait to face the requiem until Wyatt came home. And in the illusory meanwhile, Susannah had discovered that burying one's head in the sand could make it curiously easier to breathe.

As she lay the issue of the *Keystone* on her dressing table, she glanced into the mirror. Looking back at her was a girl she didn't even recognize. Her feelings for Chap were so novel, so powerful, that she couldn't help but wonder: If not for him, would she ever have known? In her new awareness, she felt an abject pity for every other girl in the world, and even the basket of letters couldn't squelch a private smile as she thought about the previous afternoon.

Chap had arrived at the boathouse a few minutes late and slightly out of breath. He'd approached with a long, swift stride, and in the sweep of an instant she was in his arms—his voice low and teasing as he pressed her against the weathered, peeling wood. "I heard there was some good fishing down here, but this is one for the wall."

A vision of an enormous sailfish—displayed in all of its prowess-proving glory over the fireplace in her father's study—rendered Susannah uncommonly witless, and her murmured response went straight down the middle of home plate: "I wouldn't like being mounted on a wall."

And at that, Chap drew back—grinning as if the bases were loaded. He had no choice but to swing. With a speculative glance at the feathery sedge growing full on the ground, he pressed his lips together and narrowed his eyes: "How would you feel about a riverbank?"

Eleven

"Behold this day—a great light shineth upon Bethlehem!" Gigi was poised in the foyer with a crystal mug of hot buttered rum, toasting the travelers upon their return. She was dark of hair and petite of frame; a passing stranger would have been hard-pressed to identify her as Frank's sister, much less his twin. Her delicate, heart-shaped face resembled that of her aunt India's . . . but her style was all her own. She was decked out in a bohemian ensemble of ballet flats, slim black slacks, and a crushed velvet smoking jacket, with a glittering stack of bangles on each wrist and a flowing scarf wrapped gypsy-style around her head.

"We've been strictly denying ourselves the least speck of yuletide cheer until you got here—I just now donned my gay apparel." It had been long enough since her last visit that the children had only an anecdotal familiarity with their aunt—they didn't really remember the actual person—and their eyes were like quarters as she swanned across the room, wafting traces of cigarette smoke and patchouli. "And I've been waiting with my mistletoe for *these* little elves." Pulling a small sprig from behind her ear, she held it over their heads. After kissing them each on both cheeks, she ran an appraising eye over Charlie's cast, which rose to his shoulder. "I heard about the broken wing." Tracing the length of it with her finger, she whistled. "That's a doozy, but it lacks"—she squinted thoughtfully—"flair. See me later and I'll get out my brushes. We'll have this sad old thing looking like a Mondrian in no time."

Moving to the doorway, she rose up on her toes to give the same European-style greeting to her brother. "You're looking very dapper, Francis." He was still in his overcoat, and she tucked the mistletoe into the lapel before turning to his wife. "And Jo—the wild Irish rose. I swear, you get prettier every year. Look at that complexion. It's positively infuriating." Holding her drink out to the side, she put her free arm around Joanna in a half-hug.

Joanna responded with a full one, squeezing her sister-in-law tight for emphasis. "Thanks so much for waiting for us—it really meant a lot."

Gigi gave a dismissive little scoff. "*Non è niente, cara.* I'm just glad you're all here now—we've had quite enough of our own squawking in this old henhouse. What we need"—she reached over and ruffled Daisy's hair—"are some little foxes to stir things up around here." Holding her mug up like a torch, she started across the hall. "The merry widows await—let the bacchanal begin. There's a scrumptious-looking hors d'oeuvres spread, and some hot cider for you tots—and we've got lots of lovely little gifts just itching to be opened."

Coats shucked, they trailed behind her, entering the drawing room to find Helen and Susannah cozied up to the fire with their own crystal mugs.

"Ah, the shepherd and his flock, returned safely to the manger," Helen warbled. "Merry Christmas, one and all!" Although her cane rested against the side of the sofa, she was settled in too deeply to try to get up, and she had to make do with a seated welcome.

Susannah stood and held her hands out to the children, who obligingly wrapped their arms around her waist, Charlie defaulting to his left one. She patted their backs, saying, "You got here in the nick of time—we were about to call the orphanage and tell them we had all these presents just sitting here, with no one to open them."

Charlie pivoted toward the tree, unable to check a mild panic even though he knew better, but Daisy was more interested in trumpeting the latest excitement. Pulling on her grandmother's sleeve, she rushed to fill her in: Santa had come down the chimney in Pennsport, yielding Daisy's dearest desire—a Chatty Cathy doll.

Joanna settled in next to Helen on the sofa, from which vantage she had her first glimpse of the abundant bright packages under the tree. As Daisy gave a full accounting of

Cathy's impressive erudition, Joanna gave Frank a gimlet eye. She had made her feelings about extravagant gifts perfectly clear, and urged him to ensure some measure of restraint on the parts of his mother and his grandmother. But he had been defensive. "You know my family has never been much for Christmas excess. Birthdays, yes—but at Christmas, if you re-member, we just exchange a gift or two. I don't think the fact that the kids live here now will change anything—Grand-mother will give them silver dollars, and Mother will give them whichever toy the clerk suggests."

But the vivid bounty crowding the bottom branches proved otherwise, and he seemed honestly chagrined. With a sheep-ish shrug, he put his hands in his pockets, rocking heel to toe. "Looks like someone got a little carried away this year—that's quite a pile." He raised a dubious brow at his mother. "Have you found a boyfriend at FAO Schwarz?"

Susannah gave him a mordant smile. "I can assure you, dear, that if I were to find a *friend*, it would not be in a shop, nor would it be a boy. You can thank your sister for the largesse. As we all know, Genevieve never does anything by halves."

"Well, I couldn't arrive empty-handed," Gigi said, refill-ing her cup from a samovar on the satinwood console. "And I have to make up for lost time. I took an extra day in the city when I landed—let me tell you, the Algonquin is not what it used to be. But I made the most of Fifth Avenue, which still puts Oxford Street to shame." She took a seat near the

Christmas tree, then set her cup down and clapped her hands. "Who's first? I'm distributing these in special order . . . saving the best for last."

That did it—Daisy forgot all about the doll, beating her brother to the foot of Gigi's chair and jigging in expectant place.

Possibly, the cavalcade that followed would have pushed Joanna over the edge on its own; but even the lavish excess of telescopes and racetracks and painting easels and musical instruments was eclipsed by the final gift.

When Gigi held out two envelopes, the children barely paid attention. They were still trying to digest the splendor of the spoils, and the plain manila was somewhat lacking in flavor. "It's something for all three of us," she said conspiratorially. "I'll give you a hint: These hold the keys to castles and double-decker buses and an enormous clock tower."

This succeeded well—they took the envelopes and tore them open, eager to solve the mystery.

"What is it?" Daisy looked quizzically at the document in her hand, unable to make out the codes and abbreviations.

Charlie lit on the words in boldest type. "It says 'Idlewild' (that one took an extra beat), and 'Heathrow.'" He looked up proudly.

"You've got it!" Gigi's smile was brilliant. "I've told all my friends in London about the two little poppets who live in the States, breaking my heart with the distance, and they're all just dying to meet you. I thought this summer would be perfect. I'm free the entire month of August, so get those raincoats ready. You'll be on your way across the pond before you know it!"

Whether the children reacted with thrilled excitement, nervous trepidation, or bland equanimity, Joanna couldn't have said. And there was certainly some response from the others, but she wasn't aware of that, either, because all she could see was a haze of red, and all she could hear was a thrumming pulse, pounding in her ears.

It wasn't until she found herself staring out the bedroom window that she even realized she had walked wordlessly out of the room. After a few minutes Frank came to find her.

"That was a hasty exit." His expression was ambiguous. "I don't think I would count it among your most gracious moments."

Joanna was stunned. She couldn't believe he was scolding *her*.

"I realize Gigi goes overboard," he said, managing to sound both weary and patronizing. "We both know that, and you should have expected it, to some degree. Yes, she should have asked about flying the kids to London, but that's just Gigi—she likes to make the grand gesture. Once you have a chance to think it over, you'll see it's a fine idea. I don't think she'll ever have kids of her own. You can't hold it against her for wanting to be closer to ours."

Joanna just stared at him, her indignation rendering her speechless.

He drew a deep breath and slid his hands into his pants pockets, a nervous habit that was becoming ever more familiar. "Well, I hope you're coming down for dinner. It would certainly be awkward if you didn't. It's Christmas, after all. Or a reasonable facsimile."

She turned to the window, silent, and Frank retreated without further comment—presumably to the more welcoming environs of the dining room.

Not only did Joanna not appear at the table, she was conspicuously absent from their bed that night, taking full advantage of the resplendent array of guest rooms at her avail. In the morning, she stayed in the room long past the breakfast hour. Someone would have told the children she had a headache, she supposed, or wasn't feeling well. In the moment, she didn't care. At about eleven o'clock, she slipped out of the house for a long walk. She needed to get away, to clear her head. She didn't admit any particular destination. She wandered first around the town, up Center and down Broad, and back to Market Street—a transparent play to legitimize her intent, to prove she simply needed space and solitude, a little distance to deal with her feelings. She wouldn't concede—even to herself—that she was headed to St. Gregory's. That she needed to talk to Daniel.

When she saw him shoveling the front walk, her relief was so palpable, she felt a conflicted sort of shame. An instinctive propriety warned her to pull the brake cord on her runaway emotions, to honor some implicit marital compact of privacy. And so, when he straightened and saw her, she just smiled.

He was smiling back. "Come inside."

Joanna was shivering, but the invitation gave her pause. "Oh, I don't think so. I wouldn't want to impose on anyone."

"It's no imposition—I could use a break. Let's have some tea. Warm up. Gran's not here—she bullied Gramps into taking her over to Pottsville to see her sister—but I make a decent cup."

There it was—the necessary information. Without acknowledging it, she needed to know that Doe and Nico were out. Thus reassured, she followed Daniel toward the house, stepping carefully across the neatly shoveled brick walk.

As they neared the back door, her eyes fell on the anonymous little grave marker that Daisy had discovered the past summer. Even half covered in snow, something about it held a strange magnetism. It wasn't alone in the yard, what with the barbecue grill and a small iron table within spitting distance, yet it was ever so lonely. BABY HAYES.

"Gran won't talk about that one. She'll tell you a story about practically everyone in here, but never Baby Hayes." Daniel had stepped back, and his shoulder brushed against hers.

"Do you think she knows? It's so close to the house— surely that means something."

"She has to know. There are records on everybody, at least for the past hundred years or so. And this marker isn't that old.

I even asked Gramps about it, but you know Nico—he just grunted and said it nobody's business but God's."

Joanna was quiet for a moment, and then she ventured a question. "Maybe Hayes isn't a surname. Are you sure your mother was their only child?"

Daniel was ahead of her. "If I ran a graveyard and my child died, that baby would have a headstone the size of a shed and a twenty-line inscription."

"Well, you know what they say about the shoemaker's children. . . ."

"But why the secrecy then?"

"You're right—it doesn't make sense."

"Anyway, it will still be here in the spring, and then you can stand here thinking about it all you want without having to wipe the frost off your lip." He took her by the arm to lead her to the house, and she had to face the disturbing fact that she liked it.

Inside, she gazed around at the kitchen. The stove was a relic, and there was still an old wooden icebox in the corner, but yellow gingham on the windows and red linoleum on the floor gave the room a sunny disposition. "This is lovely—so cheery and bright." Joanna had long been curious about the interior of Grange House, and she glanced toward the hall. "I'd love to see the rest of it. . . ." Her voice trailed off as she looked at the door, giving her apprehension away.

And Daniel was right there to gather it up and dispose of it, reading between the lines with his usual grasp. "Gran could tell you everything you would ever want to know about this place, but you'd have to wait. They won't be back for a while. I can give you the nickel tour, if you're not too picky."

There was a warm little flicker in her chest—an awareness of his awareness. "I'm not picky."

"Let me get the tea, and we can take it with us." He put a kettle on the stove, and lifted a Delft canister from a shelf on the wall. As he took the tea bags out, he looked at her evenly, imparting something more than just casual inquiry. "How was Christmas?"

She hesitated. She knew he meant Pennsport. She had told him about Gigi's imposition, and about Susannah's surprising intervention. But despite the fact that she had gotten what she wanted, things had been a bit tense. It wasn't Frank's fault. From the beginning, he had embraced her parents with familiar ease—teasing her mother with the nickname Eileen Forward, (assuring her it was better than Eileen Backward), sipping beer on the front porch with her father as the radio piped the Phillies game into warm summer nights, and—most recently—withstanding the cramped torture of her girlhood bed without so much as a grumble.

But her mother had a dowsing rod that could divine a teardrop in the heart of the Venus de Milo, and it hadn't been more than a day—while the men were off with the kids in search of a fat Norway pine—before she poured another cup of coffee for Joanna and sat down across from her.

There were holiday place mats on the table—red plastic

with a border of green holly. Joanna's hand rested on one, index finger hooked through the handle of her coffee cup. Her mother reached over and covered it with her own. "Is there anything you'd like to tell me?"

She didn't see it coming. Whenever they spoke on the phone, Joanna was conscientiously cheery—a conditioned avoidance of unsolicited concern. She hadn't considered how much she would be willing to confide if pressed. She didn't want to impugn Frank or tarnish her mother's estimation of their marriage—there was a decent chance this was just a bump in the road. Gazing at her coffee cup, she weighed the consequences. She knew she'd have to offer something. Once Eileen Rafferty had you in her sights, there was no escaping.

"Same old gypsy, same old crystal ball." Her smile was weak. "Since you asked, I'll admit things have been a little . . . tough." Tipping her head to the side, she pushed her fingers to her temple. "I guess I'm just frustrated. It feels like I don't have any . . . autonomy. I mean, I'm really just a perpetual guest. I don't have a"—she cast around the room, looking for the word—"domain." She sighed. "I don't how else to explain it. I feel like I'm disappearing. Does that sound crazy?" She didn't wait for a response. "Maybe it would be different if Frank were there more. But sometimes I don't feel like I'm even married." Suddenly her eyes welled. By giving form to her feelings, they took on extra weight, and fell on her shoulders like a thick shawl. "I just have this life now that . . . that doesn't even seem like it's mine."

Squeezing her daughter's hand, Eileen made a little tsk sound. "I know it's hard, Jo, but think about Frank. He has to be away from his wife *and* his kids. To earn for his family."

Behind the sympathy in her mother's eyes, Joanna discerned a trace of reproach. She was well aware that her parents loved Frank, and she also knew that their conventions and values were staunchly old-fashioned when it came to marriage and spousal roles. But she still felt a thud of disappointment in her chest. She had expected her mother to feel her frustration and resentment and offer some semblance of support. And then she realized something: despite her preconceptions about Susannah, she had encountered a deeper, more empathetic understanding from her mother-in-law than she had from her own mother.

"I think you need to join a club. A knitting group, maybe. Or a coffee klatsch . . . Something to make some women friends."

Did she imagine a slight emphasis on the word *women?* Joanna felt an uneasy little clutch, wary of her mother's intuition. And then, as she took a sip of coffee, her mother made a comment that stopped the cup in its path.

"Most men don't realize—until it's too late—the dangers of a lonely wife."

Now, standing in the kitchen at Grange House, the sentence echoed so loudly that Joanna wondered for a split second if her mother were in the room. In response to Daniel's question, her words were tinted a pale shade of ambiguous. "It was fine. Good to be home. Well, obviously, it isn't home anymore. . . ." She shook her head, surprised at herself. "The house seems so much smaller than it used to. And it didn't help that the kids were a little rambunctious—Frank calls it Santa Frenzy." A rueful smile crept into place. "You'll like this: Charlie got an ant farm, and then we found Daisy with it, squatting in a sunbeam with a magnifying glass. Fortunately, my mother discovered her in the nick of time and saved the livestock from going up in smoke."

Daniel chuckled. "I bet that put a dent in diplomatic relations."

"Charlie never knew. Thank God for small blessings. Other than that, it was . . ." She flashed again on the conversation with her mother, and she sounded less than convinced. "Fine."

He caught the nuance as if he had a net. His eyes questioned and waited for more, but Joanna turned away.

Wandering to the hallway, she peered into the darkened parlor. It faced north, and there wasn't much light coming through the tall, narrow windows, but she could see a few pieces of heavy Victorian furniture and the ghostly bloom of lace antimacassars draped across the backs of stuffed chairs. She understood that this was where the grieving were received, as they waited for the sad business of choosing headstones and engravings and plots. Placed on a table against the wall were several large albums—catalogs, she supposed. She was taking in a grouping of sepia portraits on the wall when Daniel appeared behind her, holding two steaming cups.

"First stop on the tour, the ominous reception room. It isn't really used for much else—Gran and Gramps have a sitting room upstairs where she knits and he watches television." He handed her a teacup and moved around her, taking a few strides forward. "Over here"—he gestured toward an archway that was bordered by a framed fretwork of oak spindles—"is the dining room, which—to my knowledge—is only used on Thanksgiving and Easter." This room was also dim in the winter's light, and a bit stuffy with a looming, carved walnut sideboard and dark William Morris wallpaper. "And over here"—they crossed back through the parlor to the front hall and a closed door—"is the office." He didn't bother to open it. "Nothing much to see in there—just an old desk and a two walls of filing cabinets."

Joanna looked at him. "Filing cabinets . . . full of records?"

"Yup." He nodded slowly as the light went on. "Full of records." Through narrowed eyes, there shone an appreciative glint. "I never pegged you for devious."

"Well, after all, you *do* work here." Her eyes widened innocently. "I'm surprised it didn't occur to you."

With a conceding shrug, he reached over and turned the knob. As he flicked on the light, Joanna brushed past him, tracing a finger along a row of cabinets and peering at the bracketed labels until she found what she wanted. Setting her teacup on the desk behind her, she pulled out a heavy oaken drawer. It was stuffed to overflowing with files, and her fingers flicked over them—Haas, Habermann, Hachette . . . until she came to Hayward. Her brow furrowed and she combed back through the names, searching again for *Hayes*. But the alphabetization was precise—there was nothing. She turned with a disappointed huff. Then, biting her cheek, she made a tentative suggestion: "We could check Janssen . . . if it's not too personal."

Daniel shrugged. "These records exist for a reason, right? If there's something in there, then it's hiding in plain sight. It's not like we're reading Gran's diary." He pulled out a drawer just to the right and started leafing through it.

There were several files of Janssens—ancestors old and young—but none were infants. "Well, that's that. No secrets there." He closed the drawer and dusted his hands together. "I guess Baby Hayes is destined for eternal obscurity." He cocked his head, thoughtful. "There's something in that, though. Somehow it makes it more . . . affecting. It could be anyone's child—like a little unknown soldier. Maybe it's better to leave it that way."

"I know. When Daisy was playing there, it really struck me. There was something sort of . . . haunting about it. For a moment, the grief just wrapped around me—like the baby was mine."

"Speaking of haunting, do you want to see the rest of the house?"

Joanna was taken aback. "Is it really haunted? I mean, Doe

talks about her soldiers and her laughing lady and the little boy on the swing, but I thought she was just being Doe. Have you ever seen anything?"

He looked a little sheepish. "Maybe Gran's craziness is contagious. Or maybe it's just . . . what do you call it . . . suggestion. But, well, I'm up in the attic, and sometimes there's a strange noise at night. Like crying. It's faint though—I'm never sure about it. I've looked at the radiator, the pipes, the shutters . . . but I haven't been able to figure it out."

Joanna was intrigued, but she also felt a disquieting heaviness pulling on her heart. The idea of some lost soul crying in the night was unspeakably sad.

"And that's not all." He hesitated, his mouth twisting. "There's a rocking chair in the corner of the attic, and I could swear that whenever I hear the sound, it rocks a little."

"Have you asked Doe about it?"

"I didn't at first. I honestly didn't want to admit that she might have been on to something all this time. But after a while, I gave in."

"And?"

"For a minute she didn't say anything. She was just quiet, which—as you know—is not like Gran. And then she said something about how spirits don't necessarily have to be from ghosts, that there can be energy that lives in a place, left over from events or . . . emotions, I think she said, that leaves a permanent . . . what did she call it? Imprint? Something like that."

"And what did she think it was?"

"I don't know. I probably never will. I mean, ghosts are one of her favorite subjects, so you'd think she would have been happy to talk about it, but she didn't seem too interested. She said something about . . . things we can't ever know."

There are some things we're just not meant to know. The sentence echoed from that day in August. It was what Doe had said about Baby Hayes.

Despite a hesitance at the propriety of wandering through private quarters, Joanna was hooked. "Could I see it?"

"Only if you happen to be here in the middle of the night." The words hung there for a moment; his expression betrayed nothing. "If it really happens at all. But if you're up for a climb, you can see the room." He glanced at his wristwatch, then swept an arm toward the stairway. "After you."

On the second floor, he took a quick detour to show her around, making a cursory effort to complete the tour. Apart from Doe and Nico's bedroom, there were two others. One was used only for storage, with towers of boxes stacked against the walls. "One of the first things I learned about Gran is that she never gets rid of anything. There are probably penmanship exercises from the third grade in there, along with any mail she's ever gotten and newspaper clippings going back to 1911."

The other bedroom retained a twin bed with a ruffled satin coverlet, and a large collection of porcelain dolls—lined in frilly exhibition on mounted wall shelves. But the most prominent feature was an elaborate dollhouse on a table in the middle of the room. "Gramps made it for my mom when she was young. All the furniture, too."

Joanna was enchanted, stepping into the room for a better look at the perfect miniatures that furnished what was clearly a replica of Grange House, down to the wallpaper in the dining room. The little house was made of wood, not brick, but the exterior was carefully painted in a trompe l'oeil of sienna and brown.

"This is amazing. Look at the detail! Your grandfather is a real craftsman." She was shaking her head in wonder as she turned to Daniel. "It's a shame that no one plays with it. Didn't your mother ever want your sisters to have this?"

His response was a bit slow in coming, as if it had never occurred to him. "I'm not sure. She never talked about her life . . . before. Once she left here, there was no going back. I guess taking a version of this place with her wasn't really an option."

He shrugged and turned away, moving on to the sitting room across the hall. It was on the snug side, with a braided rug and faded floral curtains. Doe's knitting basket overflowed from the hassock by her chair, and the aromatic smell of cherry tobacco was evidenced by Nico's pipe, nested in a large ashtray next to his well-worn recliner.

"This is where you can find them most every night, watching *Huntley-Brinkley* and working crossword puzzles out loud. I think Gran has knitted mittens for every charity case in the county."

Joanna was glad to be able to picture Doe and Nico in their places, but she was distracted by her impatience to see Daniel's room. She turned from the doorway, eyes searching the hall. "Where are the attic stairs?"

He pointed to a narrow door—it could have been a closet. When he opened it, there was a steep staircase with very shallow treads, leading up to a faint light. He let Joanna lead the way, and at the top she found an open space—it was just one big room with a ceiling that slanted on each side and a window at each end. There was another braided rug on the floor, and a set of bedroom furniture in bird's-eye maple, and in the corner, a tall Windsor rocking chair.

"This is it. The scene of the crime." Daniel stood at the top of the stairs, his hands on his hips, watching as Joanna took it all in.

She looked around at the unfinished space, which was somehow quite welcoming with its patchwork quilt and low lamps. There was a small radiator under the window. "It's very cozy—nice and warm. Did you move the furniture up?"

"No, it was here already. I'm not sure why."

Walking to the rocker, Joanna gave it a tentative push.

"Not so spooky in the daylight, I guess." Daniel seemed a little abashed.

"No—not spooky." Joanna sat down in the chair and rocked. "But there's something. . . ." As she rubbed her hand along the worn, smooth maple, she felt the same odd sadness from before—an unintentional empathy that knew no source.

And suddenly it overwhelmed her, triggering an unhappiness of her own—one which she thought she had been covering quite well. As she rocked, the facade of calm collection crumbled, and she was helpless against the tears that trailed down her cheeks.

"Are you going to tell me about it?"

He had known all along. She didn't think she had given herself away—in fact, she had suspected herself of using poor Baby Hayes as a distraction. But it was clear now that, as her mother did, Daniel knew better. And there was something so comforting, so needed, so . . . intimate . . . in his steadfast perception, that her careful restraint—worked to an exhausted lather over the past months—fell away like a broken harness. Sore and halting, the words came forth. She told him all that she felt and all that she feared. In addition to the lost and powerless portrait she had painted at her mother's table, she admitted a bleak hunch that an essential connection had been lost—that her husband no longer knew her heart, and she did not know his. And this openness, this act of complete disclosure, changed something. When he pulled her into his arms, it could have been simply compassion—nothing more than caring concern. But it wasn't simple, and it was more.

His kiss was a reprieve. It was sanctuary. It was sustenance. She kissed him back, and didn't stop. When they stumbled against the bed, Daniel drew away. He peered at her, and his words were as imperative as they were strangled: "It can only go one way or the other. Don't do this if you don't mean it."

If you don't mean it. In the clarity of mere inches, Joanna's vision was suddenly and blazingly circumspect, and the line they had crossed tightened around her chest like a cord. What did she mean? What did she want? Now that she was here, could she say with certainty it was this? Frank . . . the children . . . her family . . . her life as she knew it—everything on the table. These thoughts wheeled through her mind like a cartoon image of a printing press, rolling out pages on a desperate deadline. The bold headline was unmistakable, even in the frenzied rush, and it shouted of looming disaster. There could be no hiding now, and no going back. The convenient, protective shield of friendship had been smashed and it lay on the floor around them in glinting pieces. In the space of moments, she had become someone she had never imagined she could be. She was, officially, an unfaithful wife.

And then there was a sound. Three dulcet chimes, as jarring as a siren. Daniel swiveled toward the stairs. Joanna could see his throat move as he swallowed. "That's odd—there weren't any appointments for today." For an indecisive moment, he stared across the room. "I don't know if someone called ahead. The mortuary or . . . someone . . ." And then he met her eyes again with a long look—possibly an admonition, possibly a plea. "I have to answer it."

He left her there, standing by the bed. And as she watched the top of his head disappear, it became piercingly clear. She couldn't stay. Doe's imminent return didn't matter anymore, nor did the possibility of a customer—bereft and urgent at the door. She couldn't stay there, waiting in his room, because in doing so, she would be telling him a lie. He had been unequivocal: *It can only go one way or the other.* And in her heart, she knew. She couldn't do it. She couldn't choose Daniel.

She would go. She would simply slip out the back. Anguished apology would dishonor what they had—the truth and the beauty of their friendship. It would be more than she could bear.

In the hallway of the second floor, she paused, listening for voices. There was an indiscernible exchange as Daniel opened the door. Someone introducing himself, she presumed, explaining his sorrowful purpose. But there was something. . . . She moved forward, treading lightly. There was something in the caller's voice. Something familiar. Something recognizable. As she approached the top of the staircase, the voices became clearer, and suddenly she was rooted to the spot.

"I'm sorry to bother you." A slight pause. "I'm looking for my wife, Joanna. It was suggested I come here. I know she likes to walk in the cemetery. I thought someone might have seen her. Your grandmother, maybe? Again, I'm sorry to bother you like this."

The thoughts that could crowd the span of an instant are boundless, and in that moment Joanna's were a veritable donnybrook. Among that which jostled for elbow room was the fact that Frank was not at the office today, but out looking for her. That her absence was noticed and responded to with this level of concern prompted a small, relieved gratitude. At the same time, she had a rueful awareness that this gratitude was inherently pathetic.

Simultaneously she considered Daniel, his hand on the gates of hell. He would lie for her if she let him, and that would rob him of everything he was—the core of his being.

She processed her options. She could bluster through it, descending the stairway with an enthusiastic description of the house, exclaiming over the woodwork and the height of the ceilings and the dollhouse—all part of a spontaneous look-around . . . waiting for Doe . . . warming up a bit. She thought of her teacup, forgotten on the office desk. As a prop, it would have helped.

But over all this, she heard Daniel's words: *I never pegged you for devious*. And she knew she couldn't do it.

Daniel glanced up as she came down the stairs, and Frank followed suit. Joanna looked from one to the other: Daniel—tacitly (heartbreakingly) deferring to her lead, and Frank—visibly puzzled to see his wife emerging from the private reaches of this man's home. When she took the last step, she looked directly into her husband's eyes, offering no excuse.

The process of realization spread over his features slowly, like a dull November dawn. He looked from Joanna to Daniel, and his mouth fell open as his eyes ran down and up again. Dumbly, his gaze returned to Joanna. When he spoke, it seemed to come from some distant automation.

"Grandmother had a stroke. It doesn't . . . look good. I thought . . ." Back again to Daniel, incredulity replacing shock; and then, again, to Joanna. "I thought you should know."

With that, he turned and walked stiffly to the car.

Twelve

"There's something on your coat, dear. Turn around." Helen happened to be passing through the foyer with her evening cup of tea when Susannah came through the front door. She stepped close to her daughter, holding the saucer in one hand as she brushed at the back of Susannah's shoulder with the other. "What could this be?" Squinting at the poiret twill, she made a closer inspection. "Some kind of soot?" She gave a sharp sniff. "Your coat smells like woodsmoke." Stepping back, she gave Susannah a quizzical look. "Have you been at a bonfire?"

"Heavens, no!" Susannah gave a light laugh as she took off her gloves. "I've been studying at Evelyn's, I told you. The fireplace in the parlor backed up. It was like a forest fire in there. We opened all the windows, and I had to put my coat on. I must have brushed up on the firebox when we were fanning the smoke."

Thinking on her feet was becoming second nature, and

Susannah took a bit of unscrupulous pride in her ready response. But her fiction wasn't much of a stretch. Chap had improved their rustic environs with the addition of a stadium blanket and several plaid davenport cushions (the brothers at Chi Psi were still investigating), but the boathouse was a bit drafty, and so, in addition to supplying an extra blanket, he had gathered as much kindling as he could carry and attempted to light a fire in the rusty corner stove. What he hadn't anticipated was the presence of some kind of nest that had fully and resolutely plugged the pipe. Eventually it burned away (with no evidence of inhabitants, to Susannah's squeamish relief), but for most of the evening, an eye-watering haze had covered them more thoroughly than the blanket.

Moving toward the cloakroom, she glanced across the hall, happy to happen on a diversion. "The tree looks beautiful. It's even bigger than last year, isn't it? Ernst must have had quite a time."

The Christmas tree was, indeed, enormous, and Ernst—the beleaguered head gardener—had had to haul in a heavy, cumbersome ladder in order to reach the top.

"Yes—a veritable sequoia." Helen raised her brow dubiously. "Somehow he managed, but I wouldn't get too close. One jiggle and you could be impaled by a falling star." The precarious crowning glory of the tree was a traditional Moravian star with about twenty sharp points. "I think it would be best to place our gifts under the tree in the drawing room this year. And that reminds me: I picked up a little something for Wyatt today. I was in the city and Wannamaker's had a lovely cashmere muffler in the exact shade of Yale blue. I just couldn't resist." She pursed her lips, thoughtful. "I'll need to get something for Chap, as well. What, though?" The look she gave her daughter was enigmatic. "Any suggestions?"

Susannah blinked an extra time or two. "No . . . I . . . ah . . . wouldn't know. Maybe the same thing in brown and white?"

Helen's gaze was steady. "I think not. I've never particularly cared for Lehigh's colors. Too drab. Perhaps you can think of something else he would like?"

Susannah's bold insouciance was dissolving like chalk in the rain; suddenly she felt very warm. Grasping the cloakroom doorknob, she threw a casual response over her shoulder as she shrugged off her coat: "Sorry, I can't help you there. Kit may have an idea—you could ask him when he gets home."

"One moment." Helen stepped forward and plucked a small dead leaf from the hem of Susannah's coat. She held the bit of brown out to her daughter. "It seems the Smythes' housekeeping leaves something to be desired." Peering at Susannah's hair, she reached up and extracted another betraying fragment from the wavy bob, and her words were as dry as the foliage: "No pun intended." With that, she turned toward the staircase and walked away, teacup rattling on its saucer.

In her bedroom, Susannah sat down at the dressing table, wincing when she saw the telltale, rosy abrasion on her cheeks.

As she drew a comb through her hair, another bit of leaf fell out. She made a mental note to find a broom and sweep the boathouse floor.

It wouldn't be long now. To go public with their relationship before they broke it to Wyatt was out of the question. Compounding the injury with such an insult would be positively inhumane. But Wyatt was coming home in several days, and the evening had been spent (partially) discussing how to tell him.

"I have to do it first thing," Chap had mused, stroking his hand softly over her hair as they lay before the sputtering fire. "I just can't . . . I won't be able to take it. I'll go to the station—I can tell him in the car."

But Susannah disagreed. "I think we should wait until after the holidays. Think about it. We'll all be thrown together on Christmas Eve, and then at the country club for New Year's. It would be better to spare him until after all that. Maybe just before he goes back to school. It will make it easier if he can get away."

Chap gave a small, painful groan. "All right. But I'm not going to the club. Christmas will be hard enough." He exhaled in a dispirited puff, muttering bleakly, "What a way to start the year." For a few moments, the only sound was the crackling of the kindling, and then he spoke again—distilling the wretchedness of the situation to its essence with one grim thought: "I'll want him to be my best man. How do you think that will go over?"

It wasn't quite a proposal, but it didn't need to be. Their future together was a foregone conclusion. It was only a matter of time.

"What about Itty? She still dreams about making you pancakes. I don't imagine she'll be the most honored of maids."

Even the cold sleet of the conversation couldn't douse the gleam in Chap's eye as he moved over her, propping himself on his elbows. Through a small, pent smile his voice was throaty: "I like my pancakes with blueberries and syrup, and . . . this." And then he covered her mouth with his, and the awful complications wafted into the lingering haze.

India was the first to come home. Jimmy had been sent to the city to fetch her. It was a trip that normally took no more than two hours each way, but a picturesque holiday snowfall had Helen pacing halls and peering out windows. The late-afternoon shadows were turning to dusk as the creamy Stutz pulled up the drive, and Susannah joined Helen at the front door to form the small welcoming committee. Using every performance skill she could muster, she plastered a cheery smile on her face. "Well, look here! City mouse come to call in the country!" To her ears, the words sounded a bit forced, but her mother's bustling welcome provided a relieving buffer, and Susannah dropped back a step as Helen ushered her eldest daughter into the house and up the staircase.

After a routine homecoming exchange—the condition of

the roads . . . beastly exams . . . a new dress from Bergdorf's—
Helen drifted off to see about some floral arrangements, and
Susannah sat down on the bed in her sister's room, struggling
to maintain a semblance of the relaxed, easy bond they had always shared.

"It must seem so provincial here. I hope you aren't bored
to tears. It's too bad Harold couldn't spend the holidays
with us. But Manhattan at Christmas is divine. I suppose he
would find our little town of Bethlehem rather dull." She was
aware that she was rambling—something that had never
really been her style—but her subconscious was working
overtime pitching the big city, and—please, God—a prevail-
ing love interest therein.

India was standing before the wardrobe changing her
clothes, and her words were slightly muffled as she pulled a
gray silk blouse over her head. "I broke it off with Harold."

"Oh." Susannah's dismay was deeper than India could
know. "That's a shame." Her eyes landed vacantly on India's
suitcase, which Jimmy had deposited there for the attentions
of the new upstairs maid. "Was there . . . a particular reason?"

India gave her a weary look. "What do you think?" The
question was rhetorical, and her eyes went to the floor as
her shoulders fell. She stayed like that for a moment, lost in
the despondent futility of it, and then shook her head sharply
as she turned back to the wardrobe. "And the thing is"—
her voice thickened as she squeezed a woolen skirt tightly
with both hands—"there's nothing wrong with Harold. He's

nice and smart and handsome . . . and I couldn't even tell him why." Framed on the inside of the enormous walnut doors were long mirrors. Although India had turned her back, Susannah had a clear view as her sister tipped her chin down, pressing her eyes shut. With a deep sigh, India managed to control her emotions. "Maybe I'm delusional, but I can't help thinking that one day Chap will wake up and realize I'm the one."

Susannah hoped her cringe wasn't as pronounced as it felt, and the room hummed a little as she swallowed a good-size rock. "Well . . . um . . . Elvie's making beef Wellington for dinner . . . and Hep said he'd take us driving while you're back. . . ." She glanced rather desperately around the room, searching for another bright spot on which to focus. But nothing presented itself. "Although, if this snow keeps up, he probably won't let us behind the wheel. . . ." Her words trailed off and she stood suddenly, stroking her palms over the front of her skirt in a nervous swish. "I have a little headache—I'm just going to lie down for a bit. . . ." The vague feebleness of her voice gave credence to the words, but as she turned toward the door, India stopped her.

"Sassy, wait." There was an eager lift to her brow. "Have you seen him? Has he come to dinner?"

Susannah managed a hollow response. "What? Oh . . . you mean Chap? Ah . . . no . . . he hasn't come around. I guess he's been busy at school. . . ."

"Oh. Well." The little flicker of hope in India's voice was

snuffed to a sad, gray wisp. "I thought maybe Mother would have roped him in."

"No. Just Charles." Susannah almost made it through the doorway, but the gods weren't finished with her yet.

"Do you think he's seeing someone?" The question was more ruminative than anything—tortured speculation seeking a sounding board—but the color in Susannah's face was draining away in a swirling vortex, and she could only pray it wouldn't emit an actual gurgle as India continued her unwitting crucifixion. "I mean, I know he takes girls out, but do you think there's someone special?"

She was looking for sisterly solidarity and a reassuring denial, and in another life, Susannah would have provided it. But that was in another life. Now her hasty fib was made real. "I'm sorry. I'm really not feeling well . . . I need to lie down. . . ." And to further prove the point, her knees buckled a little as she fled to her room.

The midnight Christmas Eve service at Nativity Episcopal Church was always overflowing—packed with bodies that hadn't felt the hard seat of a pew all year. Gothic iron torchères mounted at intervals on the stone walls cast a mystical, flickering light over the nave, and the altar glowed with enormous candelabra and a tall Douglas fir decked in tiny candles. Susannah was seated—pro forma—in the front row, wedged between India and Kit. And directly behind her, emitting waves of heavy atmospheric pressure that pushed against her neck and shoulders, was Wyatt, flanked by his father on the right and Chap on the left. Her head was bowed as though in obeisance, but in fact she was staring at her hand. More specifically, at the milky, iridescent opal that was mounted in a gold ring on her finger.

Not surprisingly, Wyatt had appeared at the door the instant he got back. As Susannah came down the stairs, she registered a dim dismay at the realization that clichés are sometimes all too true: when he saw her, his eyes lit up. Harriet took his coat, and he embraced Susannah somewhat clumsily. The fact that overt displays of affection had never been Wyatt's strong suit played well for her then—her stiff, puny response didn't seem to register.

There was a nice fire going in the library, so they sat there on the small divan, where she tried her best to be warm and bright. But she was quickly realizing that Chap had been right about telling him immediately. She felt cheap and cruel, and she didn't like pretending. She had always been authentic and forthright—until the past few months, that is. But her performance to date had only been a rehearsal—this was the real thing. Looking at Wyatt's sweet, eager eyes, she found herself paralyzed with stage fright. And then those same eyes turned disappointed and confused as Susannah suddenly remembered a promise to do some last-minute Christmas shopping with India. *So sorry . . . Here, don't forget your hat. . . .*

I'll see you later. . . . When she closed the door behind him, she thought she might cry.

The following days were an awkward blur of evasions and contrivances—busy errands that just had to be done, and tasks and obligations and anything at all that would keep Wyatt at arm's length. But in her counterfeit litany of excuses, the one true thing was that she wasn't feeling well. At first she thought it had to be the flu. But it seemed to come and go, and eventually she decided that the cause of the roiling nausea was more likely emotional than physical. By Christmas Eve—despite herself—her stomach had settled; while there was still a large knot there, at least the queasiness had passed. She had finished doing her hair and was about to make herself choose a gown to wear when her mother knocked lightly and opened the door.

"I hope you're feeling better." Helen was dressed festively in a sweeping burgundy moiré skirt and a Chantilly lace blouse with a poinsettia brooch near the collar. "Alvin is serving champagne in the drawing room, and the fire is roaring." She stepped up to Susannah and laid the back of her hand across her daughter's forehead.

"Mother, really." Susannah pulled her head away sharply. She hadn't meant to be short, but jittery nerves bested her. "I'm fine—I was just going to change. I'll be down in a few minutes." She turned toward her dressing table, trying to sound casual. "Are they here yet?"

She was dying to see Chap. She needed him. She needed the grounding assurance she felt when they were together. The last days had proven it—beyond the anguish she felt about Wyatt, she had discovered another misery: the enforced separation from Chap had left her feeling adrift and melancholy. It was like homesickness—like when, as a child, she had gone to stay with Grandmother Avery in Boston. Despite weeks of eager anticipation, she had been bewilderingly sad the entire time.

"Not yet. I expect them any moment. You know how prompt Charles is. As I've always said, it's one of the best things about engineers—sticklers for precision." She looked at the small gold watch that hung constantly from a long, slender chain around her neck. "I told Elvie we would be serving at nine o'clock. There's still plenty of time for drinks and gifts before dinner." Moving to the wardrobe, she opened a door and began to survey the dresses. "This midnight velvet would look nice, I think." With a light grasp, she pulled the skirt forward, then moved on, running a hand across the hangers and making small talk as she considered the choices. "I do hope Charles doesn't feel obligated about the gifts. It's really a woman's territory, don't you think? Frances was so clever about it. Do you remember the year she brought the peanuts?"

For the first time in days, Susannah smiled honestly. "We were completely stymied. A bag of peanuts for each of us, tied up with a red bow. I can still hear Kit"—her voice went deadpan—"*Oh, peanuts. That's great. . . . I love peanuts.*" She was grinning now. "The look on his face."

"I'm afraid you all had the same expression. Frances was practically apoplectic trying not to laugh."

"And then she had to make us open them . . . *Go ahead— have some. Here's a dish for the shells.*"

"And the circus tickets were inside." Helen was shaking her head, smiling at the memory. "Oh, she was such fun." She pulled out another dress—pale green satin—and held it up appraisingly as she continued. "I tell Charles every year that he shouldn't burden himself, but I just can't let go of the gifting tradition. It would feel like one more thing gone with Frances." Examining the dress, her tone became studiously nonchalant. "Did I mention I found something for Chap? It's a new book of essays—just released. All the best of the year. Inge, Wells, Anderson . . . it looks marvelous. I hope he doesn't have it." She gave Susannah an innocuous look. "What do you think?"

Susannah was suddenly very tired of the game, and just wanted to surrender. With a small sigh, she looked directly into her mother's eyes, and her even, flat delivery spoke volumes: "I think he'll like it very much."

They stood like that for a long moment, gazes locked, and then Helen turned abruptly back to the gown. "Good. Well, then . . . I think this would be a lovely choice. It's a good color for you." She settled the hanger on top of the wardrobe door and started toward the hall. But in the doorway, she stopped and turned back, her words soft. "When I was a young woman, my father said something to me that I'll never forget. At the time, it made all the difference. He said: 'I'm never here to judge you—I'm only here to help you.'" Her smile was tender. "Merry Christmas, Sass."

"*Merry Christmas, Hedy*. I'm not much good at this—color-blind, and all—but the salesgirl tried her best." Charles gave a self-deprecating shrug as Helen opened his gift. It was a leather handbag from the saddler Hermès. "I'm told they're all the rage in Paris."

"I heard they had started producing ladies' handbags—isn't this sporty and smart!" Helen was holding the bag up, turning it this way and that. "Just think how useful this will be. I believe I could carry my entire ledger in here." She smiled broadly at Charles, and then looked coyly at her husband. "Hep, just think of all the fine purchases I can make with the checking book in hand."

Hollins rolled his eyes. "Wonderful, dear." He turned to his friend with a grimace. "Strong work, Charles. A new and efficient way to deplete the coffers."

"Always happy to help."

The Yale-blue muffler and the book of essays were both received with earnest approval, and Charles jauntily donned his gift—a plaid trilby, perfect for pheasant hunts. He gave

Hollins a bottle of aged port and a box of Cuban cigars; and for Kit, India, and Susannah, each a framed photo from a day long ago—a boating excursion on the river. It had been taken by an employee at Bethlehem Steel, eager to master a new camera. He had positioned his tripod on the shore and was trying to capture a shot of a great blue heron when the group floated by.

There was a moment of silence as they collectively regarded the image—Kit and Chap, grinning with chests puffed out and arms around shoulders; India and Susannah in pale summer dresses, waving from the bow; Charles and Hollins in straw boaters, grasping large oars; and Wyatt, seated low on a cushion next to Frances, who was leaning back as Helen held a parasol above them.

"I was cleaning out my desk at home and found the negative. Remember that fellow Fredrickson? Plant manager at Number Eight, I think. Gave it to me years ago, and I'd forgotten about it."

"I remember that day like it was yesterday," Helen remarked. "It was hot, and hardly a breeze!"

"Was that when Kit dumped the water bucket over Wyatt's head?" India's smile was smug.

"I was doing him a favor."

"Except it also soaked Mrs. Collier. That was nice work." Even years after the fact, she wouldn't let the opportunity pass.

"But Frances just laughed, if you'll remember," Helen said, gazing fondly at the copy that Kit was holding. "Even when she wasn't well, she was swell." She looked across the room. "Thank you, Charles—such a perfect gift. I think I speak for everyone when I say these will be cherished."

There were thanks all around, and then Helen stood and applauded lightly. "Well done by all. Another year of friendship and giving. Now, if we're finished here, I believe Elvie would like us to be seated before the goose starts to shiver."

"Wait—I have something."

All eyes turned to Wyatt, who was sitting on the edge of his chair, cheeks flushed and eyes bright.

"I have something else to give. I thought . . . I thought I might just as well do it now. . . ." He looked nervously at Susannah, who had intentionally chosen a seat next to India on a small settee. "I mean . . . I wanted to do it before . . . earlier, but there wasn't the chance. So, well, I have something for you." He stood and pulled a small package from his pocket.

Susannah was poleaxed. "Oh. Oh. I'm . . . I'm afraid I don't have something else for you. I mean, it has always been a family thing . . . I didn't think we were doing more. . . ."

"No, of course not. I didn't expect anything. . . ." Flustered, he thrust the package at her. "I just . . . It's just something I saw and I thought you might like it." Wyatt's aversion to the limelight had produced a telltale sheen on his forehead. "Go ahead—open it."

Susannah took the gift and held it on her lap, staring down. Finally she picked at the wrapping paper, removing it so reluctantly, there might have been a snake inside. Everyone in the room was silent as she opened the box, but when she simply sat there looking at it, Kit spoke up.

"Well, come on! Let's see what you've got. What is it, Wyatt—should we throw a pillow down?"

There was a collusive chuckle from Hollins, who grabbed a small, fringed pillow from the nearest chair and tossed it at Wyatt's feet. "Something to kneel on, son?"

"No! I mean . . . it's not like that." Wyatt was now as red as a rash. "It's just a present. Just something to have. You know, for when I'm gone. So you . . . don't forget me . . . or anything." His voice drained thinly into the air.

Because Susannah continued to stare frozenly at the small box, she didn't see the look that passed between Helen and Charles, or the way Chap bowed over, dropping his forehead to his palms, elbows on his knees.

"Put it on, Sass! Show everyone what a pretty bauble he bought you!" India had a clear view of the delicate opal ring nestled in a velvet liner. When Susannah didn't move, she reached over and picked it up, holding it out for all to see. "Isn't it beautiful? I adore an opal—they say it holds the moon inside. Here, try it on." She picked up Susannah's left hand and slid the ring onto her finger, then glanced teasingly at Wyatt. "Sorry if I'm doing your job, Wy. But somebody has to." She gave him a wink, and then lifted her sister's arm by the wrist, displaying the gift for all. "A perfect fit, and see how nice it looks on your hand."

Suddenly Helen moved across the room, taking Susannah's extended hand in her own. "It is lovely, indeed, and I think we should all give Susannah a chance to say thank you in her own way, in her own time." Her voice rose a pitch—the epitome of merry and bright: "For now, let us to the table go—the Christmas feast awaits." With that, she pulled her daughter to her feet and led her firmly across the room and through the archway, leaving the others to follow behind.

Three hours later they filed into church, some of them considerably steadier than others. Kit—embracing the celebratory opportunity with his usual gusto—had shown no qualms about signaling Alvin (on service duty in the dining room for the special occasion) with a regular sweep of his index finger toward his wine goblet; but his enthusiastic willingness to help relieve the cellar of a case of Burgundy's finest was put to shame by his best friend's bottomless thirst. When Hollins finally called for the tawny bottle of Dow's that Charles had given him, Chap—swaying a bit as he rose from his chair—had to excuse himself to get some air.

Now, as Susannah stared numbly at her left hand, Wyatt's abashment—hanging in the pew behind her like a low cloud—wasn't the only thing penetrating her daze. She also had a noxious awareness of the alcoholic fug surrounding her. When the congregation was prompted to join in on the closing hymn—"O Little Town of Bethlehem"—she had to needle Kit in the ribs as he bellowed in a terrible off-key baritone.

It was all too much, and as the service ended she wanted nothing more than to crawl into bed and close her eyes. Walking straight to the waiting car, she climbed in without a word to anyone. India slid in beside her as their father informed Kit in no uncertain terms that a nice brisk walk in the starry night would be the only way he was getting home. As Jimmy put the gears into drive, Susannah looked out the window and saw Kit and Chap—arms thrown around each other's shoulders just as they had been in the photo—swaying down the sidewalk.

She wasn't dreaming. Her sleep was deep and plenary—mercifully absent any angst. But there was a sound . . . a sibilant hushing that was pulling her from the warm, dark void. She had to force her eyes open, and when she did, she heard it again.

"Shh. Shh."

There was a figure sitting on the side of the bed with a finger to his lips. She could see his features—Apollo in the moonlight, divinely handsome even in slurry debilitation.

"Hi. Wake up. I have to talk to you." His whisper was somewhat less than discreet, and he laid his hand heavily on her shoulder. "How are you?"

Her mind was still trying to shuck the dark cloak of oblivion, but her smile was reflexive. "Better now."

He gazed at her for a long moment, then ran his finger softly across the lace strap of her nightgown. "This is. Wow. This is nice. I din't know you wore this. When you're sleeping."

His head was bobbing a little as he spoke, and Susannah giggled.

"No—don' laugh at me. I don' know what . . . I wanted to say I'm sorry. I'm sorry. You shoun't have had to go through that. I have to tell him tomorrow. Firs' thing." He picked up her hand and looked at it, but the ring was gone—she had taken it off as soon as she got to her room. "And I will get you a ring. A nice ring. And I'm gonna tell him we're getting married. Right? Getting married. And he can be the bes' man. 'Cause he is the bes' man, right? I mean, he's the *best*." He swayed forward a little, and Susannah sat up on her knees, putting a hand on either side of his face.

"Honey, how did you get up here? Where's Kit? Does he know where you are?" Her whisper was quieter than his.

"No, he's asleep. In a chair. The one tha' looks like a throne. You never called me that before. I like it."

"He's in the billiards room?" It *was* a throne—from a castle in Scotland (Brynmor Castle, to be precise)—placed as out of sight as Helen could manage, in the billiards room in the basement.

"Yesss. He's drunker than I am. I won four outta six at eight-ball. Even though we foun' the key to the gin locker."

"Did anyone see you come up?"

"Everyone's asleep. Don' worry. I was quiet."

"You're not that quiet." Her smile was tender as she stroked his face. "I think *you* need to go to sleep. Let me take you to a guest room. Hep wouldn't want you to try to make it home like this."

He leaned forward and kissed her, and she couldn't help being impressed. The kiss wasn't drunken or sloppy or by any count shy of rapturous. He was just that good at it.

"I love you." He looked intently into her eyes, as though imparting this information were absolutely vital.

Her smile broadened. Just being near him, even in his less-than-mint condition, made her feel whole and happy. "I love you too. Now go to bed." She glanced over her shoulder at the doorway. "This whole fiasco will seem like a bed of roses if Hep finds you here."

"Okay. I'm going. You stay here. I'll be fine. I'm jus' going back to the basement. I can sleep on that leather Chester . . . Chester-thing."

Susannah giggled again. "Good idea. Kit will find you where he left you. But I'm walking you down." She wasn't about to let him stumble into her parents' bedroom by mistake.

She took his arm and tiptoed across the floor, carefully pulling up on the handle as she opened the door, to relieve a squeaky hinge from the weight of the wood. They made it down the hallway without a hitch, and even navigated the stairway with a fair approximation of steadiness. On the landing, he stopped. "I can take it from here. Jus' wanna say g'night. I'll see you in the morning, and then . . . Well . . . I'll think aboudit later. I love you. Did I say that already?" He gave her that crooked, contained grin that made her heart skip, and then pulled her close and kissed her again.

For a sublime moment, Susannah felt the familiar transcendence—like she was floating on another plane. And then, high above them, a light snapped on. She wheeled around, instinctively pushing Chap away as she looked up to see Helen, standing at the top of the stairs, her hand on the switch.

And that was all it took. It wasn't much of a push, but he was stunned and off-balance, and he stumbled backward. It shouldn't have happened—Chap was an athlete, nimble and quick. He could steal a base with a slide so graceful, it looked like ballet, springing to his feet like a figurine in a music box. But he wasn't at his best. And there was a ledge—low and narrow—that ran the width of the landing, beneath the enormous stained-glass window. As he reeled, the ledge caught him behind and below the knee, and—like a fulcrum—flung him backward.

The window was rendered in a beautiful peacock motif, opaque and rich with teal and emerald. Had it been transparent, it would have provided a scene not as vibrantly colorful, but lovely just the same—of the quarried stone courtyard below.

Susannah heard it—a skin-crawling shatter—and saw the

horror on her mother's face. And then there was a crack in time—an infinite split second within which she hovered, clinging to a chimerical wisp of denial. But it slipped through her fingers, and when she turned—from a distant, dreamlike remove—there was nothing but broken glass. Shards of blue and green everywhere, and nothing else. Nothing and no one.

It wasn't much of a push.

Thirteen

"Daddy's other grandmother is already in heaven." Daisy proffered the information across the small table where the edges of a jigsaw puzzle were taking form. "Her name was Frank."

"No, it wasn't!" Charlie scoffed, irritated by the absurdity.

"Yes, it was. He told me. I'm named after a boy, and he's named after a girl, and it was his grandmother."

As Joanna entered the playroom, the children looked up from their puzzle. But Harriet, slumped in the window seat with her forehead pressed heavily against the glass, didn't move.

Daniel had offered to drive Joanna back in the old Ford pickup, but she had refused. It would have been too awful—she couldn't stomach the thought of being dropped off like a teenager who had stayed out past curfew with her boyfriend.

She just shook her head, dazed by the fact that it had come to this. In the space of an afternoon, everything had changed.

Their parting was silent. Joanna knew the obligation fell on her, but any words that might have found form stuck in her throat. It didn't matter. When she tried to speak, Daniel held up his hand and looked away. As always, he could hear what she wasn't saying. And so, she simply turned and left.

Reaching Brynmor's long driveway, she discovered that it now stretched for miles. The terrain behind the front door was uncharted and riddled with risk—jagged gorges yawning in the darkness. The closest one gaped into the infinite expanse of losing Helen.

Inside, the absence was palpable. She didn't have to check the drawing room or the library or the conservatory—the house told her: no one was there. But she wandered through the rooms anyway, finally moving upstairs to her bedroom. She was sitting on the bed, staring vacantly at the hands folded on her lap, when one of the cleaning girls—hired in from town these days—appeared in the doorway.

"Oh! Excuse me, ma'am. I didn't think anyone was here."

Joanna started and stood. "It's all right—you can come in. I didn't think anyone was here either."

"They've gone to St. Luke's." The girl cast her eyes down, uncertain about the propriety of having and sharing the information. "All but the children, that is. And Mrs. Bonner. They're upstairs." She looked up, hesitant. "I'm a little worried about Mrs. Bonner."

Joanna was confused. "You're worried about Harriet?"

"Yes, ma'am. She's not taking the . . . situation . . . too well. She looks near ready to crumble."

Joanna moved to the door, stepping around the girl and into the hallway. "Thank you . . . uh . . ."

"Jeanette."

"Thank you, Jeanette. I'll go and see. You can go ahead with your work, and"—she glanced around the room—"thank you for . . . that, too. . . ." It was still awkward for her, even after the full-butled immersion of living at Brynmor.

On the third floor, she had heard the children's voices. As she appeared in the doorway, Daisy jumped up.

"Where were you? We were looking everywhere! Grand Hedy had a . . ." She turned to Charlie. "What did she have?"

"A stroke." Charlie was somber.

"A stroke," Daisy repeated. "She went to the hospital. Grandmother told us to take care of Harriet. We're watching her, but she doesn't want to do the puzzle."

As Joanna looked worriedly at Harriet, Daisy pulled on her sleeve. "*Wasn't* Daddy's other grandmother named Frank? He said so."

Charlie rolled his eyes.

Distracted, Joanna patted Daisy's back. "You're forgetting that Daddy's full name is Francis, honey. *Frances* can be for a girl, too. There's just a different spelling." She could feel her daughter's disappointment as the little shoulders sagged. In any contest with her brother, Daisy never came out on top.

Starting across the room, Joanna looked at Charlie. "But Daisy wasn't really wrong, because she didn't have all the information. So, in a way, you're both right." The little girl brightened as Joanna approached the window seat.

"Harriet?" She laid a gentle hand on the old woman's shoulder. A pair of faded blue eyes, lost and afraid, turned slowly to look up at her. "Harriet, would you like to lie down?" Joanna's voice was tender.

The woman just shook her head, wringing her hands and turning back to the window. Joanna sat down next to her. She was almost afraid to ask. "Has there been any word?"

"No, ma'am." She looked down at the narrow, filigreed gold watch on her wrist. "They took her nearly three hours ago." Absently, she cuffed the watch, running her thumb along the bracelet.

Joanna wasn't sure what to do. She didn't want to leave Harriet here—clearly, she was in no condition to watch over the children. Joanna wasn't even sure the poor thing should be left alone. She put her arm around the hunched shoulders. "That's a beautiful watch. Is it an heirloom?

"It was a gift from Mrs. Parrish. A birthday gift. When I turned twenty-five." The words came slowly—weighted with bewildered despair.

It struck Joanna then—this woman's entire life had been devoted to Helen. She could only imagine how adrift Harriet would feel without her captain. "I'm sorry. I know this must be terribly hard for you. You've been with her for a long time. She's been so lucky to have you."

Harriet shook her head slowly. "No, I was lucky to have her." The aged voice was tremulous. "She took me on in '17, when Bertie was sent over. I was a young bride—I needed a job, a place to live. Just until Bertie got back. We would get an apartment then. I thought maybe he could come on here, in the stables or the yard." She paused for a moment, her gaze moving from the watch to the window. "It wasn't the Germans that got him. It was the influenza." Wavering already, the words grew thick: "What she did for me . . ." Hanging her head, she pulled a handkerchief from her apron pocket. "She is the finest woman to ever walk God's green earth."

Is. The word resonated with Joanna. Hugging Harriet's shoulders, she looked over at the children. They were quiet—Daisy was trying to work a piece into the puzzle, but Charlie was slumped down on the table, chin resting on his hands. She had no idea how much they understood, but Daisy's overheard remark about heaven was a pretty good clue. With an extra squeeze for Harriet, Joanna stood and went to her son.

She brushed the hair lightly off of his forehead. "Hey, handsome." Her words were soft. "Are you okay?"

He just nodded, moving his cheek across the back of his hands.

She sat down on a small wooden chair, leaning forward. "Would you like to talk about it?" Whatever the outcome, it couldn't hurt to prepare the children.

But she had misread her son. He was troubled, but not for the reason she expected. At least, not entirely. "We don't always both have to be right, you know." His mouth was set in a tight line.

"I'm sorry?"

"It's not fair. Daisy was wrong. The grandmother wasn't named Frank. Just because she didn't understand, it doesn't mean she was right."

Joanna knew it wasn't about winning the point. Charlie's sense of justice had been assaulted. It was integral—a requirement for logic, for fact. He hadn't yet developed the quality of charity; he couldn't sacrifice his conviction for kindness. She drew a deep breath. Normally, she would have taken the opportunity to instill a moral lesson—to talk about generosity of spirit and noblesse oblige. But the larger issues of the day preempted the moralizing moment. The timing was bad, and her heart wasn't in it.

"You're right. Her name was Frances. Not Frank." She looked at her daughter, whose face crumpled a little. "Sorry, honey. Sometimes, you just have to admit that you got it wrong."

The sentence snapped back at her like a rubber band, and she felt the sting of her own words. *Admit that you got it wrong*.

And then Daisy pulled on the band and snapped it again: "Like Daddy."

"What?"

"He said he was wrong and that's why you went to bed.

Last night when he tucked us in. And we didn't read any books because he was too tired. But I think actually he was too sad. Because he was wrong."

Just in case that didn't smart enough, Eileen Rafferty's voice piped into her head again (a phenomenon that had plagued Joanna for most of her life): *Think about Frank.*

Had she thought about Frank, even for a minute? Like Charlie, she had been reacting on instinct—a primal impulse that did not allow for circumspection or empathy. A septic shame crept over her, spreading the sting evenly across her skin. In all the months of feeling sorry for herself, of shifting self-pity to resentment, she had been determinedly oblivious to any need or want or fear that might have been pressing on—even crushing—her husband.

She had to get to the hospital—not only for Helen, but also for Frank. She needed to face him, to assess the damage. Rising from the tiny chair, her instructions were as distracted as they were rushed. "You're doing a great job with Harriet. She's tired and needs to rest. I have to go and see how Grand Hedy is doing. Stay right here. I'll be back as soon as I can."

She hurried down the stairs, wondering where her car keys might be. She rarely drove her Ventura these days—only when she went to Pennsport, really. She thought they were probably on the key peg by the service door, and she went to the kitchen.

As she was crossing the worn tiles, the door opened.

Frank stood aside, ushering in his mother and his sister.

Susannah looked drained, and Gigi's eyes were swollen and red. They all saw Joanna at once, but no one said a word. Gigi met her eye and shook her head—all the information required. She took her mother's arm and led her to the hall, and Frank closed the door. He stood there for a moment, holding his hat and staring at the floor. And then he wiped his shoes on the doormat and walked right past her.

Joanna grasped the edge of the big cast-iron stove. Helen was gone. The blow would have been staggering in any case—her absence would leave an abysmal hole in the house. But the fact that Joanna was standing on such shaky ground made her knees weak. Given recent events, she didn't know how to approach her husband—or for that matter, the rest of the family—and the seismic uncertainty caused her to sway.

She had to force herself back up the stairs to the bedroom. Frank was sitting by the window, still wearing his overcoat. His hands lay motionless on the arms of the chair, and his gaze was fixed on an indeterminate spot in the bleak winter landscape. He seemed so defeated, so vulnerable, that Joanna's impulse was to take him in her arms, like one of the children. And then he turned his head, and almost broke her heart with four harrowed words.

"Are you leaving me?"

Pressing her lips together to suppress an aching cry, she could only shake her head.

For a long moment he closed his eyes. The next question

was uttered with a reluctance so ragged, it might have come through a thresher. "Have you been . . . unfaithful?"

Unfaithful. The word hit her like a hammer, echoing her own thoughts, just hours earlier in Daniel's bedroom. Could she explain it to him—the sudden realization, the recognition, the decision? It was just a moment. A single conflicted interlude. Would that excuse the betrayal? But in truth, it wasn't just a moment. What about the months leading to that moment—the eagerness, the warmth in her heart, the emotional ante? She couldn't deny any of it, and there wasn't any other word for it: *unfaithful.*

She didn't have to answer—he saw it on her face. With an urgency that left a draft in its wake, he stood and strode out the door.

She didn't know how long she had been standing there when a little bird flew by. It was only in her mind, but she saw it as clearly as if it had come in and perched on the windowsill. It was her parakeet, Pete—the chirpy companion she had taken home from the pet store just before she met Frank. From the very first, Frank was troubled by Pete's cage. To Joanna, the sweet birdsong emanating from the little fluff of green seemed like happiness. But to Frank, it was terrible, tortured yearning. He was so worried about the bird's psyche that Joanna started to tease him about having an ulterior motive for wanting to come up to the tiny apartment on Lombard Street.

Despite some very compelling evidence to the contrary, she accused him of really just wanting to let Pete out of the cage.

One night Pete landed near the heat register and somehow managed to squeeze through one of the little squares. Joanna didn't have a screwdriver, and the building supervisor was off duty. Frank had gone door to door, waking people up and suffering varied abuses before finally wooing one out of the old lady in 3B. Having sworn on the woman's Bible to come back and fix her shower rod, he returned triumphant, wielding the screwdriver in the air.

Joanna could see him with his arm stretched into the heat duct, murmuring softly to Pete with a bit of peanut butter on his finger. There was a dust bunny in Frank's hair. From then on, nearly every moment he spent in the apartment found a feathered devotee hopping from one shoulder to the other. It didn't bother Frank a bit, but it was more than a little disconcerting to Joanna—Pete's peeping had taken on a whole new meaning.

The memory seemed random, but then she saw herself climbing the stairs after a long night of work at the hospital. The beatnik-type from the apartment next door was coming down as she went up. She smiled at him, grateful for the fact that he had stopped blasting his collection of Burmese folk music while he worked. She was on night shifts then, and had spent many mornings fighting for sleep while her neighbor sculpted to a wailing zither. When the days had become suddenly quiet, Joanna didn't wonder why. She just basked in the absence of twangy atonal resonance, sleeping a full night each day. It wasn't until she bumped into him in the stairwell—noting his consideration and thanking him for it—that she learned Frank had been paying the man twenty dollars a week to keep his stereo off.

She knew where this was going now. Resigned—willing, in fact—she fastened another button on her hair shirt. The next image was from some years down the road: she was at the frayed end of the rope—sleepless with a one-year-old and a colicky newborn. Waking with a start one morning, she realized she had been asleep since midnight. That was when Frank had taken Daisy from her stuporous clutch to wear a path on the living room carpet. With constant motion, it was possible to lull the baby to sleep; putting her down was another story. Joanna had looked around. Her husband wasn't in bed, and the baby was not in the cradle. Padding to the living room, she found them both on the sofa—Frank flat on his back with an arm folded over his eyes, the baby sleeping soundly on her daddy's chest, wrapped in a flannel blanket that had been secured to the upholstery with diaper pins.

There was more—a flowing stream of acts and instances, each providing sworn testimony to her husband's sweetness and constancy. The scenes ran past like a babbling brook, whose waters rushed away while calling back: *Look what you had. Look what you may have lost.*

And then she heard an engine and the muffled crunch of tires on the gravel drive. By the time she moved to the window, Frank's car was disappearing into the fading light of the day.

For the third time, Joanna started at the top of the page, trying to focus on the precocious narrative of Franny Glass instead of the precarious narrative of her own future. She was coiled on the divan in the library, unable to shake a phantom chill even under the insulation of a wool lap blanket. The children were in bed, tucked in after a sad little dinner in the kitchen. It had been just the three of them. The pall over the household had extended to the staff; when Joanna had wandered into the kitchen, she'd found Hazel, the cook, absently scrubbing at a spot on the drainboard. The woman looked up, her face puffy and tear-stained. "Mrs. Collier said just soup tonight. She and Miss Genevieve are taking supper in their rooms." She took a tissue from her apron pocket and dabbed at her nose. "I've got a nice pot of chicken and rice on the burner. I can serve you where you like—Mrs. Bonner has taken to bed." She choked a little on the words.

"Oh, thank you, Hazel." Joanna went to the woman's side, her voice solicitous. "Soup will be just the thing. But you don't have to serve us. Why don't you call it a day, too? I can feed the kids." She hesitated. "Has my husband come in?" She didn't think the car had returned, but she asked anyway.

"No, ma'am, not that I've seen."

"All right, then. We'll be fine here—you go ahead now. Consider yourself off duty." She took the scrubbing pad from Hazel and set it down. As the cook tearfully removed her apron, Joanna went to find the children.

And so it was that they ate their desultory dinner at the scarred pine worktable, over pensive talk of strokes and funerals and heaven. And when the children said their prayers that night, they invoked a new angel.

The Salinger had gone down like ice cream when Joanna had started the book a few days earlier, but tonight she couldn't digest a bite. She had picked it up as a distraction—she didn't know what to do with herself. Frank hadn't returned yet. Every creak in the house caused a little clutch in her stomach. She was staring blankly at a sentence when Susannah appeared in the doorway. The book fell to floor as Joanna jumped up. "Oh. . . I'm . . . so sorry." Her eyes welled. It was the first she had seen of her mother-in-law since the moment she learned Helen was gone, and she felt the loss more sharply for it. "I can't imagine how you must feel. It doesn't seem possible. She was . . . something special." Wavering, her voice trailed off. She wrung her hands nervously as her mother-in-law crossed the room.

"I'm going to have a brandy." Susannah sounded spent. "Would you like one?" There was a small bar in the library—a polished walnut cabinet that housed several crystal decanters and a variety of short-stemmed glasses. She opened the cabinet.

Joanna had never tasted brandy. "Yes, thank you. That would be . . . good." She sat back down.

Susannah filled two snifters generously, and then handed one to Joanna and sat down next to her. She gave her glass an appraising look. "It would appear I rather leaned on the pour." With a shrug, she sank back, resting her neck on the cushion. "Oh well. I think circumstances call for a little . . . suspension of rectitude . . . don't you?"

Suspension of rectitude. If only she knew. Or did she? She had no idea what Susannah thought. But someone had suggested to Frank that he might find his wife at the cemetery, and it hadn't been Helen.

Any suspicions her mother-in-law might have had were eclipsed, however, by grievous circumstance; Susannah's mind was on Helen as she clinked her glass lightly against Joanna's. "To Mother." She took a sip and squeezed her eyes shut, pinching the bridge of her nose. After a gathering pause, she spoke. "Yes, she was special. I've been on the telephone with Itty. We agreed we can just quit trying—we'll never rise to her standard. It's unachievable." She exhaled deeply, and took another sip of brandy. "I suppose I was lucky. I had a mother—the finest one—for over half of a century." She looked at her glass again, swirling the amber liquid. "But that doesn't necessarily make it easier. In a way, it's harder. I'm very accustomed to having her. It will be a difficult habit to break."

This perspective had never occurred to Joanna, but she saw a truth in it. She nodded mutely. Despite the sorrowful topic, she couldn't help feeling a bit relieved at the companionable tenor of the conversation.

"I haven't been able to reach Kit." Wearily, Susannah veered into the safer emotional waters of tasks at hand. "It's the same time in Peru as it is here . . . that has always surprised me . . . but no one picks up. I've got Itty trying. I hope he's not incommunicado in some godforsaken place, like before." She tapped her finger on the rim of the glass, going over a mental list. "I've spoken to most of the family—Mother was the last of her generation, but there are some cousins. Now, there's a paradox: a long life yields a sparse send-off." Her ironic expression softened then to a faraway tenderness. "She deserves all the presidents, like Eleanor Roosevelt had." It was a poignant, reflective moment, but, in the blink of an eye, it was back to business. "I believe Agnes Wright is still alive. Probably still in Pittsburgh. I don't think old Vance has given over the reins at U.S. Steel yet. I'll have to track down their telephone number . . . not enough time to send a note by post. There might be a few others. . . . I'll have to look through her book." She gazed at the window, thoughtful. "And I suppose I should notify our set. I mean, my set." She corrected herself with a sad shake of her head. "I don't think I'll ever get used to the sole possession of old friendships."

Joanna was touched by the comment. It was possibly the most personal thing she had ever heard from her mother-in-law. Susannah Parrish Collier didn't have a self-pitying bone in her body, and Joanna had never heard her utter a whimper about her widowhood. Now she realized something: the fact that some skin doesn't show scars does not mean there haven't been wounds.

"I thought Frank should say the eulogy." Practicalities again. "I hope it isn't asking too much—he's getting plenty of experience these days." She glanced around the room. "Where *is* Frank?"

Joanna swallowed hard and pulled the lap blanket close. "I don't know."

She didn't feel it coming—it was as spontaneous and uncontrollable as convulsion. As she spoke, the words were pushed from behind by a sudden, shuddering sob. It wasn't the first time she had been delivered up by her mutinous emotions that day, but the woe that had simmered over at Grange House seemed thin and watery compared to the thick misery that rose up now.

This time, however, the person who reached out to comfort her was the one she would have least expected: her mother-in-law took her hand and squeezed it—the grasp strong and steadying. "Take a drink," Susannah instructed. "It will help."

The glass trembled against her lips, but Joanna managed a sip of the brandy. It was acrid and biting, and it made her grimace. She tried again—forcing the medicine down. It burned in her chest. Exhaling the hot vapor, she regained a measure of composure. "I'm sorry. I don't know where he is." Sniffing, she dabbed the cuff of her sweater to her cheek and stared at her drink in bewildered despondency. How she could explain the betraying outburst without revealing the betrayal? How could she defend it to Frank's own mother? What mother of what son would ever understand?

But Susannah pulled a handkerchief from her pocket and pressed it into Joanna's hand, and her words were as soft as the Portuguese linen. "I don't have any illusions that I could ever possess Mother's grace. But—despite my agreement with India—I can try." She looked intently into Joanna's eyes. "When I was a young woman, my mother gave me an exceptional gift. She said it was one that her father had given her. It was just a simple sentence, but it helped me through some pitch-black hours. What she said was this: 'I'm never here to judge you; I'm only here to help you.'"

Once again, Joanna had underestimated her mother-in-law. And this benefaction—this blameless compassion—enveloped her in a warmth that finally took the chill away. Or perhaps it was the brandy. In any case, she felt the relief of her childhood confessions—kneeling in redemptive absolution at the dim, latticed window. And in response, she found herself laying open her heart.

She didn't leave anything out—not the attraction, not even the desire. By the time she came to the end, dragging the last charred scrap from the ash heap, her voice was a hollow whisper: "I don't know if he can forgive me."

Throughout the account, Susannah had been quiet. Now, when she spoke, she astonished Joanna with another gift. It was a precious and fragile thing, with a cost that was incalculable. And it had been hidden in a wrapped box for a very long time. "There's only one way to find out," she said softly, "and that's to give him the chance. You may not realize it, but this may have been a blessing. To live with deception is a terrible thing." Her gaze moved again to the window, and her eyes became as distant as her words: "Let me tell you a story about deception."

Fourteen

"I prefer Susannah." Susannah couldn't recognize herself in her pet name anymore. It mocked her, in a way that was almost jarring—like looking into the mirror to find a garish clown mask looking back.

Helen sat on the edge of the bed, hands folded on her lap. "All right, then. Susannah. It's time to come home now. Your father expects you. We can't carry this out any longer." The gentleness of her tone tempered the imperative, and she gazed tenderly at her daughter's thin form—rocking in slow, unceasing rhythm. Helen sighed and shook her head sadly. "You can't just wither away in this attic like a character from Dickens. I told your father that your train was arriving today. We can say you've decided to postpone Bryn Mawr. He'll see that you still aren't yourself. You can stay at home until . . . well, until you regain your balance."

Susannah's hand moved slowly over the smooth maple arm

of the rocking chair—an unconscious habit. "My balance."
She repeated the words absently and looked down at her
feet, bare on the braided rug. It was all she could think to say.
Nothing meant anything anymore. Simple language was in-
comprehensible mathematical theory. Life had tested her
before, but this time she couldn't pass. There was no book.
There were no answers. There was just . . . nothing.

It had been a rainy Saturday in April when Helen walked
into her daughter's bedroom to find her at the wardrobe,
dressing for the day. Susannah had her back to the door; she
turned as it opened, pulling the garment down quickly. But
not quickly enough. Against the weak, gray light of the window, the reason for her late preference for the new drop-waist
dress style was revealed in a softly curving silhouette. And
that was the beginning of another confederacy, another unsolicited compact.

The first one had been formed in the ghastly pandemonium
of the darkest Christmas hours. Assumptions had been made,
circumstances overlooked. It didn't occur to Hollins that his
wife and daughter had not just rushed out, as he had—tying
his dressing robe on the fly. The shattering crash hadn't even
reached India, asleep in her bedroom at the far end of the hall,
much less Kit, slumped in subterranean senselessness. And
so, as Susannah stood frozen amid the jagged, glistering
glass, Helen let the misconception lie. It wasn't conscious at
first, but what had begun as mute shock became tacit consen-
sus. What purpose would be served by divulging the details?

It wouldn't change anything. The accepted premise was that Chap had tried to make his intoxicated way to a guest room and had somehow fallen into the window—a horrific fluke of proximity. It was the only plausible explanation. In the aftermath, the grief that hung over the house was so heavy, it suffocated any possibility for further conjecture. No one could bear to dwell on the scenario.

After the funeral, there hadn't been any reason for Kit and India to stay in Bethlehem. The idea of returning to regular routine seemed so ludicrous as to be surreal, but there wasn't a case to be made for remaining at home to stare at the echoing walls. The dismal fact was that life had to go on. Even Wyatt went back to New Haven. It was the only thing to do. His grief was so dense that Susannah's conspicuous impassivity did not penetrate it—he couldn't see that she was now just a mannequin, posed in lifeless inexpression. He left with no more awareness than when he had arrived. And eventually he took up his pen again, reaching out to grasp for Susannah's hand as the oceanic chop slammed against him. As before, he needed her to keep him from going under. He didn't know that this time the icy waters covered them both.

Susannah was in the conservatory, a thick-bound copy of *The Age of Reason* resting on her lap, when her mother brought the letter in. Taking a seat next to her daughter, Helen held the envelope in her own lap. There was just a single page inside, but it was heavier by far than Paine's treatise, and the look she gave Susannah held volumes of its own.

"This isn't going to be easy, Sass." Her eyes brimmed with pity and sorrow. "But you can't let him sense that he has lost you, too. It would be too much. You have to find it in yourself to help him. Not just for Wyatt, but also for Chap." She held the envelope out. "As Mrs. Roosevelt said, you must do the thing you think you cannot do." When Susannah didn't move, Helen stood and laid it gently on top of the Paine, and then walked out of the room.

Susannah had no concept of how much time had passed when she finally opened the letter. She held it in her hands for so long, her fingers seemed to have frozen in a clutch; when her index finger slid under the lip of the seal, she nearly jumped. Her hand moved with a will of its own, extracting the page and unfolding it.

Dear Sass,

Are you reading this at night? If I could talk to you, I would want it to be in the dark. I don't like doing anything in the daylight now. It doesn't feel right. The sun is some kind of terrible joke. And nothing matters anymore. In class I feel like I'm just waiting for a train. Today I was watching my professor's lips moving, and I could have sworn no sound was coming out. And then he called on me, and for a minute I didn't recognize my name. I don't know who I am now. It doesn't seem possible there can be a Wyatt Collier without a Chap Collier. I had a brother. I had my brother. That's who I was.

I wish you had known him like I did. I mean, I realize you knew him as long as you've known me, but there are a lot of things you didn't know about him. Sure, he and Kit could be pretty tough on us, but he looked out for me every day of my life. Remember when I started rowing? He got up at five o'clock every morning to get on the river and call for me, before he had to get to the plant. He hated that job. And I didn't have to do anything that summer. I got to be home with our mother. But after she died, he actually thanked me. He thanked me.

You know how much he would rib me about you. He used to say, "You'd better stay on your toes, Wy. That girl will give you a run for your money." But I know he thought you were a real pip. I think he loved you like his own little sister.

I guess I just need to talk about him. I don't know what I'd do if I didn't have you. It feels like parts of me are being cut away. Having my limbs sliced off wouldn't hurt as much. I keep thinking how it could have been different. If I had gone back with them that night, I could have gotten him home. I could have looked out for him, for a change. I could have kept him from falling.

The words seeped off the page like quicksand, pulling Susannah into its depths as it pushed the air out of her lungs. How could her mother ask this of her, knowing what she knew? How could Susannah possibly be expected to continue the charade now? It was inconceivable. The weight of it had been crushing before—she had virtually crawled across the stage to the final curtain. *The final curtain.*

The book skittered across the floor as she bolted to a potted ficus and retched into the roots. When the spasms ceased, she leaned back against the windowsill, drawing her knees up and bowing her head to stifle the sobs in the flannel of her skirt. But after a while, from the smothering quagmire of guilt and pain, her conscience struggled to the surface and drew a crucial breath. And in the pale light she saw something. She could not abandon Wyatt. However battered and broken she was, she carried a debt—an essential obligation owed to both of the brothers who had loved her.

It took several days, but, after false starts and torn pages, she finally eked out a response.

Dear Wyatt,
I know how you loved him. I know how you'll miss him. And I know how it must feel to lose him. You will never know the depth of my sorrow for you. You, of all people, don't deserve this. You deserve to live in the sunlight, happy and carefree and surrounded by all who have loved you. It is an unconscionably cruel fate that could deal such a hand to someone so good as you. I know it will take time, but you have to allow yourself to let the light back into your life. It is what Chap would want. He loved you so. It would dishonor him to allow grief to steal your

future. Remember how he taught you to bat—square your
stance and keep your eye on the ball. And when you struck
out, he laughed and said there will always be another up.
I know it doesn't seem possible, but, Wyatt, you have to
heed his words . . . for your sake and for his.

There were splotches on several of the words where tears
had fallen, but she couldn't bring herself to copy it over. She
signed it hastily and put it in the envelope, licking the seal so
fast that she cut her tongue. There was nothing technically
false in what she wrote, but the lie at the heart of it glared from
the page and she couldn't look at it.

It was several weeks before he wrote again. The letter was
a rambling collection of reminiscences, and Susannah read it
in the bathtub—where the tears could fall freely and no one
could hear the ragged, stuttering breaths. Every reference
played out as though on film.

Do you remember when they won the pennant and Kit tackled
Chap on the field? And the team piled on and Chap got a black
eye?

She remembered. But she saw things now she hadn't seen
then. The film had color. She saw the lithe figure wheeling
backward as he made the winning catch, glove in the air and
cap shading his eyes. But what she could also see now was the
slant of sunlight as it fell across the angle of a cheekbone, and
the unique color of the eyes under the cap, and the hand inside the glove—strong and fine and so perfectly suited to hers.

Do you remember the time he saved Kit from Ahab?

It had been Susannah's idea. She knew her brother wouldn't be able to resist a dare from his youngest sister, and she bet him ten dollars he couldn't mount the stallion. Everyone knew it was a perilous proposition. Saddling the horse was out of the question; Kit would have to secure the lead rope and get on bareback. He needed to stay on for five seconds—India had been appointed to count. They had all watched in thrilled terror as Kit slipped under the rail of the stall gate, pulling the mounting step in behind him. The thoroughbred's head turned slowly over his shoulder, eyes wide with disbelief. His flank twitched as Kit put a tentative hand on it. Kit knew he had to be steady and assured as he slid his palm firmly toward Ahab's shoulder. But as he reached for the rope, the massive ebony chest swung toward him.

He was cornered against the trough when Chap scrambled to the top of the partition and jackknifed his body over it, leaning down to grab Kit's shirt. It must have been some kind of supernatural adrenaline that gave him the strength to yank his friend out from under the rearing hooves. Susannah remembered it well—she had been all too aware of her culpability at the time. But as she replayed the scene, she saw now what the ten-year-old girl had not: the cut of a jawline, the sinew of muscle in a forearm, the small crescent-shaped scar just below the left temple.

It was the next lines that caused her hands to drop, letting the thin sheet sink slowly in the water.

I heard a song the other day, and it reminded me of all the times he would just make up the words. They would be ridiculous, but they always rhymed.

She was late for dinner, lingering in the boathouse too long already, but he wouldn't let her go. He was singing softly into her ear as he moved her slowly around the dusty planks of the floor. It was a song they had danced to the night of her party. He got the first line right, but after that it was all imagination. *What'll I do . . . when you . . . are far . . . away . . . and I'm so blue . . . what'll I do? What'll I do . . . when I'm . . . just standing . . . here . . . not kissing . . . you . . . what'll I do? What'll I do . . . when you . . . are in . . . your bed . . . and I'm . . . not next . . . to you? When I'm alone . . . with only . . . Stan . . . and Stu . . . I'll chew . . . my shoe . . . that's what I'll do.*

She slipped under the water—an instinctive, desperate ablution—and stayed beneath the surface until it seemed her lungs would burst. But there was no relief, no cleansing. When she finally gasped for air, all she had to show for the act was the sodden, illegible page disintegrating into scraps.

It was as she rose from the bathtub that she was granted a deliverance, of sorts, from her abjection. There was a long, hinged mirror fastened to a spindle on the wall. It was designed to be positioned at any angle—a convenient accessory to the dressing toilette. And at that moment, it happened to be tilted such that when Susannah looked across the room, she was presented with the answer to the riddle of her skirt waists, buttoning ever tighter. And the dawning spread over her like holy oil.

She kept the secret to herself. It was all there was; it was everything. She didn't dwell on eventualities. It would become apparent soon enough, but until then she would cleave to the prerogative. Moving through her daily routine in quasi-isolation, she managed to maintain her studies, if not her friendships. Her detachment was attributed to the shock of the accident, of course—to the loss of a dear family friend. But her acquaintances weren't the only ones who found the change in her behavior a bit mystifying. Hollins pulled his wife aside on more than one occasion, worrying that their youngest daughter was suffering an incommensurate despair.

"I'm a bit concerned that Susannah has sunken so low—it's as if her entire personality has changed. I wouldn't have expected this type of sensitivity from her. India, yes. That's obvious. Even Kit—he has lost his other half, as it were. But I just can't figure why this has utterly taken the wind from Sassy's sails. Maybe she should see a doctor."

It was just after this conversation that Helen surprised her daughter in the bedroom. And thus, Susannah did see a doctor, but not the type her father had meant.

The ride home from Dr. Schulman's office had been a silent one, save the conventional exchanges with Jimmy. Helen followed her daughter into the house, speaking covertly. "While you were dressing, I had a word with the doctor. We have his complete confidence." She was taking off her gloves as

Susannah walked away from her, up the stairway to her bedroom. Moments later Helen appeared in the doorway. "By that I mean, no one has to know. Not even your father."

Susannah looked at her blankly. Having a baby wasn't something that people simply didn't notice.

Helen could see that her daughter wasn't following; she stepped into the room and sat down on a slipper chair by the dressing table, clearing her throat. "I'm afraid you may not be seeing things clearly, Susannah. Things that must be considered. I've reflected deeply on this—don't think for a moment that I haven't. My emotional stock may not be equal to yours, but it is immense. Chap is gone, and yet a part of him lives on. I'm not insensitive to that. But so many factors weigh in the balance. Taking them all into consideration, it becomes clear that the answer has to be the Episcopal Society. They will place the baby in an excellent home—I have assurances. Until then, I believe you'll be able to finish the term and graduate, without . . . detection." She ran her fingers absently over the fabric of a blousy frock, draped over the garment valet next to the chair. "And then, ostensibly, you'll take the European tour with Grandmother, as planned. You should know that I've confided in her. She agrees it's the only course, and she's willing to help."

The bed creaked as Susannah sat down hard, with an expression of utter disbelief. "I'm not giving this baby away." It was out of the question. It was like when Pericles had died and her father had suggested she might want another horse. But even more outrageous. Even more insulting.

Helen closed her eyes. After a moment, she drew a deep breath and looked at her daughter. "Susannah, listen to me. Chap is gone. The baby would not have a father. And you would be something less than a widow. A mother on her own, without even the history of a husband. I'm not talking about public speculation or social repercussions—that's of the least concern to me. But as your mother, I have to think of your future. It could mean a life alone, without a partner at your side. You're so young. Your whole life is in front of you. Your education, your freedom . . ." She shook her head sadly. "And, my dear, there's something else. Someone else. Think about Wyatt. It would destroy him. Everything he knows and feels about Chap . . . it would rob him of the image, the memories . . . his entire conception of brotherhood. Think of the pain. He can't suffer the loss twice. You can protect him from that. In this terrible tragedy, the one salvation is that Wyatt need never know. It is one wound you can spare him."

It was true, and it cut to the quick, but Susannah parried with a stony, penetrating question. "What about Charles?"

She had her mother there. Charles had been flattened by the loss of his son. To keep this secret from him—the existence of a grandchild, of Chap's legacy—could be considered criminal. Helen bowed her head. "I know what you're saying. I've been sleepless over that, too." She sighed. "There's nothing easy here, Sass." She thought for a moment, wringing her hands. "We don't have to make any final decisions now. But the wisest course is to leave all options open, which means we keep the situation private. We protect the possibilities." It was clear she had honed her argument. Susannah just stared at the floor as her mother continued. "There's one other person in whom I've confided—someone who's willing to help. You may have heard that Sarah Janssen married an Amish boy. Doe misses her terribly, and she would welcome you at Grange House. You can stay there until the baby is born. The timing will coincide your return from the putative trip abroad. It will give us—you—time to consider things."

Susannah's silence was taken for assent. And she did agree to go to Grange House. Keeping the secret to herself for a bit longer was a dividend; she cherished the intimacy of it. But, if Helen was under the impression that her daughter was weighing the other matter, she was wrong.

Three days after graduation, Susannah waved to her mother from the train platform, trunk at her side and carpetbag at her waist. Her father had said his goodbyes that morning, before he'd left for the office. She had returned his embrace rather awkwardly, keeping a stiff distance as he patted her back and pecked her cheek—but his parting words were a bit unsettling: "Bon voyage, darling. Good luck with your grandmother . . . and stay away from the strudel."

At the station, a sudden unspecific ailment caused Helen to instruct Jimmy to take her home, curtailing the send-off and leaving Susannah alone there . . . until Doe and Nico pulled up in the battered work truck. Since then, she had been sequestered at Grange House, while Grandmother Avery sent postcards from Paris and Florence and Vienna. That the tidings were never in Susannah's hand did not give anyone pause. Rumor had it that Grandmother Avery had been a close acquaintance of Lewis Carroll, and that Charlotte Hastings Avery was the unquestionable inspiration for the Queen of Hearts. As such, it surprised no one that the woman took the matter of correspondence into her own hands. India had walked that floor herself, having taken her tour with Grandmother two years prior. She knew who held the quill.

As it happened, the fictitious distance had a collateral benefit. As winter turned to spring, Wyatt's letters had continued to arrive. Painstakingly, Susannah had scratched out replies, but she couldn't contrive even a twig of the ready support Wyatt had known when his mother had died. Being "out of the country" meant she wouldn't have to struggle through another excruciating, elliptical effort. And because he believed she wouldn't be there, Wyatt had decided not to return to Bethlehem for the summer. He would stay in New Haven, practicing with the crew.

Though that development remedied one eminent risk, Susannah still had to keep a sharp eye whenever she was outside; almost any visitor to St. Gregory's would know her. If she wandered too far from the house, there was no telling how long she might be stranded behind the nearest monument. It was easiest to wait until the gates were closed for the night. She fell into a familiar routine—a serene stroll along the curving paths at twilight, accompanied by the evening birdsong and the scent of dew settling onto the grass—a stroll that always led to an achingly new headstone, where she would end her day in soft, solitary conversation and a reluctant good night.

Her mother came to see her often. It was the reason Helen had devised the plan—she could keep her daughter close, and no one would find the visits to the cemetery all that unusual. She brought the family report, news of the world, and clothing to accommodate the changing requirements. She also managed to sneak Susannah her bed pillow, stuffed into a shopping bag. If Jimmy wondered about the occasional parcels Mrs. Parrish was bringing to her friend Doe, he didn't ask.

Aside from the insufficient down in the pillows, the accommodations at Grange House suited Susannah. She liked the seclusion. To afford better privacy for all of them, Doe and Nico had moved the furniture from the spare bedroom to the attic, and the effect was of a cozy nest—warm and dry. A little too warm at high noon in July, perhaps, but Susannah could pass the days reading in the cool, dark parlor, or sitting with Doe in the kitchen.

Although her mother had been close to Doe for many years, Susannah didn't really know her until those long days of confinement. The ceaseless demands of groundskeeping kept the woman outdoors for much of the day, but in her downtime she taught Susannah to make sourdough bread and angel food cake and boysenberry jam. She had a way of raising Susannah's spirits. She could even raise a smile now and then too, coaxing forth the first semblance of anything like cheer in that cruel, miserable year. More than anything, Susannah liked Doe's ghost stories. In a sad, strange way, the prospect of supernatural presence gave her hope. She didn't really believe any of it, but not a night went by that she didn't stand by the window to watch and wait.

She was in the rocking chair in her attic aerie the first time she felt the baby move. Although the tap was barely discernible, it carried the emotional force of a judo kick, instantly obliterating any chance her mother might have had to advance her case for the Episcopal Society. Susannah told Chap about it that evening, lying on her side with one hand on her belly and the other on the soft, mounded grass. Until that point, she had only pictured an embryo—the tiny seed that combined them—but now she could see a child, snug in her arms, with perfect rosy lips and dark sweeping lashes and a smidgen of downy, sable-colored hair.

It was mid-July when she felt the sudden rush of wetness. In one of his routine house calls, Dr. Schulman had given her a pamphlet that described the process of labor and birth. She knew about ruptured membranes and leaking fluid, but when she stood from the rocking chair and looked down, she saw what her heart already knew: The drops spreading at her feet were crimson.

Doe and Nico had gone to bed; Susannah slumped against their bedroom door as her fist banged against it. As Doe called for the doctor, Nico carried her back up the splattered trail on the steep staircase, the soaked nightgown smearing his arms with red.

Later, she didn't have a clear memory of the pain, although she could recall the screams. What she could also recall was the tiny, perfect replica of his father. She had clung to consciousness, grasping desperately for her child through the descending fog. It was Doe who placed the still form in Susannah's arms, giving her the chance to hold her baby boy in her last moments of awareness—to see the dark lashes against the waxen cheek, to feel the fine down of sable-colored hair.

Placental abruption, the doctor had called it. For a harrowing stretch, he thought he would lose the mother, too. But Susannah survived, despite her absent will. The baby's name—Charles Hayes Collier Jr.—was recorded duly, but to the world he would be known only as Baby Hayes. His paternal grandmother's maiden name. His father's middle name. The inscription and placement of the headstone had been Helen's suggestion. To reveal the truth now would cause nothing but pain—to Wyatt, to Charles, to everyone. There was nothing to be gained. Susannah was unresponsive: What could ever be gained again?

She remained at Grange House in ghostly convalescence, a hollow shell with nothing left to give and nothing left to lose. Over the following weeks, her mother was at her side for much of each day—searching her empty eyes for the girl who once was there. Inevitably, the time came for Susannah to return home. The parameters of the invention required it. Helen stood up and closed the lid of the trunk, nearly empty, on the attic floor. All of the dresses that hung in the makeshift closet were to be given to the Salvation Army. They billowed on Susannah, and there was no point in keeping them. Helen had brought a skirt and blouse from home, and she moved across the room to take her daughter's hand and help her dress.

There was one final step in the baroque deception: Nico would take Susannah back to the train station, where she would wait with her trunk and carpetbag for Jimmy to fetch her. Helen led her daughter down the staircases and through the back door of Grange House, and there they stopped. The headstone was small—just a simple granite marker—but it filled Susannah's entire field of vision. A low moan issued from deep within; as her legs faltered, her mother grabbed her. And then Doe was at her other side, and the two women braced her up, holding her fast between them as the grief poured forth in a quaking, keening torrent. And when there was nothing left but dry suspiration, it was their strength that guided her to the waiting truck, and their strength that settled her into the cab, and their strength that would carry her forward, as Nico put the gears into drive to bring her back into the world.

Fifteen

"Wyatt never knew?" Joanna was mesmerized, sitting farther forward with each candid utterance until she was leaning over, elbows on her knees. That after all these years she was the one her mother-in-law had chosen to confide in stunned Joanna almost as much as the revelations had. But *what* revelations. They explained so much—not just the curiosities in the photo albums, but also the enigma that was Susannah Parrish Collier, and—astonishingly—the riddle of Baby Hayes.

"No. He never knew. He was away at school then." Susannah tilted her head, thinking back. "And he stopped writing after that summer. I was relieved. I didn't . . . have it in me. To be honest, I was hoping he had found someone else. But after a time, I started to worry about him. And I missed him. He had been my best friend for most of my life. I didn't see him until the following summer. It was strange, and sad. He wasn't the same person. He didn't talk about Chap anymore. I think it just dredged up too much sorrow." She set her empty glass on the side table, then slipped her shoes off and tucked her legs beneath her on the cushion, stretching her shoulders as she shifted. "And that made it . . . bearable. Any conversation like that would have been . . . Well, I don't think I could have managed it. We just went for long walks, not talking about anything at all. There were a lot of quiet walks that summer." She looked at the window; her voice was tired and starting to fade. "We were all we had. He didn't know it, but I needed him as much as he needed me."

The long hand of the grandfather clock ticked to the top, triggering a coronach of nine low chimes. Susannah waited them out, gazing pensively at the darkness outside. When the last resonant tone had faded, she continued. "Eventually, we began to find our way back . . . both separately and together. And under the bruises, I started to see some of the old Wyatt. A year later he proposed. And I said yes."

For a moment there was silence. And then Susannah leaned forward, her eyes oceans of deep blue regret. "I will never know if he could have forgiven me—if he would have found his way through it—because I never gave him the chance. It's possible that our lives would have taken an entirely different course . . . but I should have given him that chance."

Still overwhelmed by all she'd been entrusted with, Joanna also felt something like gratitude. "I want you to know that your secret is safe with me. I would never share it—not even with Frank."

But Susannah shook her head. "Don't worry, Jo—you don't have to carry my past around." With a deep sigh, she sat back, shoulders falling in tired relief. "I realized today that I don't have to live with the lie anymore. Because I wasn't the only one hiding the secret, you see. I shared the burden with someone else—someone who had risked the"—she hesitated, searching for the word—"sanctity of her marriage. And believe me, that was no small thing." She paused to let it sink in. "You have to realize, it was an enormous deception on Mother's part. Keeping something like that from my father, with such painstaking effort, well . . . if he'd ever learned the truth, it would have torn them apart." Absently, she ran a finger around the rim of the empty snifter. "Her intentions were pure—don't get me wrong. Maternal instinct will always prevail. She would have stepped in front of a train for any of her children, and she thought what she was doing was for the best. But she was wrong. It was a mistake." She reflected for a moment, watching her finger circle the glass. "It would have been worse had there been a child somewhere out there. A grandchild kept from both my father and Charles. But that wasn't to be." Her words carried a wistful sadness, but then her chin lifted significantly. "Still, it was a whopper of a lie. You have to remember, I almost died."

Joanna swallowed hard as the implications became clear. She hadn't thought about that. How would Helen have faced her husband had the worst occurred? It was a horrifying thought, and she felt a shiver run up her spine.

"And so we were both guilty," Susannah continued. "But at the heart of it, I knew I was responsible. It was for me that Mother had betrayed her husband in such a terrible way. It was for my protection. And that was why I had to protect her, too. No matter what soul-saving impulse held out a hand, I had to live with the lie."

She settled her feet back on the floor, as if to support the weight of her words, and looked intently at Joanna. "It's a wretched thing to feel like an imposter. In some fundamental way, it changed me. And the worst part of it has been knowing that the people who loved me most—my husband and my children—are the ones I have most deceived. I decided today that I don't have to be that person anymore. I don't have to hide anything. There's no one left to protect, and there's no one left to hurt."

The windows in the library were on the east wall, which faced the side drive as it wound past the house to the garages. As Susannah's words faded, an arc of light moved across one window, and then the next. Headlights. Frank was back.

But the wave of relief that rolled over Joanna crashed against a towering rock of apprehension, and it must have shown on her face. Once again her mother-in-law came to the rescue. As the headlights passed, Susannah shook her head slowly, sighing. "I don't know if I have it in me tonight." Her face was pale. "I think I'd like to speak to both Frank and Gigi together. It can wait until tomorrow." She smiled tenderly at Joanna. "But why don't you let me talk to him about what you shared with me? I think I can help. I think I might be able to provide some perspective."

It was utterly overwhelming. That Susannah would reach out like that—that from under the burden of all that weighed upon her, she could somehow summon the strength to offer her hand—left Joanna speechless. All she could manage was a simple nod. As she bowed her head, she noticed the snifter, still nearly full in her hand. Impulsively tipping it to her mouth, she drained the brandy in one long swig. And this produced a soft laugh from Susannah—released like church bells at the end of a long liturgy, clearing some of the heaviness from the air.

"Bravo. A little fortification can't hurt." There was the sound of a door closing on the other side of the house. Susannah picked up her empty glass and held it out. "Since you're up . . ."

Joanna went to the small bar and filled her mother-in-law's glass. Turning back to her, she saw that her eyes were closed and her mouth was set in a grim line. Joanna couldn't imagine the strength it had taken to tell her the story, to bring it to light after all this time. But tomorrow's tribunal would be the true test. For their entire lives, Frank and Gigi had been denied the truth. Their mother knew her liability, and she was about to own it.

Joanna set the glass next to the motionless figure on the davenport, whose hands were folded as if in prayer. She laid her hand on a taut shoulder, giving a gentle squeeze, and then moved quickly to the door. Fled, in fact. Her avoidance was wrapped in woolly layers of uncertainty—the thickest and roughest being the prospect that she would not again feel the warmth of her husband's hand on her own shoulder in the dark, empty night.

Charles Hayes Collier. She could see the name from where she was standing, given the adjacency of the Parrish and Collier plots. And next to Chap was his mother, FRANCES HAYES COLLIER. Joanna couldn't believe she hadn't noticed it before. She hadn't studied the wind-worn inscriptions; she hadn't paid close enough attention. She hadn't made the connection.

She turned her attention back to the minister, who was reciting a psalm. The family was gathered around the open grave; there was a wreath of flowers on an easel where the headstone would soon be positioned. The funeral service had been held, as a matter of course, at Nativity Episcopal. Despite Susannah's concern about a small send-off, there had been quite a crowd. Kit just made it, flying in on the red-eye from Lima without his wife and children, citing something about passport problems. Joanna was pleased to finally meet him. Until then, she'd had only the images from the photo albums to go on. He was as strapping as he had looked in his college-era photos, and his features still bore a resemblance to Susannah's. He also still called his sister Sassy, and Joanna could swear her mother-in-law lit up a little whenever he did.

India and Paul were there, of course, but there wasn't much in the way of extended family—just two cousins from Boston, along with a couple of nieces and a nephew. What filled the pews was virtually the whole of Bethlehem Steel—from the chairman to a stenographer (retired now after forty years poised with her pad at the corner of Hollins Parrish's desk)—and a heart-swelling horde of locals. Joanna stood next to Frank in the receiving line before the service, and she lost count of all the townspeople and tradespeople—dressed in their Sunday finest—who came to pay their last respects to Helen Avery Parrish.

Although the church had been filled to the transept, the interment was limited to immediate family. Accordingly, Harriet, Hazel, and Jimmy (propped up by his nephew Wayne) were there. None of them was on service today; even Wayne had turned over his duties to a couple of hired chauffeurs. And there were two others who qualified. They were regular fixtures in the cemetery, but instead of the usual overalls and apron, they were dressed today as mourners. At the church, Joanna had nearly walked right past Doe and Nico.

There wasn't much snow on the ground—the last days of December had bequeathed a tepid thaw—but when Joanna looked closely, she could see pieces of charcoal mixed into the earth piled next to the grave. What she did not see was any sign of Daniel.

For the entire morning, Joanna had dreaded the moment they would pass through the gates at St. Gregory's. Sitting next to her husband in the back of the limousine, she felt him stiffen as they rolled passed Grange House, following the hearse to the crest that overlooked the trees along the river, as stark and gray as the shame in her heart. Thus, when he put his arm around her during the committal—pulling her close as they watched the casket being lowered into the ground—her throat swelled with relief.

She had been asleep when Frank had finally come up to the bedroom on that fateful day—something she hadn't thought possible. After tossing and turning for what seemed like hours, she woke to find him sitting on the edge of the bed. In a show of hopeful optimism, she had left a small lamp burning in the corner; in the low light she could see him looking at her. And then saw something she had never seen before: there were tears in his eyes.

"I thought I'd lost you." Though the words were hoarse, they were the sweetest ones she had ever heard.

"No." Her own voice was just a cracked whisper as she shook her head on the pillow. "No. I'm so sorry. I was so stupid. So selfish."

She could see his throat move as he swallowed. "I thought . . . I thought . . . ." He couldn't say it.

Joanna knew exactly what he couldn't say. "It wasn't like that. I couldn't have . . . I couldn't." Now she was crying, and he picked up her hand as she dredged up the words. "It wasn't what I wanted. It wasn't ever what I wanted."

He closed his eyes for a moment. "It was my fault. I should

never have asked this of you. It was too much. I should have seen it." There was a gentle pressure as his hand squeezed hers. "We can fix this. We can change things. It won't be long until Burns Harbor is up and running—things will calm down and we'll get our own place. A place you can hang a painting . . . or choose new drapes . . . or buy a lamp. . . ."

"No." Joanna interrupted him, sitting up. "We're not going anywhere. I don't want to live anywhere else." With amazement, she realized the words were true. Besides, they couldn't leave Susannah here alone, not now. Not when they'd all come so far. "This is my place. You are my life. You and the kids, and your mother, too. This is where we belong."

When they had thrown the final spade of dirt onto the casket, the family moved toward the waiting cars. Kit escorted Gigi as India and Paul followed. Frank had taken his mother in one arm and Joanna in the other, the children trailing behind. But when they reached the road, he turned toward the house.

There had been just a few times in their marriage that Frank had done something completely out of character, like driving straight through a red light in downtown Philadelphia simply because it was late at night and the intersection was clear, or emptying a box of Cheerios into Daisy's crib to buy a little extra sleep on a rainy Saturday morning. As he ushered them forward, Joanna felt a rising panic that this was one of those times. For a few helpless moments she was convinced that Frank had taken a mind to confront Daniel, family in tow. Why else would he be headed for Grange House? But then he tipped his head down and she heard him ask his mother a gentle question: "It's over here?" And she knew where they were going.

"There's Baby Hayes!" Daisy skipped ahead, Charlie on her heels. She got there first, squatting down to trace her finger over the brief epitaph on the granite marker. "This is the baby with no mother," Daisy explained.

"I told you—it had a mother." Charlie wore his exasperation like sackcloth.

Joanna strode forward, taking the children in hand. "Let's go and wait in the car. Maybe we can ride in the long one." Both Charlie and Daisy had been deeply disappointed that morning when the hired stretch limo filled up and left without them, and they were relegated to the old Silver Cloud. Now they practically pulled their mother off her feet in a mad rush to secure a spot on the exotic expanses of the banquette seats.

Susannah turned to her son. "Go ahead with them—I'll just be a minute."

He understood the need for privacy, but before he stepped away, Frank asked another quiet question. "Don't you think it's time he took his rightful place?"

His mother hugged him then, wrapping her arms around

his chest to bury her face against the soft cashmere of his overcoat. And her shoulders shook. And that was her answer.

Susannah stood alone in the weak January sunlight, gazing at the inscription. There would be a new stone, one that told the truth. She heard the words of the minister, spoken just that morning: *redeemeth and restoreth*. The baby would lie next to his father now, near the place where she would someday join them.

Deep in thought, she didn't even notice that Doe had appeared, standing next to her with a cardboard box. "I don't mean to interrupt . . . but I have something for you. I was looking for a letter from Hedy this morning—something she sent me years ago, after Sarah left. It meant so much. I wanted to read it again. She was . . ." Her voice broke, and she had to take a moment to gather herself. A long stratus cloud came and went before she could continue. "Daniel likes to tease me about my filing system, but I knew right where it would be. And I remembered there were some other things in that box. Some things I've been saving for you." She set the cardboard on the cold hard ground and lifted the lid, looking up at Susannah with a sad smile. "No time like the present."

The first thing she withdrew was a plain envelope, slightly yellowed with age. Suddenly nervous, she said, "I took the liberty. I knew it wasn't my place, but I just . . . had to. I thought someday you might want . . ." Her words trailed off as she held it out.

Scrawled on the front was only one line—just a name: *Charles Hayes Collier Jr.* The envelope wasn't sealed—the flap was simply tucked under the lip of the opening. In what felt like slow motion, Susannah opened it. Inside was a tiny lock of hair. Carefully, she picked it up. For a long moment, she studied it in her palm, running a finger gently over the sable softness. And then, clenching her hand tightly, she brought her fist to her mouth and pressed her lips against it.

"Hedy didn't know. It was just before we closed the coffin." Doe was teary again, her voice thick. "It's true what they say, you know. The smallest coffins are the heaviest."

Susannah's eyes were squeezed shut, and she breathed deeply. Doe turned away, granting a private communion between mother and child. When Susannah finally opened her eyes, she looked to the old woman with an aching smile. "Thank you for this."

"There's something else." Doe stooped down and lifted out a baseball glove. "I saved this for you too. I thought you might want it back someday."

Susannah took it in her other hand. "Where did you get this?" She stared at the worn, cracked leather, smooth to the touch and heavy in her grasp.

"Right here." Doe nodded at the headstone. "Where you left it. You remember—it was about a year after . . . well, about a year later." She gave Susannah a peculiar look, registering her puzzlement. "You know Nico has a policy that we can't save all the things people leave, but this was different. I've seen a lot of sweet offerings in my time, but this . . ." She shook her head. "I had to believe you would want it back someday."

Running a finger across the insignia, Susannah turned it over to see the owner's name inked on the inside of the back strap. It was so faded that it was barely legible, but it didn't matter—she knew what she would find there: *Chap Collier.* The sight of it . . . the feel of it . . . the fact of it . . . it was like he was there—a physical presence. It made her light-headed. And in the dizzying rush, it took her a moment to process the information. The glove was left here? How was it possible?

And then, as clearly as if she were holding the page in front of her, she saw the words of a letter written long ago:

I brought his glove back here with me. I needed something of his that I could touch. Something I could hold. Whenever I put it on, I swear I can feel him standing next to me.

She hadn't left the glove on her baby's grave. It hadn't been hers to leave. But she knew who had. The realization struck with a force that nearly brought her to her knees. Like the first time she'd stood there, so many years ago, her legs faltered. And as on that raw and tender day, Doe was there to brace her up, to keep her from falling.

The letter had been signed as they all were—with just two words. They were the words that had been her salvation. They had been her future and her past. They had been her truth. But until that moment, she had not fully known the depth of that truth—and she had not known the cost.

They were just two words, but they were the story of her life:

Yours, Wyatt

Epilogue

"Mr. Collier? Can you hear me?" Betty was shaking her boss's shoulder, willing him from the slumped sprawl that covered the blotter on his desk. She had asked too many times to justify the question, but she couldn't stop. Her competence had always been unimpeachable. Mr. Collier relied on her. She couldn't fail him now.

And Wyatt *could* hear her—from a long, echoing distance. He could hear Joe Simons, too, calling out dim, buffered instructions. "Get Doc Erland! Call an ambulance! Someone find Frank!" It came in muffled snatches, like dialogue from a television playing in a room far down the hall.

He knew it was Betty's hand on his shoulder, but somehow, in the next moment, it was his mother's. "See the dragon opening his mouth?" She was kneeling next to him in the garden, bringing the yellow snapdragon magically to life with the press of her fingers. And then she was laughing—clear and bright—from the top of the porch steps as he teetered across the yard on his new stilts. She had been gone for decades, but he was just seven years old—suffused with warm relief. *There* she was. There she was. There she was.

Time had become fluid, nonlinear. Joe's voice was now his father's, hollering through cupped hands on the banks of the Schuylkill: "C'mon, Wyatt! Stay with it! You can do it!"

He could hear a siren. "Where the hell is the doctor? Dad. Dad. It's Frank. Stay with me. Just hang on. Everything will be all right."

"Look, Daddy—we found a kitten." The twins, hovering over an open hatbox. The fox was too weak to open its eyes and there was a drip of foam at its mouth, but the strike of fear was allayed by a settling retrospect. He was there in the yard with Gigi and Frank, and yet he knew: except for the poor fox, everyone would be all right.

"Clear the way, please. Everyone step out of the way." Arms hoisting him up.

Chap was standing behind him on a scruffy patch of turf, circling his arms around to clasp his hands over Wyatt's on the bat, saying, "Step into it, buddy. Like this." And then those arms enveloping him again as he shivered in the lamplight, shaken to the bone: "You didn't have to go in after her, you know."

But he did. They both did.

Chap. Ah, Chap. It wasn't your fault. How could I blame you? I know you didn't have any choice. I never damned you for it. If I had damned you for anything, it would have been for that bottle of Beefeater. But I couldn't. I can't.

And I couldn't damn her, either. My Susannah. What a price you paid.

There was a sound, a repeated beeping, that somehow transmuted to a chime—the bell at Brynmor's massive door. He had come to surprise her, carefully timing his arrival to coincide with Susannah's return from Europe. It was a prize he had clutched all summer long, as firmly as he clutched his oar—pushing down the pain with every grueling stroke, fixing his gaze on the distant shore that was Susannah.

But she wasn't there. *They expected her anytime,* Harriet said. *Come right in, Mister Wyatt. She'll be so happy to see you.* Only he hadn't been back to Chap's grave. It was something he needed to do. It was a step he had to make himself take. He could do it now, while he waited.

The Center Street gate was closest. He could cut across the grass to the rise overlooking the river. It was a familiar path, though more rugged now—his step burdened by the added weight of an extra grave. The cemetery was quiet—hundreds of souls, not one in sight. But as he reached a paved walk, he heard something. Despite the trees and monuments that rose out of the undulating lawns, he had a clear sight line to the back of Grange House. His glance was reflexive—he expected to see one of the Janssens. Absently, he registered that it *was* Mrs. Janssen coming out of the house, but then there was an odd, disjointed moment where he was certain his eyes were deceiving him. Because behind her emerged two figures that didn't fit the picture. In dreamlike disorientation, he looked on as the three women stopped not far from the door. And then the stillness was pierced by an agonized, gut-wrenching wail. It was the cry of an animal caught in the razor prongs of a trap; it was the cry of a prisoner on the rack; it was the cry of a mother who has lost her child.

And he watched as Susannah crumpled.

How long he stood there, he couldn't have said. He was frozen in place long after the truck pulled away, and Helen moved toward the Church Street gate, and Doe went back into the house. His mind was numb to any processing, to any explanation. Instinctively, he pushed all speculation away. He wanted to refuse it outright. He needed to refuse it. Because there wasn't really any question, and he knew it in his heart. It wasn't just that something was wrong. Everything was wrong.

Finally, slowly, his feet took him to the spot where the women had stood. And there he saw the headstone, and he knew. He knew it as though he had written the story himself— assured and fully fledged. A handful of small, fragmented slips fell together to form a whole—slivers of torn pages that had been scattered here and there, bits of stray inklings that drifted against the edges of perception, intently ignored, steadfastly denied. As he stood looking down at the grave, he knew exactly who lay there. BABY HAYES.

"One, two, three, lift!"

The voices were growing ever dimmer—it was all becoming a soft white hum. He thought he heard Frank again, shouting "Someone call my mother!" but he wasn't sure if it was happening now or if it was something from before. Everything was oddly simultaneous. Anything that had ever happened was happening now, but it was all draining away . . . all but the image of sapphire eyes, dancing across the ripple of the river as he struggled in his fool's mission to save her. *My Susannah.*

Should I have risked it all and told you that I knew? I didn't have the guts. I was afraid to let it out of its cage. I was afraid of its size. I was afraid it would eat us alive.

There was silence now—peaceful, enveloping. *No, I couldn't take that chance. Oh, Sass, how I have loved you. I never had a choice, any more than he did. I hope you can forgive me.*

The last image he had was of the first time he'd seen her, eight years old and sitting at the table in the unfamiliar splendor of the dining room at Brynmor. She'd looked across at him and smiled that smile. "Welcome to Bethlehem," she had said.

It was all she had to say. He was home.